The Prisoners
of September

www.randomhousechildrens.co.uk

Also by Leon Garfield:

THE PRISONERS
OF SEPTEMBER

Leon Garfield

RED FOX CLASSICS

THE PRISONERS OF SEPTEMBER
A RED FOX CLASSIC BOOK 978 1 782 95077 6

Published in 2015 in Great Britain by Red Fox,
an imprint of Random House Children's Publishers UK
A Penguin Random House Company

Penguin
Random House
UK

1 3 5 7 9 10 8 6 4 2

First published by Viking Kestrel, 1975

Copyright © The Estate of Leon Garfield, 1975

Penguin Random House is committed to a sustainable future for our
business, our readers and our planet. This book is made from Forest
Stewardship Council® certified paper.

MIX
Paper from
responsible sources
FSC® C018179

Set in Bembo 12/17pt by Falcon Oast Graphic Art Ltd.

Red Fox Books are published by Random House Children's Publishers UK,
61–63 Uxbridge Road, London W5 5SA

www.**randomhousechildrens**.co.uk
www.**totallyrandombooks**.co.uk
www.**randomhouse**.co.uk

Addresses for companies within The Random House Group Limited
can be found at: www.randomhouse.co.uk/offices.htm

THE RANDOM HOUSE GROUP Limited Reg. No. 954009

A CIP catalogue record for this book is available from the British Library.

Printed and bound in Great Britain by Clays Ltd, St Ives plc.

To my wife and daughter

CONTENTS

PART ONE

Liberté

CHAPTER ONE

O who will o'er the Downs so free;
O who will with me ride?

THE SONG FLOATED out, clear and joyous, across the Sussex Downs where they dipped and rose towards the road to Preston. It was a fine, blustery afternoon at the beginning of July in 1789; and the solitary horseman, despite the burden of his song, did not seem much in need of company. Indeed he galloped so easily and swiftly that the most obliging companion would have been hard put to keep him in sight.

O who will up and follow me
To win a blooming bride?

A melodious but rhetorical question. Young, vigorous and in radiantly good spirits, the musical rider's appearance suggested irresistibly that he would have scorned assistance in such an enterprise, even if, as he continued to sing:

> *Her father he has locked the door,*
> *Her mother keeps the key;*
> *But neither door nor bolt shall part*
> *My own true love from me!*

His voice was a light but strong baritone, and as harmonious as everything else about him, so that it was hard to believe that any parents, however choosy, would have put obstacles in his path to their daughter. He was just eighteen years old and was full of that intense happiness that seems possible only to very young or very selfish natures. It was his birthday and he was possessed of a new horse and sundry trinkets that twinkled as the sun caught them.

Presently he reached the brow of a hill that overlooked the road. He reined in his horse, admired its glossy brown flanks, then turned to contemplate the wide landscape that folded down towards Brighton and the sea. He strained his eyes, hoping to catch a distant sparkle of sunlight on water . . . when a sound from the opposite direction distracted him.

He looked down to the road; a carriage, drawn by two black horses, was approaching rapidly. In fact, it was approaching far too rapidly. The vehicle was rocking from side to side and the horses seemed panic-stricken.

As the carriage drew near he saw the reason for this. The coachman had collapsed; he was slewed across his seat and the horses were galloping free.

The carriage was now level with him. He saw a white face at its window; he heard a woman's voice screaming. In a moment, the vehicle had dashed past. Alarmed and tremendously excited, the young man rode down the hillside and set off in pursuit of the runaway.

His horse was swift – swifter by far than the carriage horses – yet for a time he did not seem to gain on them. It was almost as if he was deliberately savouring the situation to the full before bringing it to a commonplace end. His own mood of intense happiness, combined with the sudden apparition of the bolting yellow carriage and the white face at its window, had produced so powerful a feeling of romantic excitement that the young man felt himself to be quite translated into the fantasy world of his sisters' monthly novels.

A thousand thoughts and dreams teemed in his brain as he followed: thoughts of heiresses to be rescued . . . princesses and God knew what! Whirling thoughts of boundless gratitude and applause – of assembled multitudes – his family, friends and neighbours!

The carriage leaped and jolted; the wheels made

furious splintering sounds; again the woman's voice screamed. He drew close, then level; glanced through the window – caught a confused glimpse of staring eyes, red lips and a flash of white bosom. He was equal with the coachman's seat; he saw the man himself: a jolting pile of clothing containing a slice of red cheek and a jerking hand . . .

He attempted to stretch down and grasp the reins. Impossible! The furious motion of the horses had flung them out of reach. He rode ahead, now galloping side by side with the carriage horses, whose steaming nostrils and black-blinkered eyes turned them to blinded dragons in full career.

He shouted to them; leaned over and perilously reached out. He seized a bridle strap – was all but dragged from his saddle. He felt his fingers being squeezed and crushed by a buckle. He scowled ferociously but held on. Little by little the pace diminished. The confused, continuous roar of hooves separated out into a broken rhythm of single beats. The carriage slowed down . . . and halted on the outskirts of Preston.

The young man dismounted. His heart was beating violently from the exertion of his ride and the excitement of the hopes he couldn't help nourishing. He ran his fingers through his hair that the wind had tugged from its mooring, and went to open the yellow casket that would contain his heiress, his princess, his lovely noble-woman – or, he smiled wryly to himself, the raddled ladies' maid who'd fainted away.

'Rich woman . . . poor woman . . . beggar woman . . . thief . . . rich—' He shortened his pace and just managed to accommodate 'woman!' as he reached the door.

There was a crest on the panel: a silver shield containing three golden fleurs-de-lis. His optimism returned; but even as he opened the door he had taken the precaution of preparing himself for the worst—

'Good God!' he said, as a small avalanche of beauty in blue silk tumbled out and overwhelmed him with gratitude in a strong French accent.

'So brave! So young! So – so dashing! How can I reward – recompense you? Tell me – tell me!'

'Miss – Madam – I – I—' stammered the young man. He stood, foolish and open-mouthed, while his thoughts, bolting like the beauty's horses, galloped on resistlessly to applauding multitudes . . . his amazed family . . . his admiring friends . . . He beamed in a dazed fashion, half unable to believe in his own good fortune.

Meanwhile the lady had recovered herself; she glanced back into the carriage where an elderly maid sat gazing rather wistfully at the absurdly handsome young man who had rescued her mistress.

'At least,' smiled the lady, courteously putting an end to the young man's hopeless silence, 'you must tell me your name . . . that is,' she added mischievously, 'if you are able to remember it!'

'Boston! Lewis Alexander Boston . . . er . . . Lewis.'

'Is it Mister? Is it Sir? Or is it – Milord?'

'Oh, Mister! Mister Boston! But – but *Lewis*, please!'

'Already? You travel as swiftly as your horse, Mr Boston!'

She laughed at the young man's obvious confusion. She seemed accustomed to the effect she was creating.

'Now I must tell you my name. It is Jeanne.'

'Miss? Lady? Or Princess?' asked Lewis, with a sudden explosion of gallantry.

She laughed again. 'None of them! Alas! I am only a countess. The Countess de la Motte-Valois.'

'Good God!' said Lewis for a second time. It was impossible! But it had happened! He had actually rescued a beautiful noblewoman! Ma! Pa! he longed to shout out: I've done it! I've really done it!

The countess looked momentarily puzzled. She glanced again at her maid and imperceptibly shrugged her shoulders.

'Tell me, Mr Boston – is there no way I can reward you? You have saved my life, you know.'

'Come to my home!' burst out Lewis ecstatically.

'Visit my family! That will be reward enough! Oh do come, ma'am! Please!'

The lovely countess was taken aback. Her lively blue eyes widened. The reward the young man asked was so – so – she couldn't quite find the words to fit it. Being somewhat more worldly than this provincial Adonis, she'd imagined something rather different.

'But your family, Mr Boston!' (There was the hint of a chuckle in her voice.) 'Will not they be – be inconvenienced?'

'Oh no, no, no! They'll be honoured! Delighted . . . I promise you! They'll be – *enchanted*!' he finished up with a triumphant rush.

'Very well. I will come.'

'Now? Right away?'

'Oh no, no! I was on my way to visit with a gentleman in Brighton. I had arranged, you understand . . .'

'Tomorrow, then!'

'Not so soon—'

'The day after?'

'Please! Give me a little more time—'

'Saturday, then?'

'Next week.'

'Monday?'

'Tuesday. I will come on Tuesday.'

'Promise?'

'I promise!' (Again, the chuckle.)

At this point there came a groan from the coachman's seat. Totally ignored by his mistress and forgotten by his dazzled preserver, he had been left to make his own recovery. He dabbed at his head tenderly where a low-hanging branch had struck it and knocked him unconscious. Dazed and confused, he gathered the reins and was about to drive on when he became aware that his mistress was outside and that various things must have happened of which he had no knowledge. Conversation floated up to him as inconsequentially as in a dream.

'On Tuesday, then?'

'I promised – I promised.'

'Wait! My home! You don't know where! It's in Lancing. We – we are well known there.'

'Lancing. Tuesday. The house of Boston. I will remember.'

'At – at two o'clock?'

'So early?'

'Half past, then.'

'Half past two o'clock. It is agreed.'

'You promise?'

'Oh Mr Boston! I promise, I promise!'

'My name is Lewis, you know ...'

'Charming! Like the poor king!'

CHAPTER TWO

TUESDAY, 14TH OF July, and another magnificent day. What a summer it was! The Downs glowed and the sea sparkled like a trayful of diamonds.

Another young man was riding – but slowly, pensively, with eyes downcast, looking only occasionally in the direction he was travelling as if it mattered little to him whether he arrived or not. He, too, was handsome; but in place of Lewis Boston's flushed health was a pallor and a lean severity. It would be hard to imagine this young man with a song on his lips . . . still less in his heart.

Presently he passed between a pair of stone gateposts beside which stood a small lodge. The gatekeeper came running out, saw who it was and touched his cap with respect. The young man nodded and rode on, his brows drawn down and his lips curled in faint contempt.

After some hundred yards between well-kept, high-growing shrubs, the house came into view – a Gothic mansion in the latest style: a folly, a dream, a nightmare, perhaps, or a child's fantasy complete with soaring turrets

11 WITHDRAWN

for the immuring of beauties and battlements for the repelling of invaders. Above the massy door was a stone inscribed: A.B. 1785. This was not a mistake on the stonemason's part; the A.B. stood for Alexander Boston, Importer of Fine Wines and Lewis's father.

The young man turned his horse towards the stables when a groom came quickly to hold his bridle and assist him to dismount. For God's sake, thought the young man with weary exasperation, must you all be so slavishly fawning? Have you forgotten the dignity of being men?

Nevertheless, he accepted the assistance and rewarded the groom suitably. He walked to the front door, but before he could knock it was flung open and Lewis Boston, blazing in a new waistcoat and striped stockings, rushed out to greet him.

'I'm so glad you could come early, Dick!'

The young man frowned imperceptibly; he disliked the abbreviation of his name.

'You insisted, Lewis. You always do, you know.' There was the merest hint of criticism in his voice – perhaps intentionally so – that was immediately taken up. (With the faintest suggestion of effort, the young man responded to his friend's childish boisterousness.)

'Next time we won't ask you at all!'

'Then I shall come in disguise. You won't know me.'

'No one admitted without an engraved invitation!'

'I'll forge one.'

'What? A Mortimer turn criminal?'

The cloud — if cloud it had been between the two young men — had vanished; good humour reigned supreme; thanks, Mortimer felt, to himself.

'There was a Mortimer in Elizabeth's reign who was hanged . . .'

'And there was a Boston who was fined five shillings last year!'

'Then we've both got bad blood!'

'So let's go inside and purify it with some of Pa's best wine!'

It was half past one and the first guests were not expected until two. As the friends entered, the house was heard to be in a state of agreeable agitation, which manifested itself in a pattering of feet, a slamming of doors and a distant rattle of glass and plate.

'Who's coming today?' Mortimer spoke carelessly.

'We've sent out cards to everyone!'

'The same as usual, then.'

Lewis flushed. Whether he intended to or not, Richard Mortimer always managed to make him feel uncomfortable.

'No! It's not the same at all!' he began indignantly; and then, as if remembering that this was to be a day of days, softened. 'You haven't seen her yet . . . my . . . the countess – my Valois! Oh she's lovely!'

Mortimer smiled as Lewis struggled to unburden his overflowing heart; the countess, who had never left his thoughts, was now in sole occupation of them.

'I can see you don't believe me,' he ended up, observing his friend's continuing smile. 'You're a cold fish, Richard Mortimer! Come and drink some wine and warm up!'

'The best? You said it would be the best! I won't have anything but the best.'

'Yes, it's—' began Lewis, then, realizing that his friend was making fun of him – and this time perhaps maliciously – stopped and frowned.

It was a strange friendship between these two young men. Neither ever felt really at ease in the other's company, yet somehow the attachment survived; and if either had been asked, in all truth and solemnity, whose good opinion he valued most, he would unhesitatingly have answered the other's.

The Mortimers were an ancient family, though not the titled branch of it. They were discreet, gentlemanly and almost painfully refined in their tastes. The boisterous display of the Bostons was utterly alien to their nature: and this display was seen at its most painful in Lewis. He was absurd, he was ridiculous, he was an impossibly vulgar young man ... yet Richard Mortimer felt himself deeply bound to him as to a curiously vulnerable part of himself. Frequently ashamed of him, often witty at his expense, Mortimer was instantly filled with remorse when he perceived his humour had struck home.

He was about to disarm his friend – as he knew he so easily could – by a frank apology for his jibe, when Mrs Boston's voice, quavering and petulant, called Lewis from upstairs. Somewhat coolly Lewis excused himself and left Mortimer to find his own way to the principal drawing-room where 'the function' – as Mr Boston chose to call his frequent entertainings – was to take place.

'I'm sorry,' whispered Mortimer hopelessly towards the angular staircase, up which the unmistakably offended Lewis had stalked like an animated stained-glass window.

As the image occurred to him, Mortimer lapsed into his faintly contemptuous smile. Mockery of the Bostons seemed inevitable. Their mansion was even more Gothic inside than out. Pointed arches and fretted woodwork confronted the eye at every turn; the whole place so resembled a cathedral that it was to be wondered that the Bostons hadn't dressed their servants in vestments instead of livery.

Although not five years old, the mansion was

rumoured to be haunted – not by a headless monk or ghastly, walled-up nun, but by the ghost of the architect who had been killed by falling from a turret while inspecting the carving. His gloomy, battered visage had been seen – notably by Henrietta, Lewis's younger sister – peering in at various windows with an expression of gloom and dismay. It was possible that he was upset by what the Bostons had done to his design. In particular, the principal drawing-room. Here the architect had made his masterpiece and created a thorough-going chapel that might not have been out of place in Lincoln or Canterbury. One couldn't but admire the vaulted ceiling and the severely ecclesiastical windows with their delicate tracery of stonework. Mr Boston had been second to none in his appreciation; but alas, it would seem he had loved not wisely but too well. It had been utterly devastated by an explosion of his own personal taste.

He had filled it with his most treasured purchases, the ransackery of the Haymarket, the Strand, and various ships from the Orient (or thereabouts) that had come into Shoreham Harbour when he'd happened to be there. Screens, urns and busts vied with one another in gilded splendour, and, by reason of several large mirrors in the Chinese style, multiplied themselves so hysterically that one felt that King Midas had come to dinner and hiccupped. Beside a heavily inlaid harpsichord ('the more you show the inlay, the more you show the outlay,' was Mr Boston's principle in furnishing) stood a monster vase, decorated with the arms of Schleswig-Holstein, that had been bought by Mr Boston to honour a German gentleman he had met in Shoreham and had invited to dinner under the unshakeable conviction that he was a count.

'Very 'andsome, sir, don't you think?'

A footman had come in with a goblet of wine for Mr Mortimer.

Mortimer accepted the wine and transferred his gaze to the object of the footman's admiration. It turned out to be a large porcelain pineapple liberally endowed with bees and butterflies.

'Oh yes . . . handsome . . . unusual . . . one might say, unique.'

'Mr Lewis bought it,' said the footman, approaching confidentially. Mortimer shrank away from him – and at the same time condemned himself for doing so. He was a much perplexed young man. Having come under the influence at a very early age of one Mr Archer, a private tutor with strongly republican sympathies (he had once been a friend of Tom Paine), Richard Mortimer had become that paradox, a youth with all the advantages of class who felt nothing but contempt for the indignity of it all. This same Mr Archer had been Lewis's tutor, too; but Lewis, bone-headed Lewis, had somehow failed to benefit to the same extent; and not all Mortimer's gentle mockery had been able to rid him of the ostentation and delight in social climbing that was the plague of all the Boston tribe.

'Ah! I was going to show it to you!' said Lewis, coming into the room briskly so that his watch-fobs chimed faintly as he moved. He came and stood beside Mortimer who seemed to be lost in awe at the pineapple.

'It's a surprise, you know.'

'It certainly is,' agreed Mortimer gravely.

'No, no! I mean what's inside.'

'Is there more, then?'

'Of course! It's to be in *her* honour! A sort of *coup-de-théâtre*.'

'Oh yes. The Valois lady.'

Mortimer glanced quickly at his friend's excited face, marvelled at the innocence thereon, and drank off his glass of wine.

'At least,' he said, turning away, 'here's something good that's come out of France!'

'The best – the best! Nothing but the best in this house!'

Mr Boston had bustled in, and, catching the praise

for his wine, expanded with pride. He was a resplendent, beaming little man with a tremendous number of fingers. He had once been a fair performer on the fiddle, and in his humbler days had given small music parties, accompanied on the harpsichord by his daughters' music teacher. But with increasing prosperity the fiddle had faded away, leaving only the ghost of itself behind, on which Mr Boston seemed to be playing wistful dances with inconceivable dexterity.

'Three pound the dozen. Full-bodied wine, that. Take care you ain't tipsy before Lewis's countess arrives!'

He laughed as Mortimer gravely promised he would try not to disgrace the function. 'I didn't mean it − I didn't mean it!' he said, and, playing a succession of trills on his ghostly fiddle, prattled on about his wine and the mountains of extravagant food that waited in the dining-room.

Mortimer smiled and listened, striving to restrain the expression of faint disgust that he knew was becoming almost habitual with him. Little by little, he felt his smile turning to stone. He found himself wondering why he had come. To oblige Lewis. His friend. His only friend. He felt oppressively empty and lonely; he half wished a calamity might befall Lewis to drive him to share in his own bleak loneliness.

★ ★ ★

The mirrors – in the Chinese style – had the effect of multiplying the guests as well as Mr Boston's treasures. By a quarter to three o'clock, a murmuring tide of wigs, feathers, pale shoulders and embroidered smiles seemed to be coming in and out, in and out, through the various ornamental openings in the walls. A dozen servants, all identical, brought wine in unison, and the tinkling crash of a dropped glass provoked flurries as far as the eye could see. The geometry of reflection was forever confusing the eye and teasing the mind; could that glamorous back belong with this raddled front? And could this dignified gentleman, conversing with his hostess, be the owner of those hands urgently scratching at a private place? Mirrors are the windows of the devil, overlooking nothing but a landscape of lies!

Already, everybody who was anybody in the district had arrived – together with a fair sprinkling of nobodies. This was an odd quality in Mr Boston, much deplored by his wife; no matter how high he aspired, he never forgot the lower rungs of the social ladder and always invited them. However, by way of compensation, he always promoted them out of their lawful station when introducing them. Nobody was a nobody at a Boston function.

The countess had not yet come. Mortimer, more

lonely than ever, moved among the throng, dispensing nods and smiles but finding no one to attract him. At a great distance, or in a mirror – it was hard to say which – he saw his father exchanging what were no doubt unpleasantries with Lady Bullock, ancient widow of Lancing Manor whom everybody kept thinking was dead and whose appearance did little to dispel the idea. And yet how sadly young her back looked – with her gown fiercely dragged in to fit her shrunken form; it might almost have been the back of a child parading in its mother's dress. Mr Mortimer, on the other hand, suffered no change from the mirror; he was immaculate all round.

Ah! there was Mr Archer! Eagerly Mortimer made his way to the sideboard where his old tutor was ensconced.

Mr Archer: saturnine man; high-principled moulder of the local young. Private tutor only to such as could afford him. ('Give me the pearls and I'll cast them, privately, before the little swine of your choice!')

'I understand we are to be honoured with a Valois,' said Mr Archer, spilling a little of his wine in his cravat. He smirked at his pupil who responded with an expressive glance round the room.

'All this – all this vulgar and lavish pantomime!' muttered Mortimer.'And for what?' He spoke with great freedom to Mr Archer. Although a world of class divided them, they met on the common ground of ideals, and Mortimer felt that with his tutor he could be his truest self. 'Here we all are,' he went on with a sense of relief, 'crammed into uncomfortable clothes, ready to stuff ourselves with enough food and drink to keep a family of labourers for a year, because – because some highborn whore from Versailles is about to honour us with her presence!'

Mr Archer nodded approvingly; he derived immense satisfaction from seeing his teaching blossom so vigorously. As if to check his pupil's exercise, he, too, glanced round the teeming room.

His gaze, crossing one of the mirrors, was caught by a tight, pompous back hurrying away towards a sour-faced shabby individual leaning beside a singularly bored-looking youth. An unappetizing pair.

'Ah! Archer and young Mortimer!'

With a distinct shock, Mr Archer recognized himself and his pupil now being addressed by the front of the tight, pompous back. It was Dr Stump, his arch-enemy. Together they represented opposite poles of political thought ... if Dr Stump's opinions could be dignified by the term thought. The doctor was a royalist to his heart's core and wore a black mourning band every January 30th to commemorate the execution of Charles I. Mr

Archer responded by wearing a similar band each May 29th to commemorate the Restoration of the Monarchy: Death of Liberty, Burial of Equality, etc.

'How's your mother, young man?' asked the doctor. 'Ha – ha! I should be telling you! Much the same – much the same! No cause for concern. Look at this, Archer! Fascinating, eh?'

He held up a small, leather-bound book and obligingly read out: '*Mémoires justificatifs de la Comtesse de la Motte-Valois.*'

Mr Archer and his pupil exchanged glances.

'Her book, y'know,' went on Dr Stump. 'Thought I'd get her to sign it. Remarkable lady, from all accounts.'

'And an outrageous one, I may add,' said Mr Archer coolly. In the hope of being engaged in conversation, the tutor had been at some pains to make himself familiar with the great scandal of three years ago when the countess was reputed to have been publicly tried in Paris for stealing the Queen of France's diamond necklace.

'My dear fellow – my dear fellow, we don't understand the half of it!'

So far as Dr Stump was concerned, this was absolutely true. The countess's memoirs were in French and the doctor had been baffled. All he'd been able to gather had been a quantity of high-sounding names, some of which had lodged in his memory.

'People like the Duke of Orleans, y'know, and that Cardinal what's-his-name . . . and the Queen of France and that Princess Polly something. You can't talk of ordinary scandals where a Valois is concerned. These are great folk, Archer. Mortimer, here, will understand what I mean. They're playing for stakes way out of our scope. I'm looking forward to meeting her, I can tell you! A Valois, descended from an ancient line of kings! It's all in here, y'know . . .'

The countess had still not arrived. Lewis Boston, like a troubled dragon-fly, flitted and hovered, flitted and hovered, darted outside, hovered for the sound of a carriage . . . then back again. The possibility of the lady's not turning up had struck him forcibly. He staggered. What would he do? Suicide was a coward's way out. Perhaps he could turn hermit and write passionate, melancholy verses?

She! His whole being ached to behold her again; his very soul got down on its knees before her. Besides, if she didn't come, he'd look such a fool . . .

Bemusedly, he saw the back of Richard Mortimer's head; he saw his sister Henrietta, ribboned like a flagship, arguing with Eliza; then everyone turned away from him and he saw the door suddenly burst open and catch his pa on the side of the head. He saw Mr Boston staggering, with an astonished look on his face; he saw—

'The Countess de la Motte-Valois!' shouted a footman.

A wind seemed to breathe down the back of Lewis's neck. He trembled. The room grew dim with shining as the small avalanche of beauty that had emerged from the yellow casket on the Brighton road advanced to greet him.

Ah! Breath of Versailles – perfume imperial . . . rustling, smiling . . . eyes endowed with more than natural brightness, cheeks of cream; hand outstretched, the other lost in a cloud of blue silk. The best – the best the house has to offer!

Mr Boston, dazed by the door and what had come through it, tottered after, playing what seemed to be the ghost of a cello . . .

'You came . . . you came . . .' breathed Lewis, feeling unaccountably that his ears had caught fire and were now burning like torches.

'You CAME!'

'Oh Mr Boston! I promised – I promised!'

She promised, she promised! How sweetly the words fell from her soft lips! How widely her silken eyes opened – and engulfed him! He bent to kiss her wrist . . . strange aromas reached his brain. She moved away – and he all but fell.

He was gossamer, he was thistledown, he walked on air in the beauty's rustling wake. 'May I present . . . May I present . . . my – the Countess . . . May I present . . .'

Ha! May he present, indeed! He'd not have parted with her for heaven and earth!

'May I present . . . ?'

Briefly taken at his word, he lost her to his ma and sisters; then he took back his gift, only to lose her again, to Mr Boston, who was walking backwards and appeared to be performing on a double-bass.

Still walking backwards, Mr Boston reached the sideboard and trod on Mr Archer's foot. Instantly he made an inspired promotion.

'Madame! May I present the Very Reverend Dr Archer?'

She curtsied. Oh my God! Collapse of wine-damp tutor within himself. Tongue like glue. Forgot Tom Paine . . .

'And Professor Stump, the eminent physician—'

'Enchanted!'

'Madame! Madame! This book! If you'd be so kind?'

'A pleasure!'

Book changes hands. Lewis scowls.

'What shall I write with?'

A pencil! Panic. Who has a pencil? Mr Archer

searched himself to the bone; Mr Boston instituted wholesale inquiries. Richard Mortimer, until then retired, gracefully offered his own. Lewis glared and cursed himself. Had he thought of it, he would have cut off the tip of his finger and let her sign her name in his blood. But he hadn't thought of it; and now it was too late. Mortimer of the high ideals had won the lady with his pencil. And it wasn't even gold.

She wrote, putting the tip of her tongue between her teeth. A crowd pressed; watched her signature being formed. Awed admiration. Dr Stump absolutely overcome.

'Look, Archer, look! She's written me name in it as well! What a woman!' He dabbed his dazzled eyes. 'Look, Lewis, look!'

Impatiently Lewis lingered to stare at the doctor's most prized possession, then turned to follow his dream when he saw, with a sense of outrage, that Richard Mortimer had forestalled him.

'Madame!'

The lady paused, then turned in wide surprise.

'Sir?'

Mortimer felt suddenly out of breath — as if he'd run a great distance instead of having taken half a dozen sauntering steps. You and I, he thought — and at the same time bitterly rebuked himself for thinking it

— are closer together in blood and breeding than to any others in this room. We should understand each other . . .

'Sir?'

'M-my pencil—'

'Oh! Forgive me! Here! Here it is! Charming instrument. So elegant.'

'Keep it! A – a remembrance!'

'Of what?'

'Of . . . me.' He smiled.

Out of the corner of his eye, he glimpsed Mr Archer staring at him mournfully. He carefully avoided seeing Lewis.

'Why, Mr Mortimer! You travel as swiftly as your friend!'

'You lend us wings!' The compliment was neatly turned; Mortimer felt a glow of pleasure . . .

'Pardon? I do not understand? Wings?'

'You are very beautiful—'

'*Oh là là!* I am old enough to be your mother!' she chuckled, and added: 'Come. I shall show you something interesting.'

Imperceptibly she seemed to beckon and create a little circle of seclusion about herself.

'Now,' she murmured. 'This should interest a young gentleman.' She drew a small roll of paper out of her purse, unfurled it and showed it to Mortimer. It was the patent of her ancestry.

'You see?' she said, running her finger across the paper. 'There is Henri II – a Valois. And there is the Baronne de Saint-Remy Valois. Here is Henri III, and see! Only five generations – one, two, three, four, five! – and here am I: Jeanne de Saint-Remy Valois. That is me!'

There was a smile of almost childish pride on her face. She put her head on one side and peered at Mortimer. She nodded, rolled up her ancestors and put them back in her purse. She tapped Mortimer lightly with her fan. 'Come,' she said, as one might speak to an importunate child, 'we must mingle with the others.'

Mortimer followed her. It was impossible for him not to be gratified by how easily he had displaced his friend.

'Silence! Silence everybody!'

Lewis was shouting, shouting at the top of his voice. He was standing by the porcelain pineapple. He had been following the queen of his heart and the viper in his bosom with increasing rage. Bloody thief! He wept inwardly. I hate you, Richard Mortimer! I hate you – I hate you! He felt himself on the verge of childish tears. He had withdrawn to the pineapple and helplessly watched in all of the mirrors as all of the countesses and all of the Mortimers smiled and sauntered and exchanged intimate murmurs regardless of the terrible eyes that watched them.

He'd seen the paper unrolled and immediately got it into his head that a tryst was being arranged and Mortimer was being shown where. He'd challenge Mortimer to a duel. That's what he'd do! No! Better! The grand surprise – the *coup-de-théâtre*! He'd have it now. He'd show his Valois what *real* gallantry was! Something rather finer than a cheap silver pencil!

'Silence, *please!*'

Half resentfully, the room quietened down. Mortimer shrugged his shoulders and stationed himself as close to the countess as he was able. Still he avoided his friend's eyes.

'Fetch me a candle!'

A stir of curiosity. What was it to be? Fireworks? Anything was possible with the Bostons. The candle entered.

'Draw the curtains, Henrietta!'

Cries of mock alarm as the room went into a jerky darkness. Frantically Lewis glared to see what Mortimer might be doing. Perhaps he'd taken the lady outside? He knew he was being perfectly ridiculous; but he was so *angry*. His father approached, bearing the candle which glimmered and danced in all the mirrors like a troupe of fireflies. Mr Boston's face, lit from underneath, looked eerie and devilish. Lewis was momentarily appalled. Then he lifted the pineapple and revealed what seemed to be a painted paper egg nestling on a dish. What was it?

Lewis deposited the pineapple on the floor and raised up the paper egg. It proved to be a balloon. Silken cords unravelled and concluded in a tiny wicker basket. Now Mr Boston advanced the candle to touch a wick inside the basket. Lewis's hands were trembling. Something was bound to go wrong. It always did for him.

But no! The candle flame appeared to give birth; it divided and the newborn flame spluttered, as if crying sparks; then it gathered in strength.

Lewis, feeling like a master magician, peered over the top of the glow at the dim, watchful host. Where was she? Surely she ought to shine in the dark? His heart was dark, and she shone there!

Mr Boston extinguished his candle. Lewis felt the frail balloon grow warm under his hands. It seemed alive. He began to release his hold.

He became aware that he was no longer holding the balloon. It was floating in air. It was rising; it was going up!

Higher and higher it rose, a drifting yellow moon in a vaulted night. Fascinated, Lewis watched it growing brighter and brighter as fluted shadows rushed down as if to embrace it. When would she notice . . . ?

'Look! Look! The arms of Valois! My family in the sky!'

Lit from within, the balloon's decorations glared forth unmistakably. Shields, fleurs-de-lis . . . shields, fleurs-de-lis . . . They should have been silver and gold, but the light turned them black. Black shields, black lilies . . .

'Look, look, my queen!' breathed Lewis ecstatically. 'I've put a moon in the sky for you! I've dressed it in your livery! Your moon, your sky! What more can love do?'

It was indeed the countess's moon, and would have been even more so if Mr Boston hadn't seen fit to have painted round the lower half: *A. Boston and Son. Importers of Fine Wines.* But still, thought Lewis, it was an added tribute. Match that, if you can, Richard Mortimer!

The moon began to wander, dispensing a doll-like radiance in drifting patches, pausing every now and then to admire itself in a passing mirror; then, with a toss of its head, it would be off again, bosomed in nothingness, floating in a cave of faces – marble, flesh, bronze and gilt . . .

'Ah! See how the little moon dances for me!'

A fan, briskly used, had caused the tiny planet to hop and jig.

The countess clapped in childish delight, and Lewis's heart swelled. At once another fan set up in business; gentlemen, having no fans, began to puff and blow – the universal darkness rendering their antics invisible. Everyone was laughing and clapping; the function was turning out to be a tremendous success. The balloon was quite tipsy now . . . a powerful advertisement for the Importers of Fine Wines!

Happily Lewis blundered his way towards the countess, blowing as he went with the best of them and provoking little squeals of surprise as he inadvertently puffed in a heated face. The swinging light tipped strange visions all around him. Fans fluttered like great black moths and swollen-cheeked faces huffed up a dark wind. Dr Stump was nearly exploding; Mr Archer, his mouth wide open, seemed to have blown himself dizzy . . . Now Lewis glimpsed the countess. She was radiant with delight; her lips were parted, revealing teeth like diamonds.

'Look out! Look out!'

My God! What had happened? The balloon basket had tipped too violently. The flame had touched a silken cord. A thin golden worm was crawling up it. In a moment the moon was a sun – engulfed in fire!

An uproar had broken out. Shouts, cries of alarm, stumbling of feet, crashing of furniture and glasses as everyone fought to avoid the blazing object that was dropping downwards, tearing itself asunder as it came.

'Water! Fetch water!'

But the fire, rapid in its growth on account of the varnish employed in the balloon's decoration, was equally rapid in consuming itself. Down, down, down came the poor moon, dwindling into a sullen, cobwebby ghost. It seemed to have vanished altogether, when there was an abrupt explosion of sparks.

A woman screamed. God in heaven, what a scream! Like an animal! A sense of panic instantly swept through the room. Every man feared for his own wife or daughter. A scream is anonymous; no one screams with an accent. A great rush began in all directions, accompanied by an urgent calling of names. Then someone had the good sense to draw back the curtains.

Sunlight streamed in. The air was full of patterns of smoke and swarming black specks. Who had screamed?

It had been the countess. The falling fire had brushed against her delicate muslin cape and set it smouldering. Although she could not have been much injured, there was a look of ghastly terror on her face; it was as if fire was her deepest and most terrible fear.

Lewis flung himself towards her. Among many

turbulent emotions was the entirely natural thought that he must reach her before Mortimer did. He had rescued her once – he would rescue her again! It was his destiny. He was a born rescuer. Earnest and serious was his face; bright were his eyes with all the unreasonable hopes of youth.

He reached her. He seized hold of her cape, meaning to snatch it away with one grand gesture. Perhaps he was being a little ostentatious, but no Boston could have been otherwise. He pulled at the cape; he tugged it; he tore it. It refused to come away, and there followed a brief but ignominious struggle between Lewis, the countess and the cape.

He cried out in sudden distress as he felt a sudden sharp pain in the third finger of his left hand. Pins, pins! Why do they use so many pins? Suddenly he succeeded. The cape came away. He flung it to the ground and stamped on it with a St-George-and-the-dragon-like zeal. He felt wonderfully happy.

He did not seem to be aware that the countess was staring at him. Her eyes were blazing far more dangerously than had the ill-fated balloon. She began to sway. People moved aside to give her air. As they did so, the sunlight rushed through and lit up her nearly naked back and bosom. She screamed again.

Two livid marks had been exposed: one on her

shoulder and the other just below the swell of her breast. Puckered and hideously unsightly, they were unmistakable. They were the scars of a branded criminal. Small wonder she had screamed at the touch of fire: a public executioner's iron had burned her and marked her for ever with a 'V'.

'V for *voleur*,' said a voice contemptuously, that Lewis instantly recognized as Mortimer's. 'That means thief.'

'*Voleuse*,' corrected Mr Archer helplessly. 'But thief all the same.'

The countess said nothing at all. She had done the only thing possible in the circumstances. She had fainted.

Dazedly Lewis picked up the remnants of the cape. He knelt and, with confused notions of gallantry, attempted to cover up his own and the lady's shame. He looked up; he looked round, as if hoping that in one of the Chinese-style mirrors – just one! – the awful calamity would not have taken place.

CHAPTER THREE

THERE ARE CERTAIN individuals, generally of striking presence and volatile nature, who have the ability to become detached from their private calamities, leaving them to stink out other people's houses. They resemble lizards, who, caught by the tail, abandon that limb and rush away to grow another, leaving the severed member, at first wriggling with residual energy, to fester and smell. Whether such individuals are put on earth by God or the Devil is a political rather than a theological question. Such an individual was the Countess de la Motte-Valois.

Already, as a consequence of her greed for a fortune in diamonds, she had left behind in France a ruined cardinal, a discredited queen and a throne undermined. And the infection was still spreading.

Now, in humbler Lancing, she had bequeathed a smell of disgrace to the Gothic mansion of an Importer of Fine Wines whose only sin had been a passion for social success. Like the lizard, she had rushed away, leaving her tail to rot in the house: the luckless Bostons were unjustly neglected by their friends and avoided by their neighbours. It was as mysterious and as inevitable as sickness. Only Dr Stump, being of that noble profession that scorns danger to bring comfort to houses stricken with the plague, continued to call. He had a patient in the mansion.

The sharp pain Lewis had felt in his finger on the day of the calamity had not been caused by a pin. Teeth had done it. The countess had bitten him; she had bitten clean through his glove and drawn blood. He was very worried about it.

Apparently disregarding the house's seeming collapse into ruins and his family's wandering distractedly from room to room as if in search of buried guests, he kept producing his finger for Dr Stump's inspection – the good doctor having stayed to attend his hysterical hostess.

Actually Lewis had been so distraught by the total overthrow of his fortunes, the nightmarish rushing away of everybody, his mother screaming senselessly about all the uneaten food, that he thought he'd go mad. His painful finger was the only thing he could fix his thoughts on.

At first Dr Stump had flatly refused to believe him, had told him to stop talking nonsense and had kept pushing him out of the way. He declined even to spare the finger a glance. But when at last he did, and saw the actual marks of teeth, he became quite fascinated. He had never seen anything like it. Right through the glove. (Obligingly Lewis had produced that bloodstained item.) Amazing. He touched the finger respectfully . . . almost as if the Valois teeth were still embedded in it.

'It hurts,' said Lewis, withdrawing his hand sharply.

'You may not lose the nail,' said Dr Stump. 'But then again, you might. I'll call and look at it tomorrow.'

All that night it hurt furiously and kept Lewis from sleeping. He got up several times and wandered about the house, holding his finger upright, like St John the Baptist. Henrietta, his younger sister – a plain child of fourteen with a huge literary appetite – had once read a grisly German romance and was able to warn him about vampires who, by sucking their victims' blood, leave them fatally infected. Although she admitted that the great vein of the neck was the usual site of operations, she did not think that fingers could be ruled out altogether. Irritably, Lewis had dismissed her; but now, in the midst of the mansion's Gothic night, with every sculptured arch a tomb of shadows, with uncanny rustlings proceeding from the rooms downstairs – doubtless the work of banqueting mice – and his mind in a turmoil, the possibility of there having been something unnatural about the countess did not seem so improbable. Anxiously he sucked the tooth-holes and produced exquisite torments in the base of his nail.

Early next morning, without waiting for the doctor's promised call, he hastened to Dr Stump, had his finger examined and dressed, and his arm put in a sling.

As a consequence of this, his acute shame and humiliation diminished and presently sank into a state of gloom that found its expression in a desire to be alone. He spent many hours staring in his mirror, in an effort at self-examination.

What had become of him? He was pale; he was hollow-eyed. His hair looked a wreck and even his tongue was unhealthy. He touched his injured fingertip and produced a feathery convulsion of nerves ... When it died down, he imagined he could smell the countess's perfume ...

He sighed. What could life still hold for him? One or two grim possibilities suggested themselves, but were rejected. At length he approached Mr Boston with the request that he be sent to the vineyards in France on family business. He was sure he would do better abroad.

Unluckily, any mention of France was taken as an indirect reference to the countess. His request was curtly denied and he was asked, somewhat unreasonably, never to mention 'that woman' again.

For a time it had been supposed that the lady had been an impostor and not a countess at all, and that they'd all been cleverly taken in. They were almost ready to be amused by the woman's effrontery; but Dr Stump, no doubt protecting his autographed volume, denied them even this crumb of comfort. He was able to assure them that the Countess de la Motte-Valois was well-known to have been branded in the manner they had all observed. There was no question of her not being a Valois. Nor, for that matter, was there any question that she'd been treated inhumanly and unjustly.

'Then she *was* guilty!' said Mrs Boston with bitter satisfaction.

'No, no!' exclaimed the doctor, eager to justify the daughter of the Valois. 'You misunderstand! I meant she *has* been treated monstrously! I assure you of it. I have read her book – or, at least, parts of it. She was a pawn, ma'am, a hapless pawn crushed between a prince of the Church and the Queen of France. We are dealing here with great folk. Tremendous concerns. The necklace was a trifle – an excuse. People like the Valois don't pilfer trinkets! Descendant of ancient kings, y'know . . .'

'A branded woman is a marked woman,' said Mrs Boston obstinately. 'And that's the disgrace! She must have been a thief, or they wouldn't have branded her like that!'

'I don't care if she nicked the queen's necklace or not!' said Lewis hotly (any discussion of the countess caused his blood to become heated). 'She bit my finger to the bone!'

His nail had at last come off. He had been able to lift it out of its bed, watched by the fascinated Henrietta. It seemed that in the basements of certain castles in the Black Forest – with which she was unwholesomely familiar – the pulling out of fingernails was almost a nightly occurrence. She had a scholarly interest in seeing it being done.

The resulting raw pink patch, though no longer painful, was weirdly tender, producing disembodied sensations when touched. It was also unsightly. Mrs Boston couldn't bear to look at it and ordered Lewis to wear a glove. It reminded her of 'that woman'.

'I don't deny,' said Dr Stump defensively, 'that she's a lady of strong passions—'

'And strong teeth!'

'But think of her position,' went on the doctor, ignoring Henrietta's pert interruption. 'Suddenly exposed! Her terrible humiliation revealed to all! She is at bay! She turns, desperate – not knowing how to defend herself. Yes! This royal lady – this daughter of kings – this Valois! Terrible in her rage . . . like the lioness – the queen of nature—' Here Dr Stump paused, pleased by the aptness of the comparison. 'Like the queenly lioness, she bites! Yes – she bites! I see nothing shameful there,' finished up Dr Stump, having convinced himself to his own satisfaction.

'But don't you think,' said Henrietta, who made up in wit whatever she might have lacked in feminine grace and charm, 'that in the circumstances, discretion would have been the better part of Valois?'

Dr Stump looked at her sharply; was met with wide-eyed innocence. However, the doctor was sufficiently human to allow the corners of his mouth to twitch and turn up.

Henrietta's witticism had the honour of being repeated wherever Dr Stump thought it might go down well. It was by means of the doctor – who betrayed his patients' confidences as readily as he obtained them – that interesting news was carried from household to household over a very wide area. Though the Bostons were still not visited, news of them was freely available wherever there was an invalid in the house. A stranger, unaware of the busy doctor, would have supposed that it was Nature herself, compensating the bed-ridden with a mysterious sense of what was going on inside the Gothic mansion on the hill.

Three and a half miles to the west of Lancing, on the

outskirts of the village of Salvington, the Mortimers lived in a fine, red-brick house built in the time of Queen Anne. Every afternoon, after visiting the Bostons, Dr Stump would drive up in his gig, drawn by an animal as sleek and tightly filled as himself. Scarcely waiting for his vehicle to halt, he would bounce out of his seat, bounce into the house and up the stairs as if he'd been struck by a racket; it was impossible not to feel that, if he met with a wall or a closed door, he would strike it and bounce all the way back.

He came to attend Richard Mortimer's mother, who had been an invalid for many years. No one, least of all Dr Stump, really knew what was wrong with her; she had been ill, in one way or another, since the birth of her only son. It was as if the effort of producing another life had drained her of some vital fluid, leaving her a weary, lustreless lady, with the remains of beauty clinging to her like a cobweb. Her malady, though always mysterious, had never seemed grave to Dr Stump. Her life was not despaired of; it was only the living of it that gave cause for concern. Lately he'd introduced into the house a respectable nurse by the name of Mrs Coker; but this was more for appearance than necessity.

'And how goes the busy world today, Stump?' enquired Mr Mortimer when the doctor had descended after inspecting his patient and finding her 'no better, no worse'. Mr Mortimer was an exceedingly tall, pleasant-faced gentleman who, though he invariably enquired about the world, was not deeply interested in it.

Dr Stump, seating himself in the small, graceful parlour that the Mortimers inhabited every afternoon, beamed and repeated Henrietta's witticism. It fell a little flat. Mr Mortimer smiled faintly.

'I'm delighted,' he said, 'that they can make a joke of it.'

'Oh really, sir!' exclaimed Richard. 'I think it's very witty! Give credit where it's due!'

As Dr Stump had spoken, a picture of the Bostons had risen vividly before him. Suddenly he saw them, utterly impossible . . . being hysterical, ludicrously dignified, distracted, laughing, shouting up and down their fantastic house . . . and then overwhelming one with gladness and affection.

He felt a sharp pang of regret for having neglected them for so long. He had fully persuaded himself that delicacy had dictated this. He really hadn't wanted to face Lewis after the calamity. He felt his friend would have been even more distressed by his presence. Had he for a moment thought otherwise, he would have gone directly; but he knew himself well enough to fear his own uncontrollably mocking tongue.

Had anyone suggested to him that guilt had kept

him away as much as delicacy, he would have been much surprised.

'I have no doubt,' said Mr Mortimer quietly, 'that in the – the atmosphere of *that* household, the remark must have seemed more sparkling than perhaps it would, say, here?'

Dr Stump reddened, and Richard, observing the doctor's discomfiture, came to his rescue with an enquiry about Lewis's finger.

'As you know, the nail is off now,' said Dr Stump with a look of gratitude to Richard. 'But there's no sign of infection. Clean as a whistle. A remarkable injury. Right through the glove. Amazing . . . one might almost say, unique!'

'Not quite,' said Mr Mortimer smoothly. 'I understand that the lady has bitten through leather before. I heard from a friend of mine in town that she bit the poor wretch whose task it was to apply the – the iron to her. She bit through his jerkin and drew blood. It would seem the lady has quite a taste for leather! I assume Master Boston was wearing kid and not cotton?'

Mr Mortimer smiled broadly at the neatness of his own expression.

'What would you have had her do, Mr Mortimer?' demanded Dr Stump, with barely suppressed indignation. 'Submit meekly to the great disgrace? Remember, sir, she is a Valois! And even if there was not a soul standing by to raise a finger—'

'Do you blame them?' put in Mr Mortimer. 'They might have lost it!'

He laughed with the utmost good humour and flashed a glance at his son as if to demonstrate how easily Henrietta's witticism had been eclipsed. Richard sighed, reflecting how much he'd inherited from his father, and how little he was grateful for it.

'I shall call on Lewis tomorrow,' he said abruptly. He had been consumed with a sudden longing to escape from his home.

When Dr Stump had gone, Mortimer looked at his father.

'I take it you have no objection, sir, to my calling on the Bostons?'

'I neither approve nor disapprove,' said Mr Mortimer coolly. 'All I ask is that you spare me their wit.'

Chapter Four

THE BOSTONS HAD fallen victims to a new panic. They were a family much given to sudden alarms; in moments great excitement changed to oppressive gloom, laughter to tears, affection to violent recrimination. Like most families who'd risen in a single generation, they worried painfully about the sturdiness of the ladder they'd constructed and climbed themselves. Would it continue to support them – or would it break and cast them ignominiously back into the depths from which they'd risen? They never thought of falling halfway; it was the depths or nothing.

The new panic was financial. The captain of a vessel bringing in goods for Mr Boston had also brought some unsettling political news from France, where a great part of the Boston fortune was invested in high-interest loans. At once Mr Boston had rushed off to Drummond and Coutts – his bankers in town – to arrange for his capital to be converted into gold and pulled out. In a flash the whole family saw themselves destitute and Mr Boston in prison for debt. When Mortimer called, they were at breakfast in 'the office', wondering if and when Mr Boston would return.

The office was not a place of business; it was the breakfast-parlour and the one retreat in the mansion where the architect had relented from the Gothic. To enter it was like stepping inside a gaily papered box in which, perhaps, the rest of the house had arrived, been unpacked and set up in all its toy-like grandeur. It had begun as the architect's office, and the name had somehow survived.

Here, among furniture the Bostons no longer admired, stood a set of ugly, throne-like chairs in which, with dynastic anarchy and hysterical solemnity, the children had played at kings and crowned each other to rule for a day.

'Who's monarch today?' asked Mortimer, seating himself in response to a preoccupied invitation. He was hoping to revive memories of more carefree times and to avoid any mention of the unlucky function. He was unaware that the strained atmosphere of the breakfast-table proceeded from another cause entirely.

'The monarchy's fallen,' said Henrietta curtly. 'We are now a republic of unequals.'

Mrs Boston rose. The sight of the assured, well-born Mortimer boy upset her. He and his family would be the first to turn away from them when they were begging in the streets. She remembered with a shudder that the Mortimers had been among the first to desert them after the countess had been assisted away by her coachman.

'Pray excuse me,' she said. 'I must go and have a headache – that is, I have a headache and must go and lie down.'

She hurried from the room with the sudden idea of sorting through her jewels and offering them to Mr Boston on his return so that he might sell them and keep the family afloat.

'It's the French trouble,' said Lewis evasively. Knowing how ready Mortimer was to mock any concern over money, he was particularly anxious not to discuss the family's affairs in detail. 'Pa's gone to town to see what can be done.'

He hoped this would suffice and perhaps convey a better class of impression than the facts warranted.

Mortimer looked surprised. 'I don't see how—' he began, when Henrietta, who had no particular scruples about anything, informed Mortimer that they were all about to be ruined unless Mr Boston could achieve prodigies of financial dexterity. They would have to sell the house, of course—

'Be quiet, Henrietta!' snapped Eliza, her older sister, who, at seventeen, was an almost vulgarly pretty girl who had inherited her father's lively brown eyes and her mother's nerves. Mortimer often found himself thinking about her, but always recoiled.

'Henrietta's exaggerating,' said Lewis, furious to find himself blushing. 'It's just that my father had some news yesterday of a new uproar in Paris. You know the sort of thing,' he went on, endeavouring to sound easy and unconcerned. 'Crowds wasting their time round the Palais-Royal, reading rubbishy pamphlets and listening to the usual mischief-makers. My father says the trouble is that they've got no firm hand at the helm. He thinks that until some sound businessman advises their king and puts everything on a solid financial footing, it's impossible to have any confidence in France. That's why he's gone to Drummond and Coutts – to arrange about calling in some loans. He says it's the only sensible, responsible thing to do: pull out until things settle down. He really feels,' finished up Lewis, feeling pleased with his lucid grasp of finance, 'that unless that king of theirs acts quickly and firmly, the whole country will go to the dogs.'

'Go to the dogs?' mused Mortimer, unable to keep the irony out of his voice. Listening to Lewis's arrogant and selfish exposition, Mortimer found himself getting angry. Lewis was a fool. He knew nothing and cared less about the lofty idealism that was striving to put an end to the age-old agony of France. Rubbishy pamphlets and mischief-makers! How dared he! All that mattered to the Bostons was profit – no matter who paid it or how.

'Go to the dogs. Just what does that expression really mean? Will packs of wild dogs really inherit the land? Will they run about biting legs and eating babies? Will they rush through the streets of Paris with the private parts of princesses in their jaws?'

'What a horrible thing to say!' exclaimed Eliza, putting down a piece of toast and reddening.

'It's your brother's expression – not mine.'

'It was just an expression,' said Lewis. 'You know perfectly well!'

'But it still meant something. When you throw something to the dogs, you throw it to be eaten.'

'You know quite well I didn't mean dogs literally. And anyway, I don't want to argue about it,' he added with a frown. Mortimer was irritating him. Mortimer was so much more astute than he was, and so much better able to twist words.

'Why don't you want to argue about it, Lewis?' pursued Mortimer, who resented Lewis's off-hand dismissal of ideas. He found himself becoming more and more heated.

'Who *are* the dogs you meant, then? You can only

mean the poor. Yes! They're dogs all right! They're certainly dogs when they clamour for justice and their rights! But of course, when they're meek and obliging, then they work like horses, they're as strong as oxen, they're as busy as bees! In fact, they're anything but human beings, like you and me!'

'What about rats?' said Henrietta, feeling that her brother was not equal to combating Mortimer's eloquence. 'You left out rats, Mr Mortimer. You know, the little creatures that desert sinking ships. To change the subject, we were sorry you and your father left us so quickly after the countess's accident. And we were even sorrier that you waited nine days before seeing fit to come back!'

Mortimer felt his face burning with shame; his eyes filled with stinging tears of anger as he stared at plain, dumpy Henrietta. To have his own behaviour thus exposed and criticized was extraordinarily painful. He then said something he regretted even as the words were leaving his lips.

'Oh yes – the rats and the sinking ship. I would have thought they were more like the financiers who pull out until things settle down.'

Lewis half rose from his seat; he clenched his fists and gave a sharp gasp of pain as he inadvertently pressed on his raw finger. Henrietta, her mouth open in eager terror, wondered what she might be about to witness ... when her mother came back into the room.

Mrs Boston was now wearing a pair of ruby earrings that Mr Boston had given her on her birthday. If everything else went, she hoped she might be allowed to keep them. She looked at the distracted table with some uncertainty.

'We were talking about France,' said Lewis, sitting down with a savage scowl at Mortimer, as if enjoining him to keep the peace for Mrs Boston's sake.

'I've asked you never to mention that subject again,' said Mrs Boston ungratefully. As far as she was concerned, France and the Countess de la Motte-Valois were one and the same thing. Ever since that woman had come into their lives, there had been nothing but grief, trouble and disgrace. She was unshakeably convinced that the countess was directly responsible, not only for her son's injury, but for the dreadful uproar in Paris and Mr Boston's present worries. While seated at her jewel-box, she'd felt like screaming and tearing the countess's hair out.

Mortimer, controlling himself rather more deftly than Lewis managed, asked courteously after Mrs Boston's headache, and shortly after left the house.

He began to ride away, then paused to glance back at the great vulgar mansion with the sun blaring out of the turret windows. It really was like a brutish medieval castle built on the flesh and bones of the voiceless oppressed. How many poor wretches in distant France were being bled white to keep such a place in luxury?

He set off again, this time at a gallop – as if to blow out of his head all the feelings of sick anger and regret that were stifling him. But he was glad he hadn't compromised his ideals. He'd held to his own convictions even at the risk of offending his friends. That at least was something. It would have been cheap and easy to nod and smile and seem not to care ... as his own father was so adept at doing.

Unconsciously he slowed his horse to a walk. He was in no great hurry to reach his home. What if, as Henrietta had declared, the Bostons were really in danger of being ruined? Not very likely; they were always panicking. And even if they were, it would be in a good cause ... Mortimer frowned, momentarily uncertain of his own feelings.

He shook his head and allowed his horse to choose its own pace and find its own way back. He would have to make it up with the Bostons. He would give things a day or so to blow over, then he'd call again. He could rely on them having forgotten the argument. He'd make an effort; he'd put himself out and really charm them out of their trees!

When he reached his home, his father was reading the *London Chronicle*. Mr Mortimer looked up at his son.

'What news from your Bostons? What epigrams today?'

'They are a republic of unequals,' said Mortimer, remembering Henrietta's expression and falling into his father's slightly indolent tones. 'What news in the *Chronicle*, sir?'

'Poor de Launay's been killed in Paris. In the street. That means Philippe will be a marquis now. He's not much older than you ...'

Mr Mortimer gazed at his son with a small spark of interest. 'Yes ... a marquis at nineteen ...'

He handed Richard the newspaper. 'Read it for yourself.'

He stood up to his considerable height and left the room, murmuring again, 'A marquis at nineteen,' as if, somehow, it was a singularly bitter blow.

How or why the Marquis de Launay, Governor of the Bastille, had met his end did not remotely concern him.

CHAPTER FIVE

MR ARCHER HAD once had a cold – a bad, heavy, thick cold that had lain on his chest like a wet blanket. Then fever had stalked into his monastic rooms and laid him even lower. He'd summoned Dr Stump, who, setting aside political differences, had dosed him and arranged for Mrs Coker – Mrs Mortimer's attendant nurse – to visit twice a week and maintain the feeble flicker of life.

Mr Archer recovered from the cold – but not from Mrs Coker. She kept up her visits, on Fridays and Mondays, and enriched Mr Archer's mind with details of life in a high-class establishment like the Mortimers'.

Reluctantly he paid her a small stipend for her offices, which she always received with the glassy discretion of an official taking a bribe. If, for any reason, he forgot, or was absorbed in a book, she came and stood at his elbow and stared at the back of his head until he became aware of her. She never asked.

As Mr Archer was unmarried and Mrs Coker a seasoned widow, it was commonly supposed that she had designs on his liberty as well as her meagre wage.

Now, towards the end of July, Mr Archer fell victim to another cold, and Mrs Coker brought him, on her Friday visit, a copy of the *London Chronicle* she had 'tidied away' from the Mortimers' parlour. She knew that gentlemen liked to read the newspaper and she watched red-nosed, red-eyed, chesty Mr Archer with maternal indulgence as he endeavoured to hide himself behind her thoughtful gift. Suddenly he put it down. His eyes were bright.

'At last!' he exclaimed. 'At last – at last!' (His actual expression had been 'Add last!' – his nose being totally obstructed.)

Mrs Coker folded her arms and put her head on one side. There was a gentle smile on her broad, fleshy face.

'Something cheerful in the newspaper, Mr Archer?'

'Subthig wudderful, Bissus Coker!'

'That's nice.'

'Great dews frob Paris!'

'Have you got relations there, then?'

Mrs Coker was one of those souls whose interest in foreign parts was confined to the affairs of relatives and the nuptials of royalty. Beyond these two areas of interest existed a curious limbo that, for all Mrs Coker knew, might have been the place people went to when they died.

'They've risedd at last, Bissus Coker!' spluttered Mr Archer, banging his fist on the newspaper. 'The people have risedd! They've storbed the Bastille! This is trebeddus dews! My fred Bister Tom Paine will be overjoyed! Here – listedd to it, Bissus Coker! Listedd and rejoice!'

He sat bolt upright in his bed and, with intense excitement, read aloud to Mrs Coker the brief account in the *London Chronicle* of the great event. Breathlessly (in every sense), he read how, on the evening of July 14th, a crowd of armed citizens had demanded the surrender of the Bastille – the ancient royal fortress and symbol of tyranny and oppression. Under a flag of truce a party of forty citizens had been admitted to parley with the governor, Marquis de Launay. Once within, the drawbridge had been raised and the whole party treacherously massacred by the guards. Whereupon the crowd, incensed beyond all endurance, had stormed and taken the fortress, executed the luckless de Launay and carried his severed head round the city, fixed on a pike.

'Mr Mortimer's been to Paris, of course,' said Mrs Coker; 'and I rather think Mrs Mortimer has a married cousin living somewhere in France.'

She said this with some complacency, as if bestowing on Mr Archer a piece of news quite overshadowing the rowdiness of the French capital.

'Good God, Bissus Coker!' cried Mr Archer. 'Do you doh what this beans? It's the fall of the Bastille! Do you *doh* what it sigdifies?'

'Oh, I expect it will blow over, Mr Archer,' said Mrs Coker comfortably.

Speechless, the one-time friend of Tom Paine sat in his ruthlessly tidied sick-bed and glared at this woman of the people with savage contempt. She exasperated him. He felt a ridiculous desire to awaken her, to shock her, to make her cow-like eyes start from her head at the violence that was erupting on behalf of penurious souls like herself. He wanted to make her scream.

'They cut off the goverdor's head!' he exploded. 'Cut it off with add axe . . . or a dife – it doh't say which! Thed they stuck it, *pourig* blood, odd a pike! Id the *street,* Bissus Coker!'

He gestured frantically to the window as if inviting Mrs Coker to go and witness, if not a severed head, at least a street.

'Now I come to think of it, Mrs Mortimer's married cousin lives in the south,' said Mrs Coker uneasily. 'I expect it's all right down there.'

Whether or not Mr Archer would have leaped from his bed and inflicted actual bodily injury on Mrs Coker will never be known. At that moment a visitor appeared. Richard Mortimer had come to see his old tutor.

Mrs Coker, feeling obscurely that she had been apprehended in a felony, stood motionless and became almost transparent.

'Dear Mr Archer! I heard you were ill – oh! good morning, Mrs Coker – so I came as soon as I could, sir. Have you heard the news? The Bastille has fallen to the people! I meant to bring you the newspaper, but I couldn't find it! Ah! I see you've managed to get one!'

Mrs Coker stood, if possible, more motionless and became even more transparent. There was, on her face, an expression of innocent curiosity, as if, although she'd *heard* of newspapers, she had never laid eyes on one until that very moment when a mention had brought the fact to her notice. At the same time, she managed to suggest that, were anyone to accuse her of anything, she would be hurt and offended.

'These are great days, Richard, my boy!' said Mr Archer, delighted to see his pupil. 'The world is throwing off its chaids. First Paris – thed who dohs?'

'How splendid it must be to live in Paris now! To be present at such a beginning! Even to help – to work – to give oneself to such a cause!'

'Were I a yugger bad,' said Mr Archer, almost incomprehensibly, 'I would be there! I would be tearig down that fortress with my bare hads!'

'I've brought you some brandy, Mr Archer! Let's drink to the new world!'

Silently, Mrs Coker materialized glasses, inadvertently providing three – two of which were placed close together, and the third at a respectful distance, like a disinterested spectator.

'I'll take mine in the other room, Mr Archer,' she murmured; and, as the woman of the people executed a notional curtsey and withdrew with her filled glass, the master and pupil drank enthusiastically to the overthrow of tyranny, to liberty and equality among all mankind.

Eagerly they debated the causes of the revolt, dwelling on such aspects as had always interested them in their discussions in the past: the merciless taxation to repay high-interest loans, the insane extravagance of the queen, the general corruption of the nobility and the Church ...

Mr Archer sneezed and smiled with pride and pleasure to observe how his teachings had borne fruit. This aristocratic young man seemed to him to be genuinely inspired by the glorious explosion of liberty. He was so passionate in the way he inveighed against the criminal selfishness of bankers and financiers ... He felt almost that he was Richard Mortimer's spiritual father.

'And don't you feel, sir, that there's something deeper

to it all? Isn't it possible that a great human anger is at work here? It seems to me, sometimes, that all the political reasons we find for great events are really only external to something much, much more profound. There's been royal extravagance before; there's been high taxation before – and corruption and poverty have been with us always. But nothing happened. Yet now – ? There *must* be something deeper . . . some natural impulse to destroy, to wipe away everything rotten . . .'

'What a piddy,' said Mr Archer, 'that you dever met by fred Tob Paine.'

Mortimer put down his glass.

'That's one reason why I came to see you, sir. I've made up my mind. I mean to go to Paris. I cannot bear to remain at home.' His expression darkened as if the very mention of his home, with its refined inhabitants, weighed on his soul like lead. 'I can't bear to stay here while men are fighting for liberty scarcely a hundred miles away!'

'But your father,' began Mr Archer uneasily. Although he was proud of the extent of his influence, he was, nevertheless, alarmed at the thought of being blamed for it. He had a living to earn.

'My father,' said Mortimer coolly, 'neither approves nor disapproves. As usual.'

'Thed – thed what do you wad be to do?'

'Write a letter for me, sir. Your old friend, Tom Paine, is in London now. Please write me a letter of introduction. He must know everybody in Paris who really matters. He can help me – to help them! A letter from Tom Paine, the great revolutionary, will be better than gold! Please, Mr Archer! All my hopes for the future rest on such a letter! For both our sakes – write it!'

Mr Archer looked remarkably uncomfortable.

'It's fifteed years,' he mumbled, drawing his blanket up round his chin. 'I've dot seed him for fifteed years . . .'

'But you were old friends!'

Mr Archer looked even more uncomfortable, and seemed to be making an effort to disappear under his blanket. His total claim on the great man's friendship rested on an hour and a half's acquaintance in a Lewes alehouse, fifteen years before. It had been just before Tom Paine, in sore domestic distress, had gone to America. He had been in a mood to talk to anyone and had actually asked Mr Archer – half jokingly – to join him in his great adventure. But Mr Archer, timid, vacillating Mr Archer, had passed the opportunity by. Since that time, the incident had grown and grown in his mind till he'd come to believe that he'd spurned destiny and that all his subsequent penury and distress had been visited on him as a punishment.

'Oh yes, we were freds . . .' It was impossible for the tutor to destroy his pupil's faith in him. It would break young Mortimer's heart.

Their relationship was suddenly immensely important. Mr Archer thought he perceived that his pupil was at the self-same crossroads that he himself had been at, that evening in Lewes, long ago. He was determined that Richard Mortimer should not make the same mistake that he had made. Everything now rested on maintaining the young man's faith in his teaching. He *must* take the right road. He must fulfil his, Mr Archer's, cherished dreams. There, he said to himself, gazing at the bright-eyed youth, but for my own feeble cowardice, stand I!

'I'll write you the ledder,' he said. 'But doad be put off if Bister Paine has forgodden me.'

Excitedly Mortimer fetched writing materials and watched while Mr Archer laboriously composed the fateful letter.

'Dear Tom Paine,' he wrote. 'Although it is many years since last we met in that alehouse in Lewes, I hope you remember me still. I am writing to introduce the bearer, Richard Mortimer, who is a pupil of mine. He longs to join the popular movement in Paris and hopes you will be kind enough to give him a letter of introduction to people in Paris whose cause we all support. He is an admirable young man of an old and honourable family who longs for nothing better than to help his fellow men to throw off the chains of slavery. For the sake of our old friendship, and, indeed, for the sake of suffering mankind, I beg you to receive him kindly and render him such assistance as you can. I remain, dear friend, your old companion and devoted admirer, Jonas Archer, M.A.'

'I'b afraid,' said Mr Archer, folding the letter, 'that I doad know dear Tob's address.' Having committed himself, Mr Archer felt an entirely irrational bond with the great philosopher; and had Tom Paine professed complete ignorance of Jonas Archer, M.A., he would have been extremely surprised and angry.

'I've heard,' said Mortimer, taking the letter as reverently as if it had been a communication from Mount Sinai, 'that Mr Paine's to be found in a tavern in Fleet Street – The Cock. He's there on Fridays when one of the revolutionary societies meets. I'm certain to find him there, sir.'

When his pupil had gone, Mr Archer found his eyes full of water. He sighed and attempted to dream, until he became aware of a presence at his elbow. He blinked and looked up. Mrs Coker was regarding him with her look of bland discretion.

'Bister Bortiber's goig to Paris, Bissus Coker.'

She nodded. 'The change will do him good, Mr Archer. I always said he needed a holiday.'

She smiled and continued to stare at the top of Mr Archer's head until he awoke to the disagreeable necessity of giving her her money.

CHAPTER SIX

THE COCK TAVERN in Fleet Street was a tall, narrow, elderly structure, with a tipsy nod to its upper storeys. It was supported on one side by a tallow-chandler's and on the other by a cabinet-maker's, both of whom ought to have known better. All three resembled a party of drunken tradesmen out long past their grave-time.

Although The Cock was narrow – having a frontage of scarcely ten feet – it was surprisingly deep; rather like the gentlemen who met on Fridays, in an upper room, to promote the interests of liberty and equality in France. In an atmosphere thick with tallow and tobacco smoke and the aroma of burnt wine, news of the French capital buzzed incessantly while comely barmaids flitted from table to table, bearing tankards of inspiration.

Here, at midday on Friday, 30th of July, came Richard Mortimer, his eyes bright, his cheeks flushed and his soul on fire with destiny. The access of energy that had come to him following his quarrel with Lewis Boston and his subsequent visit to Mr Archer had not deserted him.

Clutching his tutor's letter, he mounted the stairs and entered the foggy, raucous room.

The sheer volume of voices and bewildering number of arguing faces for the moment appalled him. He felt utterly insignificant; he wished with all his heart that Mr Archer had come with him. Suddenly the whole enterprise seemed outrageous, impossible! What was he, Richard Mortimer from a tiny village in Sussex, doing in this place among these sage philosophers? For to him, in those first moments, every flushed face seemed to conceal a mighty brain. They would laugh at him . . .

'There's an empty chair yonder,' said a barmaid, taking pity on the obviously bewildered youth.

'Is Mr Tom Paine here today?' asked Mortimer, holding the precious letter close to his chest.

'I heard of him,' said the barmaid. 'But I can't say I know which one he is.' She indicated, with a sweep of her steam-reddened arm, the ocean of customers who bobbed and seethed and broke against the walls of the room. Obligingly she asked of a near-by table, but was answered by shrugs and the shaking of heads.

'You'd best enquire around yourself,' said the barmaid, and departed with a sympathetic smile.

Mortimer felt like flinging his letter away and running for his life. He was sure several people were grinning at him already. He bit his lip and made his way towards the empty chair the barmaid had pointed out. He thought he might sit there in some obscurity before quietly making his escape. When he reached the chair it was no longer empty. He glared down at the occupant in dismay. The man looked up enquiringly.

'Is – is Mr Tom Paine here today?'

'Haven't seen him,' said the man. 'But try over by the window.'

Mortimer moved on; but now, having actually opened his mouth and spoken and finding that he had been answered civilly, he discovered it was possible to enquire again. This he did, and was directed to yet another part of the room, then another and another . . . till he became quite familiar with it and even found himself exchanging smiles of recognition with philosophers he'd passed before.

One man in particular kept attracting his attention. He was sitting quite close to the door and seemed to be more of a listener than a disputer. He had a smooth, rosy face, black curled hair and alert brown eyes. Time and again his look met Mortimer's and each time his smile grew more encouraging. Mortimer began to wonder if *he* was Tom Paine; but there was something about the man's smile and neat black attire that didn't accord with his notion of the great thinker. Presently a chair beside the man was vacated, and, smiling quite openly and revealing even, white teeth, he beckoned Mortimer to join him.

'I'm afraid,' he said, with the trace of an Irish accent, 'that our friend Mr Tom Paine is not here today. But sit you down and take a drink with me, young man.'

He waved a white hand and seemed to pluck a barmaid out of the air. He ordered wine and Mortimer sat down, feeling suddenly gloomy and deflated. His journey, his high expectations had all been in vain. The barmaid departed and the stranger leaned forward.

'Have you come a long journey to meet with Mr Tom Paine?'

'From Sussex.'

'A pity . . . a pity. Is that – a letter for him?'

Mortimer reddened and began to put Mr Archer's letter into his pocket.

'May I see it?'

The stranger was holding out his hand and watching Mortimer with the utmost kindliness and interest. 'That is,' he added, 'if it is not private. But then,' he went on, still holding out his hand, 'reason tells me that it cannot be so. I observe that it is not sealed. I observe that you do not know Mr Tom Paine personally – else why should you ask instead of looking for him? Therefore the letter is not personal. Further, I observe that you have been holding it in your hand as if to present it the moment you should find that gentleman. Now you do not look, to me, to be the sort of young man to be burdened with a mere message. Therefore I deduce that it is a letter of recommendation, of introduction! Am I right? Am I right?'

He snapped his fingers delightedly and gazed at Mortimer with eager triumph.

Mortimer was not sure whether he had given the stranger the letter, or whether the man had actually drawn it out of his fingers by that same mysterious power that had summoned the barmaid. At all events, Mr Archer's letter was in his incredibly white hand (he wore skin-tight cotton gloves that followed the folds of his flesh minutely) and his liquid brown eyes were racing across the lines. He was smiling.

'I see we are of a mind, Mr Mortimer – Mr Richard Mortimer,' he murmured, glancing up brightly. 'And now that you have been introduced to me – by Mr Jonas Archer, M.A. – let me return the compliment. My name is Dignam-Browne. With a hyphen and an "e". But don't burden yourself with the "Dignam". It was my mother's name and we never saw eye to eye. Call me "Browne"; but don't forget the "e".'

He extended his gloved hand to be shaken; Mortimer was surprised and relieved to find his grip firm. Somehow he had expected something slippery and cold.

The wine arrived, was paid for by Mr Browne out of a purse of many compartments, and a toast was drunk to Mr Tom Paine and 'our friends in Paris'.

Obscurely Mortimer felt he would like to leave as soon as possible. To be honest, he was not particularly pleased with his new acquaintance. Mr Browne, on the other hand, seemed remarkably pleased with the young man. He was also remarkably curious about him. He asked him about his family, his home, his early days with Mr Archer. He wondered where he was staying in London, and whether he had many friends in the metropolis?

Mortimer answered coolly and, at times, even sharply when he considered Mr Browne was trespassing on his privacy. He did his best to turn the conversation to politics; but Mr Browne always smilingly turned it back again. Mortimer grew irritated, although he did his best to conceal it. He wondered if Mr Browne considered him too much of a country bumpkin to be concerned with such London things as ideals?

Presently a well-dressed, intelligent-looking gentleman passed their table. He saw Mr Browne and greeted him respectfully. Mr Browne barely acknowledged him. Mortimer was undeniably impressed, and was even a little flattered that Mr Browne seemed more interested in him.

'Let us leave this place and continue in the parlour downstairs,' said Mr Browne abruptly. He rose and led the way; Mortimer followed, feeling curiously lost, as if destiny had suddenly abandoned him. He could not make up his mind about Mr Browne at all; but he knew he would have to be extraordinarily careful not to make a fool of himself, or worse.

Mr Browne hurried downstairs into the long parlour, investigating nook after nook rather in the manner of a brisk black dog sniffing out a fox-hole. At length he discovered one sufficiently secluded, summoned a barmaid by the same almost supernatural gesture and proposed the toast as before: 'Mr Tom Paine and our friends in Paris.'

'Now, Mr Richard Mortimer,' he said, wiping his lips on an expensive-looking handkerchief, 'talk to me about politics to your heart's content. I want to hear all about your ideals. I want to hear how you would arrange the world.'

There was not the ghost of a smile on his face. He was deeply serious. Mortimer felt his energy and enthusiasm return; he finished his glass of wine and at first diffidently, and then with increasing passion, poured out to Mr Browne all his anger against oppression, tyranny and inequality. He hated the abuses of wealth and rank and longed to see them swept away.

'What of the laws that protect these abuses?' asked Mr Browne quietly.

'The laws are as corrupt as those who administer them!' answered Mortimer hotly. 'There must be a clean sweep! Nothing can be built on rotten foundations!'

'You are speaking, of course, of France?' murmured Mr Browne.

'I'm speaking of the world!' cried Mortimer, thinking of a great many things at once: of his quarrel with the Bostons – of Henrietta humiliating him – of his deathly home, reeking of indolence and mysterious sickness. Perhaps his exposition to Mr Browne had been a little vague, a little lacking in sound political thought, but there had been no mistaking the sheer romantic force of it, and the passionate sincerity with which it had been delivered.

'I observe,' said Mr Browne, studying Mr Archer's letter which he still held, 'that Mr Jonas Archer, M.A., considers you high-minded and honourable.'

It was an oddity of Mr Browne's that, though he amputated his own name leaving himself with an anonymous stump (always remembering the 'e'), he chose to embellish everyone else to the fullest extent, down to the last full stop.

'With this opinion I fully concur. But honesty is not enough. Nor, even, is enthusiasm. We require intelligence.

Now, before you fly into the air, Mr Richard Mortimer, and protest that you are another Sir Isaac Newton, let me tell you that I have made up my mind. All this time that I've been listening to you, I have been asking myself a simple question. Would a man like Mr Jonas Archer, M.A., commit himself to paper and not only acknowledge but actually *recommend* a pupil who was not exceptionally intelligent? Now at last I have the answer. Of course he wouldn't! *Of course he wouldn't!*'

'You mentioned *we*,' said Mortimer carefully. 'You said, "*we* require intelligence". Who are *we*?'

Mr Browne looked surprised, then he leaned back with a look of remarkable astuteness.

'Ah! Now you *show* me that intelligence I had deduced! And powers of observation, too. And a mind capable not only of enthusiasm, but enquiry. All these qualities must be used.'

'You still haven't told me. Who are *we*?'

As if in answer, Mr Browne summoned the barmaid again. Of all his many curious attributes, this mysterious power of his was perhaps the most fascinating. It was as if the white, visible portions of his fingers were but the beginnings of immensely long tentacles that were able to roam and search out a whole room.

The wine arrived and once more was paid for out of the purse of many compartments. Absorbedly Mortimer watched the spotless fingers twinkle down into the leather darkness and come up with a coin. There was something about the action that suggested a bird pulling up a worm ... even to the brisk little tugs.

'*We*, Mr Browne. Who are *we*?'

Mr Browne looked up, his fingers poised above a compartment as if waiting for some reckless worm to betray itself.

'Very well, Mr Richard Mortimer; as you have told me a little, I will tell you a little. There are certain people, noblemen I might add – very highly placed – who think as you do. Do not imagine that you have a monopoly of ideals. I assure you, there are many of us who want the fourteenth of July to prosper.'

'Are you a club – or a society?'

'You may call us that, and you wouldn't be wrong. You may even call us a poor relation of His Majesty's Government – and you wouldn't be wrong. You might even call us a small room in the neighbourhood of the Foreign Office – and you wouldn't be wrong. But you would not be right, either! Now, Mr Richard Mortimer, I have told you enough. Come and see me next week; on Friday again. Here is where to find me.'

The white fingers dived down again and came up with a card. He handed it to Mortimer.

'You will observe there is no name; only an address.

Number eighty, the Haymarket. You will find it is a snuff-merchant's shop. No; I will not be there. Upstairs. There is a door beside the shop leading to the apartments of Mrs McMahon. She is not concerned. She is a charming Irish lady who takes an interest in charity. We do not like to trouble her. Tell her servant that you are for upstairs, and give him this card. About midday. I will expect you.'

He rose to go and then, as if recalling something trifling, said:

'I hope you will not speak of our little meeting?' He raised a hand as if in protest. 'No. I don't ask for vows. I ask for discretion and the word of a gentleman.'

On his way back to Sussex, Mortimer was both excited and disturbed. He was much divided as to whether he would keep the appointment. He dozed off in the rocking coach and dreamed that he had somehow fallen into Mr Browne's purse. He was in a singularly deep compartment, like a leather chasm. He saw huge white fingers above him, snapping like a great beak. He cowered away into the evil-smelling leather dust; the fingers approached and, in a desperate bid to escape, he bit one of them.

He woke up abruptly with an unpleasant taste in his mouth. He smiled ironically. Everyone seemed to be biting fingers these days! Then he remembered Lewis and the circumstances of the quarrel. At once he felt angry again. He *would* go to town on the following Friday; but not to keep the appointment. He would go back to The Cock and try to find Tom Paine. It was only then that he remembered Mr Archer's letter. Mr Browne had not returned it to him.

Chapter Seven

MORTIMER FELT HUMILIATED; Dignam-Browne's urging of discretion had been as offensive as it was unnecessary. He was not a child to go prattling in the marketplace about everything that happened to him. Even if he'd held on to the letter of introduction it was doubtful if he would have confided in Mr Archer; he was not proud of his new acquaintance, and had begun to wonder what sort of figure he had really cut with that uncomfortable man. The only thing he had to show for his journey to London was a card with an address: number eighty, the Haymarket. Though he had reason to hope that something would come of it, he would not know for certain until the following Friday. He felt in a suspended, irritable state that made him avoid company and leave his friends to imagine what they would.

Mr Archer, now partly risen from his sick-bed, heard that his pupil had returned and was bitterly offended that he'd had no visit. Knowing nothing of Mr Dignam-Browne, he had no course but to assume, shamefully, that

Mortimer hadn't called because the letter to Tom Paine had fallen flat. He felt acutely mortified and then angry; he tended to lose interest in Paris and its struggle for liberty and justice. Temporarily the rights of mankind yielded before the wrongs of one of them. In addition he was very unkind to Mrs Coker, who, when she came on Monday, was thoughtful enough to ask him: 'And how are all your goings-on in France today, Mr Archer?'

'They can go to the devil!' he snarled. But later, when Dr Stump called, he was sufficiently master of himself to wax enthusiastic about the glorious fourteenth of July. He declared that no man with a heart and soul could fail to be stirred and uplifted by the thought of the people of Paris tearing down with their bare hands the fortress that had so long threatened and oppressed them. Were he, Jonas Archer, a younger man, he would be there himself, tearing down the ramparts till his hands were in ribbons; and he hoped Dr Stump would be at his side. Dr Stump's indignation at the suggestion afforded Mr Archer a sense of moral satisfaction that amounted to victory.

Unfortunately, although the spirit was willing, the flesh wasn't quite up to it – neither in Shoreham nor in Paris. The ancient fortress obstinately resisted the most strenuous efforts to dismantle it and the task had to be given over to a shrewdly patriotic builder who made fairly short work of it and sold off the stones as souvenirs, making a handsome profit.

On Wednesday, Mr Boston was offered two such souvenirs by the captain of a ship that had come into Shoreham harbour. Sorely tempted, Mr Boston haggled briefly – and made the purchase. The stones were historic.

The Bostons once more were on top of the world. The cloud of ruin that had hung over their heads had blown away; the French business was settled to everyone's satisfaction and Mr Boston, as adept at one sort of fiddling as another, had actually emerged with a small profit which he intended to reinvest just as soon as French interest rates should be stable. All talk of selling the house was at an end and, far from disposing of his wife's jewels, Mr Boston bought her a fine diamond ring from Grey's in New Bond Street. The gem – a round stone of eleven carats – was almost certainly from the Queen of France's famous necklace that the de la Motte woman and her husband had stolen and subsequently sold. Mr Boston had been shown the actual receipt. Mrs Boston, slipping the ring on her finger, felt obscurely that she was being revenged on the countess.

And now came the stones from the Bastille itself. There seemed something fateful about it all.

'I fancy your friend, young Mortimer, will be pleased,'

said Mr Boston to Lewis, 'to see we take an interest in such things! I'm inclined to agree with him, you know, that it was a great occasion. I rather think that, when we set the stones up, we should have some sort of function . . . small, of course—'

He beamed and played something *pizzicato* on his ghostly instrument as if to indicate the diminutive nature of the function he had in mind.

'Haven't we had enough of that sort of thing?' muttered Lewis ungraciously; but he was overruled by his family who at once began arguing about where the stones should be placed and how celebrated. At length it was decided to cement them on either side of the front door and, if the weather held, to give a garden party to mark the event.

Henrietta was agog to set eyes on the stones, hoped they were from one of the more interesting dungeons, and dreamed of them being stained with blood or marked with dying fingers. However, when the cart from Shoreham arrived, and two nondescript grey blocks were deposited in the stable-yard, they refused to yield up any secret, even to the most prolonged scrutiny. In fact, they might just as well have come off the side of Shoreham quay; and everyone couldn't help wondering if Mr Boston had been taken advantage of.

But, as so often happens, the reason for an occasion

was obscured by the occasion itself; had the stones been from Brighton beach the Bostons were not to be cheated of their garden party.

Excitement mounted and Lewis was commissioned to go to London and purchase parasols, scarves and ribbons. He took an early breakfast on the Thursday, meaning to catch the midday coach. Henrietta and Eliza joined him in 'the office' and Mrs Boston appeared with last minute alterations to the list. Henrietta – who cared little for adornment, as it failed to improve her – demanded perfume. Mrs Boston unthinkingly said it was unsuitable – and then regretted it. Henrietta was at a difficult age and sensitive about her appearance. One never knew which way she would fly off if thwarted. To Mrs Boston's relief the child shrugged her shoulders, then announced that, as she was in the monarch's seat, it was her day to rule the house. She stared round as if defying anyone to forget their ancient childhood custom.

'Do be kind to Henrietta,' murmured Mrs Boston apprehensively – and left unstated the obvious fact that poor, plain Henrietta had little enough else to look forward to.

Lewis and Eliza sighed and exchanged glances; nevertheless they passed toast, preserves and sugar in response to imperious demands with every show of deference.

'Pour my tea!'

'But really!' protested Lewis gently. 'It's right next to you – Your Majesty!'

'Revolution! Revolution! Off to the Bastille with him!'

'Go on, Lewis,' smiled Eliza. 'Off to the stable-yard and sit on the stones.'

'Do be kind to Henrietta, dear . . .'

So Lewis went and breakfast continued under the eye of the avenged queen. But, being rather new to the office, Henrietta couldn't forbear leaving the table to see for herself if her dread command had been obeyed.

Lewis was dutifully sitting on one of the rough, grey blocks.

'Are you repentant?'

'Forgive me, Majesty!'

'You will not disobey again?'

'On my honour – as a Boston!'

'Then bring me back some perfume – and don't tell Ma!'

Lewis laughed and Henrietta, momentarily relinquishing her royal dignity, sat on the other stone.

'*She* was there, you know . . . in the Bastille.'

'Who?'

'The countess.'

'What made you think of her?'

He glanced at his sister. Her face was subdued and dreamy. The countess had fascinated her. In the beautiful Frenchwoman poor Henrietta had glimpsed the true *femme fatale*; and nothing could be more haunting to a fourteen-year-old *femme* singularly un*fatale*. And had not the countess been imprisoned in the legendary Bastille? Perhaps her tears had moistened the very stone on which Henrietta was sitting. And she had been brutally branded by the public executioner – her glamour was endless!

'I often think of her. Don't you?'

Lewis nodded; she had never really left his thoughts, and now, the prospect of another function brought her vividly before him.

'Buy her book!' said Henrietta suddenly. 'I want to read about her.'

Lewis nodded again.

'And Lewis—'

'What?'

'Please ask her to sign it.'

Lewis's heart contracted. The thought of calling on the lady filled him with alarm.

'I don't know where she lives,' he said evasively.

'I do. Pa was going to send her a case of wine, so I asked. She stays with a friend. A Mrs McMahon. Number eighty, the Haymarket. You could call on Friday.'

CHAPTER EIGHT

FOR THE THIRD or fourth time Lewis sauntered the length of the Haymarket; his good looks drew many eyes and his splendid costume the occasional wondering smile. He kept glancing at number eighty, quickening his pace as he passed it and slowing down to a casual amble when it was safely behind. He resembled a singularly gaudy butterfly, mesmerized by a poisonous leaf.

Already several carriages had stopped before the door and elegant visitors had been coming and going. This put him off; he would rather have approached the countess on her own. He was by no means sure he'd be kindly received; after all, she'd bitten his finger in Lancing – God knew what she might do in London!

He had bought her book from Coup's in Bond Street and now had it tucked under his arm. He wondered if Henrietta would know if he forged the countess's signature? He frowned and turned for yet another parade. This time he'd summon up his courage and knock on the door. After all, she couldn't *eat* him!

He stopped at number eighty; he paused — then compromised by going into a snuff-merchant's next door.

An acrid, pleasantly sneezable atmosphere engulfed him and he had the sensation of having stepped inside a tobacco-jar. The snuff-merchant himself came forward. Would the gentleman care for light or dark snuff? Or would he sample one of the establishment's superior mixtures?

Lewis, not being a snuff-taker, shook his head; then, observing a flat-topped glass case on the counter, cleverly said that he'd come on behalf of a friend who was interested in snuff-boxes.

The merchant compressed his lips. He knew only too well the 'friends' of idle shoppers. He knew how they had to be consulted; how they had something very like this or that, and as a last resort, how they had to be met with at a near-by coffee-house so that wretched shoppers might make an easy escape after he, the merchant, had slaved and fawned to no purpose.

'A friend; yes,' he said bitterly, and added under his breath:'Doubtless waiting at a coffee-house for you.And you'll have to go and consult him. And that's the last I'll see of you.' Nevertheless, he opened the case and left Lewis in peace.

'Beautiful objects, are they not?'

Lewis looked up in surprise. Another customer,

materialized from the shop's deep recesses, approached and joined him over the snuff-boxes. This gentleman, dressed in black, with black curling hair and a rosy face, stared down at the rows of brilliant little boxes resting on dark velvet.

'Do you take snuff?' He spoke with the trace of an Irish accent.

'No – no,' said Lewis. 'I – I'm here for a friend.'

'Ah yes,' said the stranger. 'A dirty habit – snuff-taking. One cannot keep one's fingers clean.' Here he exhibited his hands which were encased in dazzlingly white cotton gloves. 'If they made white snuff – snow-white, you understand – then I'd be an addict. For I love snuff-boxes. See – that little gilt one, with the miniature on the lid: Marie Antoinette, I imagine . . .'

He made a rapid gesture, more with his fingers than with his whole hand, and the merchant seemed drawn out of air to wait at his elbow.

'Sir?'

'That little gilt box. Is the painting of the Queen of France?'

'I believe so, sir.'

'How much is it?'

The merchant picked up the box and examined it with an air of wondering whether it was too precious to part with.

'Ten guineas, sir.'

Another gesture and the merchant retreated to the front of the shop where he seemed to be held in abeyance. The box was now mysteriously in the stranger's white hand.

'Lovely . . . lovely . . .'

'She *is* beautiful,' agreed Lewis, peering at the woman on the lid.

'You are a sympathizer? With the French queen, I mean?'

Damn politics! thought Lewis. He didn't understand them; they baffled and irritated him.

'I hadn't really thought,' he said honestly. 'But she's a very pretty woman.'

'Yours for ten guineas!' smiled the stranger, holding out the box.

Lewis stared at the box and reflected that if he bought it for Henrietta – to keep her beauty patches in – she'd forgive him for not getting the countess's autograph.

'All right,' he said. 'I'll have it.' He walked to the front of the shop where the merchant was still held in abeyance. 'I'll take—' began Lewis, when suddenly he stopped.

'Forgive me!' he said hurriedly. 'I've just seen a friend of mine!'

'No!' cried the merchant involuntarily. This was too cruel! Right at the last moment!

Lewis hastened to the door, colliding with the stranger who had also decided to make his departure.

'Excuse me!' muttered Lewis. 'There's a friend of mine! I want to catch him!'

Of all people in the world, he had seen Richard Mortimer crossing the street and approaching. It was an extraordinary coincidence. As he ran outside, the stranger withdrew into the shop and watched curiously.

'Dick! Dick!'

Mortimer, his pale cheeks flushed with excitement, stopped abruptly and almost glared at Lewis.

'Dick! How wonderful it is to see you!'

In the surprise of the meeting, Lewis forgot the estrangement and felt nothing but pleasure at the un-expected sight of his friend. They stood outside the door of number eighty.

'What are you doing here?'

'I – I have an appointment . . .' muttered Mortimer.

'With a lady?' Lewis beamed. He believed he'd come upon a secret part of his friend's life. Certainly the strange look on Mortimer's face and the brightness in his eyes suggested something quite new about him.

'No. Not at all! Please, Lewis – I'm in a hurry!'

'All right, all right! I've got an appointment myself . . . well, not really an appointment, but—'

'Goodbye, Lewis!' said Mortimer distractedly,

and hurried away, leaving his friend much puzzled.

Lewis shrugged his shoulders and, remembering the snuff-box, returned to the shop. The stranger was still there. Lewis completed his purchase and stood waiting for his receipt. He glanced through the window onto the street and saw, to his considerable astonishment, Mortimer return and knock quickly on the door of number eighty.

At once a surge of indignation rose within him. He stalked outside. Mortimer, seeing him, went as white as a sheet.

'You're going to see *her*, aren't you?' demanded Lewis, furiously.

'Who? Who do you mean?'

'*Her! Her!* My countess!'

'I don't know what you're talking about!'

'Then what are you doing at her door?'

'I didn't—'

'Liar! Damned liar!'

'Lewis—'

At that moment a servant answered the door and put an end to the argument. After a moment's hesitation, Mortimer muttered 'Upstairs,' and offered Mr Browne's card.

'This way, sir.'

'No you don't!' suddenly shouted Lewis, thereby

causing a minor sensation among passers-by.

'For God's sake, leave me alone, Lewis!'

Lewis had seized Mortimer's coat in order to prevent him going inside. Mortimer wrenched free and made to mount the stairs. Beside himself, Lewis pushed past the servant and ran after Mortimer. He was entirely convinced that Mortimer had succeeded in making an assignation. He was wildly, savagely jealous. Mortimer was a sly, arrogant pig! All that bloody pretending of his!

'Come back!'

He flung himself at Mortimer's ascending form; and Mortimer, desperately kicking backwards, caught Lewis in the chest with his foot. Lewis cried out and tumbled to the bottom of the stairs. By the time he'd recovered himself, Mortimer had vanished and the appearance of two more servants rendered further pursuit out of the question.

Miserably Lewis returned yet again to the snuff-shop. His clothing was rumpled and his shirt a little torn. He took his receipt in silence. It was made out grandly to 'Lewis Alexander Boston; of Lancing.'

'I see you've had a small accident,' remarked the stranger. Lewis did not answer. He was panting heavily.

'Have you acquaintances next door?'

Lewis shook his head. 'I – I was going to call on the Countess de la Motte-Valois.'

'You know her?'

'A little. I wanted her to sign her book.'

'This book?' The stranger picked up the volume Lewis had left on the counter. Lewis nodded unhappily. The stranger looked at him sharply.

'My dear Mr Lewis Alexander Boston! If you'd but looked inside you would have seen that it's signed already! I understand the lady has autographed all the new edition!'

Mortimer stumbled up the stairs, inwardly cursing the servant who preceded him for being so slow and stately in his ascent. Any instant he expected to hear Lewis pounding up at his heels.

What a fool – what a stupid, stupid fool he'd been for not waiting and watching to see where Lewis went! To be caught out like a guilty child!

He heard the front door closing and heaved a sigh of relief when it became apparent that Lewis was on the other side of it. But almost at once he was gripped by a sharp anguish over what had happened. Because of his own panic he'd isolated himself completely. Were he now to go down on his knees before Lewis he doubted if he'd be forgiven.

He was utterly alone. Alone! Please God let something come of today! he prayed. Let me plunge into

wild action somewhere far, far away! Let me lose myself
– and maybe find a better self.

His original purpose in keeping the appointment
with Mr Browne had been to get back his letter. Now
that was forgotten. He wanted help.

What had Lewis meant about the countess? Surely it
was Mrs McMahon who occupied the first floor; Mr
Browne had said so, and her name was on the door.

As he mounted past the obviously sumptuous
apartments in the servant's wake, he enquired if the
Countess de la Motte-Valois was known in the house?

'Why yes, sir. She often stays with Mrs McMahon.'

'Oh God!' whispered Mortimer. 'So that was it!'

He cast a look of loathing towards the closed doors;
he blamed the countess entirely for his break with the
Bostons. He fancied he could smell her perfume on the
landing, and felt himself sweating as he remembered his
own helplessness and ridiculous attempt at gallantry in
that woman's presence. He hated her for having reduced
him to the level of an animal, panting in her wake.

'If you would be so good as to wait here, sir,' said
the servant, opening a door on the next landing, 'the
gentleman will be with you directly.'

Mortimer found himself ushered into a small, barely
furnished room with a small window overlooking the
backs of opposing houses. There was a table in the room

and three chairs, one of which was occupied by a short, yellowish-skinned gentleman with singularly bright black eyes. He nodded to Mortimer.

'Good day, Monsieur.'

Mortimer acknowledged the greeting with a faint thrill of excitement at the stranger's French accent. He felt that this quiet Frenchman might well be the instrument of his destiny. He seated himself, but, to his disappointment, no further words were exchanged. The stranger seemed to lose interest in him and stared out of the window. Presently Mr Browne arrived.

'Well, Mr Richard Mortimer,' he said, seating himself behind the table and edging back his chair in order to cross his legs, 'I observe you have been hurrying. You are quite out of breath. And your clothing, I note, is a trifle disarranged.'

He picked up the card that the servant had deposited on the table, examined it and dropped it into his mysterious purse. He glanced up at Mortimer and the young man instantly knew that Mr Browne was aware of his meeting with Lewis, but would say nothing until he, Mortimer, volunteered the information.

'I – I met a friend . . . downstairs – by accident,' he muttered, trying to see how the Frenchman would take the news. 'It was a – a horrible coincidence! I swear it was!' he ended up vehemently.

'I believe you,' smiled Mr Browne, nodding at the Frenchman as if to reassure him. 'I really do believe you. And what is more, I believe everything you told me about yourself last Friday. For, do you see, we have enquired.'

Mortimer looked as if he might be angry when Mr Browne held up a white hand to stave off any outburst.

'Last week I paid you the compliment of recognizing that you were probably intelligent. Now I ask you to return that compliment. Although your word, as a gentleman, was not to be questioned, you must surely see that we had first to be certain that you *were* a gentleman. The whole enquiry – and I promise you it was discreet – was undertaken at the command of my masters who doubted not so much your breeding as my ability to gauge it.'

As Mr Browne talked, rapidly and good-humouredly, Mortimer sensed that his exposition was chiefly for the benefit of the seemingly disinterested Frenchman. He kept glancing at him, as if to make sure he was following the conversation. Mortimer also watched this man, feeling that his whole future, the realization of his great need, rested with this yellow-skinned gentleman who had said no more to him than 'good day'.

'Now listen to me, Mr Richard Mortimer!' Mr Browne's voice had changed; it had become quiet and decisive. He uncrossed his legs and leaned forward over the table. His face was close to Mortimer's; his breath smelled vaguely antiseptic.

'We want you to go to Paris with certain sums of money – in gold – and distribute them among certain people whose addresses will be given to you. Do you understand that?'

Mortimer nodded, but at the same time a vaguely disappointed frown settled on his face. Mr Browne saw it.

'Oh yes! I forgot. The ideals. Well – as I told you last week in the Cock Tavern, you have no monopoly of ideals. We also have our share. But we are practical. We know that words are not enough. We are prepared to put our hands in our pockets and provide our ideals with something to live on. I promise you the addresses you will be given will be of such Frenchmen beside whom Mr Tom Paine is but a dawdler on the road to liberty! Ah! I see you smile! I see you nod! Good! Very good! How does it feel, Mr Richard Mortimer, gentleman, to be enrolled as a – er – servant of the people?'

'You are right, Mr Browne,' muttered Mortimer, catching a faintly approving smile on the Frenchman's lips. 'One must be practical.' The Frenchman was on his side, thank God!

'Is there anything you would like to ask me, Mr Richard Mortimer?'

'Yes. Who are your – our masters?'

Mr Browne chuckled. 'I like the "our". I like it very much! But all I will tell you is that they are gentlemen in whose company you would not feel ashamed. To know more than that would expose you to unnecessary danger. For let me be open with you. Although the sums of money you will carry will not be great, they will be regular. You will be, in effect, a courier. And couriers are subject to risk. The present government in France is a ruthless tyranny – as doubtless you know. Were they to capture you and were they to torture you to betray us, is it not better that you should have no names to give up? Oh! I know you would withstand perhaps three nights and days of agony; but when the fourth dawned? Believe me, Mr Richard Mortimer, those heroes who died in agony rather than betray their cause did so because they didn't really *know* their cause. Ignorance is the only safeguard. Flesh is weak; discretion is but skin and fingernail deep. No one would applaud, say, the three days you endured (I am generous, there), but all would revile you on the fourth! *That* is human nature. Now: are you still willing to work for us?'

'When do I leave?' The threat of danger produced an extraordinary joy in Mortimer.

Mr Browne leaned back from the table and recrossed his legs. He glanced once more at the Frenchman who gave an imperceptible nod.

'Would Monday be too soon?'

'Why not now! Why not today?'

CHAPTER NINE

ON SATURDAY, 28TH August, the Bostons held their garden party to distinguish the setting up of the two Bastille stones which had been cemented on either side of the doors leading onto the terrace and where they were of irresistible interest to the household's dogs.

Among the thirty or so summery silks and muslins that bloomed among the tables on the Boston lawns, Mr Archer contrived to be outstanding. Attired in leaf-green and white, he insinuated himself among the tables, expanding and contracting like a large caterpillar to ease his linen which had shrunk from frequent washing. He was in unusually high spirits. Having quite recovered from his sickness, and with no more than a small cloud on his horizon, he felt heart and soul with the occasion. Not only did his well-known friendship with Tom Paine, and therefore the revolutionary cause, bestow on him a sort of authority over the Bastille stones, but he had, the day before, received a letter from his favourite pupil

– Richard Mortimer – who was at this very moment in Paris, working for the cause of liberty.

The small cloud on his horizon was Mrs Coker. Her principal employer – Mrs Mortimer – had taken a turn for the worse following the sudden departure of her son; and, while not coming out with anything definite, Mrs Coker had discreetly intimated that the time might be approaching when she would be in a position to offer him one or two more mornings a week. She hoped not; but she feared it might be the case.

Mr Archer had been frightened to tell Mrs Coker that he couldn't bear to put up with any more of her, and now consulted Dr Stump as to whether Mrs Mortimer was really approaching the melancholy state in which she would no longer require Mrs Coker.

Dr Stump – rose-pink waistcoat and dark-green coat – puffed out his cheeks professionally as Mr Archer put his question.

'As I see it, Archer,' he said, implying that if there were other ways of seeing it, they were beneath contempt, 'this sudden sinking is of a nervous origin . . .'

'Then there's no immediate danger?'

'Ah! I wouldn't say that. The loss of the son has been a great shock.' Here Dr Stump looked rather accusingly at Mr Archer.

'She's lost a son and gained mankind!' retaliated Mr

Archer, who couldn't help feeling a little guilty. There was no doubt young Mortimer's departure had been inspired by his teachings. He'd said nothing about the letter of introduction to Tom Paine and, under the circumstances, felt it best that way.

'Nonsense, Archer! Her son's just gone off into the blue—'

'Ah! The red, white and blue!' interposed Mr Archer, expanding and contracting vigorously; he was referring to the colours of the French National Assembly whose cause Richard Mortimer had selflessly espoused. 'As you know, I had a letter from him yesterday. He tells me he has already been received by a great many fine people and he has thrown himself heart and soul into the cause of liberty!'

'Insurrection, you mean!' snapped Dr Stump, bending down to remove a piece of mud from his shoe.

Mr Archer stared contemptuously at the doctor's fat little satin arse parting his coat tails like a bride coming through curtains. He longed to kick it and justified the schoolboyish impulse by reasoning that he might be kicking sense into its owner. Dr Stump stood up, red in the face, and continued:

'I don't see what's to be gained by overthrowing a tried and settled order. If change must come, let it come from within, little by little, without violence, without bloodshed . . .'

'True enough,' said Mr Archer, lifting a jellied chicken leg from a near-by table and dropping fragments of it down his waistcoat; 'it's true enough that when men, women, and children starve to death, they don't bleed. Certainly that is a good way of avoiding bloodshed. I presume that is the sort of change you find acceptable? You consider it right and proper that a fat king' – Mr Archer, who was thin, naturally equated portliness with evil – 'and a bloated aristocracy should be supported on the misery of the people?'

'If my foot pains me,' said Dr Stump, feeling some retreat into professional wisdom was called for, 'I don't cut off my head.'

Mr Archer looked at him blankly; and Dr Stump, realizing that he had not quite done himself justice, changed the subject by remarking that the Bastille stones looked rather handsome surmounting the terrace.

So the two green gentlemen, still disputing, still arguing – but at bottom not unfriendly to one another – strolled across the pleasant lawn under an impossibly blue sky.

They mounted the shallow steps and gravely inspected the rough, ancient blocks that, if they hadn't come from Shoreham quay, had actually once threatened the people of Paris.

'I suppose,' said Dr Stump, 'that this wilful destruction

of royal property is going to bring down the price of bread?' He laughed ironically and considered he had demolished Mr Archer as completely as the Bastille itself.

'It was symbolic,' began Mr Archer with dignity, when he was interrupted by the approach of several Bostons.

Dr Stump greeted Lewis with excessive cordiality as being the good son who had remained as a support to his family. Lewis frowned slightly. The obvious reference to Mortimer pained him. Actually he missed his friend and had been disconsolately wandering among the guests, thinking what a gap Mortimer's absence made.

The memory of Mortimer vanishing like a thief up the stairs of number eighty, the Haymarket was still strong; but he had got over the worst of his anger and would willingly have made up the quarrel. It had occurred to him that Mortimer might really have been in love with the countess. Lewis could have understood that. And he understood that love was a horrible, delicious emotion that robbed a man of reason and even made him turn against his friends. From this premise, Lewis had supposed that Mortimer had fled to Paris following some violently bitter disappointment over the lady. It was even possible he'd come face to face with her husband, had been challenged to a duel and had decamped to avoid the public disgrace. This latter explanation had been Henrietta's, and Lewis privately thought it not unlikely.

He listened with an attempted show of interest while Mr Archer proudly related parts of Mortimer's letter.

'Here, let me read it to you,' said the tutor at length; and taking out the letter, which he evidently treasured, read aloud:

'So you see, sir, we are determined that the glorious fourteenth shall not be forgotten. There is much, much to be done. Misery and poverty are, everywhere, existing side by side with obscene extravagance. The abominable Marie Antoinette—'

'Does he say that?' queried Dr Stump angrily. 'The insolent young—'

'He is referring to her mad spending.'

'A drop in the ocean, Archer! Do you or he really imagine that the queen's pin-money would provide even a single slice of bread for each of her people?'

'The ocean, Dr Stump, as any man of science should know, is composed of drops. And one slice of bread, as any mathematician should know, is many million times better than none!'

'Talking of Marie Antoinette,' said Henrietta, who, like her brother, found politics dull and incomprehensible, 'look! I've got her picture!'

She produced the gilt snuff-box that Lewis had bought her. Dr Stump inspected it reverently.

'A lovely woman.'

'It looks more like that countess of yours,' said Mr Archer ungraciously.

'Ah! The Countess de la Motte-Valois!' said Henrietta; and, gently kicking the stone on which she was sitting, remarked: '*She* was here, you know. She was a prisoner of the Bastille. Isn't it a coincidence? Our last function turned out to be for a Bastille prisoner, and this one is for the stones of that very prison. And here's another coincidence,' she added. 'Our last function was on the very day the Bastille fell. Now we've set a seal on it!'

Lewis smiled and Henrietta looked dreamily intense – as if she were receiving mysterious intimations from the stone on which she sat.

Presently Dr Stump and Mr Archer strolled away. 'Amazing!' murmured the tutor. 'The sheer vanity of it! To reduce such an event to mere – mere functions! To personalities!'

'I wouldn't call it "reducing"!' replied Dr Stump, and, still disputing, the two green gentlemen strolled back to the tables, the food and the perambulating guests.

The sky grew more and more intense in its blue, till it verged on the grey. The towers and battlements of the Boston mansion seemed to be holding themselves up with difficulty against the increasing weight of the atmosphere. It was as if heaven and all its angels were coming down in so thick a multitude that their blue robes had turned to black, to visit the Bostons' garden party.

Huge, blood-warm drops of rain began to fall, splashing into cups and glasses. A breeze sprang up and the guests, like leaves and petals, began to scurry hither and thither, picking up belongings and hurrying for shelter.

Suddenly a vein of lightning opened up in the sky and was followed almost at once by a terrific explosion of thunder. Then came the downpour – a silver forest of rain and hail. Again and again the lightning flashed and the thunder coughed and roared until the guests, assembled in the drawing-room and gazing through the windows apprehensively, began to wonder if the Gothic mansion, the folly, the childish dream could survive the storm.

They looked across the running terrace, the streaming Bastille stones and the sodden lawns to where the Boston servants ran through the deluge with heads down and collars up to rescue the glasses, china and the drowned remains of the feast.

PART TWO

Egalité

Chapter Ten

HENRIETTA WAS IMPROVING. Her heavy, circular face had begun to condense into an oval, and her thick, bulky limbs -- admirable in a tree but deplorable in a female − now slipped into sleeves and stockings with scarcely any effort.

But this change was being wrought so gradually that the only person who remarked it was her uncle, Mr Boston's younger brother, who saw her only once a year.

'Why dammit!' he exclaimed, when the first signs began to show. 'This can't be fat little Henrietta? Why! She's turning out good enough to post on company orders!'

He was a military man – this dashing, hand-pumping, upright Boston; he was quartermaster to a Midland Regiment of Foot. Mr Boston had bought him his commission both as an act of brotherly affection and a business investment. All the regiment's wine affairs were now conducted through the House of A. Boston and Son.

Previously Henrietta had always despised her uncle and made him the butt of her sharpest wit. He was a great lounger in best chairs, a pompous boaster and an insufferable teaser of little girls. But now she had to admit that there was more to him than she'd supposed in the blindness of her youth.

As soon as she could, she escaped into the drawing-room, shut the door and twirled about among the Chinese-style mirrors to catch unfamiliar glimpses of herself and confirm the soldier's judgement. He was right – he was right! She saw pleasing profiles, the beginnings of a waist, the flash of an ankle and a knee that was losing its dimple! She dropped her skirts and whirled faster, her petticoats flying out and her thoughts overreaching them to where she was dancing on a mess-room table and driving the officers frantic with desire.

Perhaps it was a little sad to see so promising a bluestocking and so neat a wit seduced by a mere mirror; but Henrietta didn't abandon her scholarly pursuits entirely. She moved them upstairs, transferring her imagination from the dungeon to the bedroom where she played the intoxicating courtesan to cruel counts, haughty marquises and, above all, to Richard Mortimer for whom, since his departure for Paris, she had been nourishing a grand passion.

There was no doubt that distance had invested her

brother's pale, lean friend with a striking glamour. The few letters Lewis had had from him, describing the exhilaration and brilliant excitement of living in a city in revolution, where hope sprang up at every street corner and flamed in every public place, made Henrietta ache to be at his side, in his arms . . . He had actually mentioned her in his letters, had asked to be remembered . . .

Remembered! She smiled dreamily. She supposed she had always really loved him . . . which accounted for her previous dislike. Her reading informed her that it often happened that way. She studied the memoirs of the Countess de la Motte-Valois with assiduity, believing that Richard had admired that tempestuous lady. She attempted to model herself on her and when, in August of 1791, came the bewildering news that the countess was dead, having fallen from a third-floor window, screaming drunk according to some and attempting to escape from relentless agents of the Duke of Orleans according to others, Henrietta wept and wore black. A bright light had gone out of the world. Such a fatality overtaking a *femme fatale* seemed a violence inflicted on the secret heart of nature itself. She should have ended in blood-red silks, not on cold grey stone. In the privacy of her turret bedroom, Henrietta drew a 'V' on her breast in rouge; then had the utmost difficulty in removing it when she found it showed above her bodice. Mrs Boston thought the resulting redness was a rash and threatened to call in Dr Stump. Henrietta retaliated with something of her old rudeness so that Mrs Boston wisely washed her hands of her and so the incident passed.

Warrior Boston generally came towards the end of August and, since his first great flash of vision, Henrietta actually looked forward to his arrival. At last he came and she awaited his soldier's judgement with flushed cheeks and bated breath. How was she now?

'Why! Dammit!' he exclaimed. 'This can't be our fat little Henrietta? Why! She's turning out good enough to post on company orders!'

So far as the military man was concerned, there was no sense in trying to improve on a previous success and he was surprised to catch Henrietta's look of dismay; and the following year when, in the brightest of bright regimentals, he greeted her with precisely the same words, he was quite taken aback when his undeniably handsome seventeen-year-old niece regarded him with something very like hatred.

Nor, as it turned out, was the quartermaster in much higher favour with his wealthy brother. Mr Boston was angry with him; he was also angry with himself, with treacherous, unreliable France, with Drummond and Coutts, but above all with the warrior member of his tribe whose advice he had unwisely taken and which was proving ruinous.

Although Mr Boston regarded his younger brother as being feckless, he'd always been sneakingly proud of him in his showy uniform and had often boasted of 'my brother in the army, you know'. In consequence of this he tended to regard him perhaps more highly than he ought; and whenever the quartermaster had talked finance – about which he knew nothing – Mr Boston had been obscurely pleased and surprised. He even took notice of him because he felt his brother was making an effort to be one of the family.

This was absolutely true; the quartermaster felt quite strongly that he needed some sort of standing with his rich brother and accordingly passed on choice items of information about the financial dealings of his superior officers.

'French assignats, old boy,' he had confided to Mr Boston at the beginning of 1790. 'You know – that paper money they're printing now. A good thing. The colonel's going in for them in a big way. Can't lose. Buy 'em at a five per cent discount. They're tied to the land. You're really getting a stake in the country itself – soil – bricks and mortar and all that. The colonel's no fool . . .'

Mr Boston, undeniably impressed by his brother's colonel – who was a peer of the realm – beamed indulgently at his brother, and bought assignats. He bought a great many of them; he even boasted about them.

But alas, though the quartermaster's colonel may have been no fool, Mr Boston had come to the conclusion that his quartermaster was. No sooner had Drummond and Coutts made the purchases than disaster after disaster struck France. Riot, rebellion, flight of the king and queen, recapture of that hopeless pair, ministries rising and falling like the flanks of a sick mare, mansions pillaged and burned by roaming madmen . . . all this, together with senseless France declaring war on Austria, had its inevitable effect. Mr Boston's assignats plummeted in value, taking with them the smile from his face and the tune from his ghostly fiddle.

He really didn't know what was the matter with France. It was as if the whole country were conspiring to ruin him. Whatever he did seemed to turn against him. He called in the last of his loans in order to escape from the madness; but the scoundrels round Bordeaux retaliated by putting up their rents so high that the price of wine was rising to almost undrinkable heights. The very house of A. Boston and Son was in danger.

However, it seemed there was a chance of recovering something from the wreckage. Mr Boston had heard that it was possible to get a better price for his assignats by dealing directly with Drummond and Coutts's agents in Paris. He was sending Lewis there. All the boy had to do was to present himself at the bank, hand over the assignats and take what they gave him. Nothing more. Mr Boston considered Lewis quite capable and even thought the travel would broaden his mind. Lately he had come to have a good deal more faith in Lewis than he had in the boy's uncle . . .

The day fixed for Lewis's departure was Monday, 27th August, 1792. With reasonable weather, he should be in Paris by the beginning of September. He himself was scarcely able to believe it and it was only when the family sat down to a late dinner on the Sunday and kept gazing at him with more affection and regard than was usual that he really felt he was going to leave them on the morrow.

It seemed so dreamlike, so improbable, so unlike what he'd supposed the future might hold for him.

Eliza was in London, visiting with an aunt; but her place was substantially filled by his uncle who was now in the second week of his yearly stay.

Mrs Boston was frankly frightened for her son's safety; lately she had heard so much about blood running ankle-deep in the Paris streets and perfect strangers being set upon, murdered, their heads cut off and stuck on pikes, that every time her gaze fell upon her son's handsome face she regarded his whole head with mournful apprehension. Mr Boston laughed and reassured her that Lewis was going on business, not politics. The boy really wouldn't be concerned in that sort of thing.

'You will be careful, Lewis?' said Henrietta, gazing at her brother anxiously. She was very attached to him and even proud of him; but somehow she did not think him as capable of confronting danger as Richard Mortimer, whom she loved, but didn't worry about.

'Don't be frightened, little charmer!' said the military Boston confidently. 'It'll all be over before he gets there! The Austrian army will have put an end to all that nonsense! The sight of a few well-drilled soldiers will soon restore order all round!'

Grateful for the comfort and the 'little charmer', Henrietta smiled at her uncle, who promptly lost all by winking and wondering:

'Can this *really* be our fat little Henrietta?'

'I think he should take a warm coat,' said Mrs Boston down the length of the table. 'It may get cold at night over there.'

'He won't be sleeping out,' said Mr Boston, but found himself contradicted by his brother, who declared that a good soldier travelled with everything on his back.

Mr Boston countered by observing that his son was destined for better things than the army and didn't have to carry his belongings on his back. Thank God he was well able to afford a carriage.

Mrs Boston wondered about the cleanliness of French carriages and shouldn't Lewis take a blanket and cushions? Mr Boston observed that he wasn't going among naked savages. He was going as a businessman to meet with businessmen. The military Boston sided with his sister-in-law: it was sensible to travel with bedding. A good soldier never relied on the terrain . . .

'Do you suppose you'll see Richard?' asked Henrietta, blushing helplessly.

'I'd like to, Hen,' answered Lewis sincerely, 'I'd like to very much.' The thought of meeting with his friend appealed to Lewis strongly. The old quarrel between them had grown into a sort of bond, as far as Lewis was concerned; he couldn't imagine that Mortimer felt otherwise. He wondered if Mortimer had heard about the death of the countess? He felt he would like to break that news to him himself. He visualized a moment of great tenderness and consolation. Lewis was still convinced that blighted love had been the true cause of Mortimer's departure so soon after their meeting in the Haymarket. He could imagine no stronger reason. Although Mortimer's letters had contained no word of the countess, Lewis believed he could detect in them a hectic energy, a feeling – as Henrietta had put it – of a soul escaping self-torment.

'You will – remember me to him, Lewis?'

'I don't think he'll have forgotten you, Hen.'

His sister smiled. 'Tell him I've changed, though.'

'I'll say his fat little Henrietta is—'

'Pig! Don't you dare!'

'Henrietta!' said Mrs Boston sharply. She had caught the word 'pig'.

Henrietta, crediting her mother with penetrating her secret passion, blushed again and lapsed into silence. She wondered if Lewis, too, had guessed, and promised herself a long, private talk with him in the darkest recesses of the night. She felt she might even unburden herself.

'Lewis,' said Mrs Boston. 'Your uncle thinks you should take a sword rather than pistols as he's heard French powder don't go off.'

'He's to take no such thing!' cried Mr Boston. 'He's not to get mixed up with any unpleasantness. An armed man attracts armed men. A sensible businessman goes unarmed, troubles nobody and looks after his own business.'

That night Lewis had a strange and disturbing dream. He dreamed he had walked into a coffee-shop – most likely in Paris as everything looked foreign and odd. His father was there, sitting at a table by himself and drinking coffee from a steaming cup. Lewis greeted him in surprise, but Mr Boston didn't answer. He just smiled rather feebly and continued to drink. Again Lewis greeted him, when he observed that everyone else in the room was lying in pools of blood. This made Lewis angry. He spoke sharply to his father who continued to smile and drink. So Lewis emptied the steaming cup over his father's head and hit him in the face. He was amazed by how easily he accomplished this. His father never stopped smiling. Lewis hit him again and again in a furious temper – and then ran away with a sense of shame and guilt . . . and also of relief.

'Lewis! Lewis!' someone was shouting out.

He stopped running and woke up. Henrietta was in his room, looking dreamlike with her candle.

'You were twisting and turning so,' she whispered. 'I thought you were having a fit!'

'Just a dream . . .'

'Can we talk?'

'I must go early in the morning—'

'Only for a little while.'

'What about?'

'Paris . . .'

'What about Paris?'

She hesitated. It never seemed the right time.

'Oh, bring me back … something, Lewis?'

'What?'

Richard, said her eyes, lowered to stare at the candle-flame dancing in its pool of wax. 'Oh, anything – anything.'

'I'll bring you back the finest "anything" money can buy!'

'Promise?'

'I promise.'

CHAPTER ELEVEN

THE WEATHER WAS reasonable, the roads were dry and Lewis Boston, equipped for every hardship and attired for every festivity, reached Dover on the Tuesday morning and crossed the Channel to Boulogne-sur-mer on the very same day.

In addition to all his belongings, he carried news for Richard Mortimer from Mr Archer and Dr Stump: Mr Archer's was full of hope; Dr Stump's was not. Mrs Mortimer was sinking. She lay in her bed, her pallor rendering her almost indistinguishable from her sheets. It seemed remarkable to the doctor that the flame of life bothered itself to remain in so disheartening a refuge where its vital warmth was expended to so little effect. In a way it was like a child, left in an abandoned house, creeping from room to room and wondering what all the cobwebby grandeur was for.

'Tell the young man his place is at home,' Dr Stump had said sternly. 'Let him put his own house in order. He has obligations . . .'

★ ★ ★

At first slowly and then with tremulous speed England dwindled away, the stout cliffs shivering into mist and finally dissolving into no more than a light veil cast between heaven and the sea.

Lewis, standing on the deck of the packet-boat, securely encased in a many-caped greatcoat with enormous silver buttons, gazed forlornly down at the speeding water. He followed every twist, every white-topped hillock as it rushed back home.

From time to time he glanced up, shading his eyes for a glimpse of mysterious France. What would it be like? He tried to imagine the violent land; tales clamoured in his head of innocent bystanders butchered out of hand. Melancholy fears gnawed at him, undermining the excitement he'd felt on embarkation.

He fumbled inside his coat for the solid gold saint's medal Henrietta had given him and begged him to wear. His fingers closed round it passionately; and he looked up to the marvellous sky.

Sea-birds dipped and screamed, sometimes passing quite close with savage eyes. Were they French birds? Someone threw them a crust and they pounced down in the water like revolutionaries.

He thrust his hand in his pocket and felt the reassur-ing letter in French that Mr Boston had given him, entreating whosoever read it to guide the bearer to the Paris coach and thence to Drummond and Coutts.

A slight feeling of indignation overcame him. After all, he was not a complete fool. He was a grown man with a tongue in his head – and *someone* would understand English.

What would it be like – what would it be like? Mr Archer had said the greatest event in human history was, at this very moment, being unfolded in Paris. He had declared that were he a younger man he'd have been at Lewis's side. 'Tell Richard I'm proud of him!' he'd murmured emotionally, clasping Lewis's hand in the absence of Mortimer's. 'Tell him my heart marches with him always!'

Visions of Mortimer invaded his mind: Mortimer marching, Mortimer laughing in the face of danger, lean, pale Mortimer leading the people's army, eyes aflame and clutching a perfectly enormous flag.

Lewis scowled and clenched his fists as wave after wave of envy soured him. He became aware that he cut rather a poor figure beside his friend. O monied Boston, first-born of a wine importer, beloved brother and idolized son, standing on deck with a saint's medal, a letter of assistance, a bag full of money – and on your way to make more – what use are *you* to the world?

Gloomily he unwrapped a piece of veal pie his

mother had pressed on him and threw it to the sea-birds; at the same time he wished he had the courage to dispense likewise with the letter of assistance and stand on his own young feet.

Lewis had lost his trunk. Bewildered and frightened he stood on the quayside. Boulogne was a madhouse – a Bedlam of shouting, arguing, pushing and, above all, a Bedlam of French. It was as if a cork had been taken out of France and everyone, everything, was rushing out by the force of gravity alone.

His trunk had vanished beyond recall. He'd seen it disappear down a street and had been helpless to follow. 'Papers! Papers!' Blue-coated soldiers had been everywhere, demanding passports. He'd stopped, and lost his trunk. He had failed. In the very first moments he'd failed. Everything went wrong for him. He felt like sitting down in the middle of everyone and weeping.

'Papers! Papers!'

Dully he obeyed, offering his papers yet again. The soldier examined them, looked up, shrugged his shoulders and returned the papers. Abruptly he reached forward, seized Lewis by the arm and began to drag him along the street, shouting at him impatiently.

Good God! Was he being arrested? Gloom and humiliation gave way to terror as every sort of torment and indignity presented themselves to him. Suddenly the soldier released him and gesticulated:

'*Le coche! Le coche! A Paris! Voilà!*'

With overwhelming relief, Lewis saw he had been brought to the coaching yard. He saw his trunk standing beside the coach. He went to sit down on it to recover himself. Presently the relief subsided; he realized the soldier had acted on his father's letter of assistance. He felt acutely mortified.

On Saturday, September 1st, Lewis reached Paris and presented his credentials at the Porte Saint-Denis. He was tired, a little dilapidated, and full of unease. He had had a terrible journey, staying in inns of unbelievable squalor where he had been robbed of two of his buttons and one of his watches. But that wasn't the worst of it. The few English travellers he'd met seemed to have taken a delight in disturbing him. They were rumour-mad. The Revolution was done for; the king was back on his throne chopping up heads like cucumbers; Paris was in flames and the people frying like onions; money was worthless; the few souls who hadn't been fried were burning assignats in the streets; and all the prisons had been broken open and thieves and murderers were roaming at large. This last fear was perhaps the most disquieting of all, having a sinister, domestic terror of shadowy figures murdering in alleyways and slipping through unlatched windows to redden the city's beds.

'*La maison de Drummond et Coutts? Ah! Rue Saint-Honoré. Allez tout droit, M. Boston.*'

The blue-coated soldier handed him back his passport and letter and displayed no further interest in him. He passed through the gate into the mysterious cobbled maze of the city.

The House of Drummond and Coutts, which occupied the ground and first floors of imposing premises on a corner in the Rue Saint-Honoré, was in a state of great excitement, not to say panic. The rumours which had beset Lewis were also distracting the bank. Tales of the fall of town after town to the invading Austrian army came in thick and fast from no clearly discernible source. Exchange rates rose and fell with wild abandon; and in addition to these financial tremors, these fevers of the body economic, were the antics of an unstable and irresponsible government. For the last two days every business-house in Paris had been shut while soldiers searched for weapons to defend the city. This was ruinous; it interfered with the banking houses taking advantage of the situation; investors throughout Europe would suffer. Now at last they were permitted to open their doors and M. Paré, in his little brass cage, looked out anxiously for the arrival of *l'Anglais*.

The yellow-skinned, dark-eyed Frenchman from number eighty, the Haymarket had received intelligence from his good friend Mr Browne. It would seem, Mr Browne had implied, that if certain events were to take place, matters would inevitably arise to their mutual advantage and to the advantage of their masters. But speed was of the essence; no time was to be lost.

M. Paré was very edgy and sharp with his clerks. He was worried. National Guardsmen kept passing the door and gazing over the partly obscured windows very threat-eningly. Bloodthirsty scoundrels – dregs of humanity!

One in particular frightened and angered him: a fat, greasy little corporal with a huge moustache and eyes like fire. Several times he'd pushed open the door and poked his musket and head simultaneously inside, grinning and offering a contemptuous salute.

'What-ho!' he'd called in a mockery of gentleman's English. (It was surprising how English M. Paré felt in Paris, and how French in the Haymarket.)

Once the corporal had actually had the impertinence to clump inside, breathe wine and tobacco through the bars of the little brass cage and ask hoarsely if M. Paré knew a 'Mister 'oskins of 'umpshire?'

M. Paré had smiled thinly and shaken his head. One couldn't afford to offend National Guardsmen; in fact, these days one could scarcely afford to offend anyone.

A clerk came up to him. An Englishman had just arrived. No – no! Not *l'Anglais*. A different one. Very substantial young man. Father with large account at London house. Wanted to convert assignats. Name of Boston . . .

'And how is the dear Haymarket looking now? And Wills's Coffee-house, and the Cocoa-Tree? Ah! I love that city, M. Boston!'

M. Paré chattered away, pausing only to smile nostalgically up through his bars at Lewis as he counted the assignats, examining them closely. There had been forgeries, he explained; not that M. Boston of London, etc., etc. . . . .

Silently Lewis watched the unhealthy-looking Frenchman in his cage plucking at the notes like some bird of prey rending feathers.

Paris had frightened Lewis. Perhaps it had been no more than the creeping rumours he'd heard combined with the unfamiliarity of the land that had produced this feeling; but he was unable to shake it off.

Few people had been about; groups of ragged-looking soldiers had been congregating at corners . . . then a street with no one – nothing moving but a huge poster flapping off a wall as if the skin of the house had been half torn away. 'The country's going to the dogs.' The memory of his own expression and Mortimer's comment on it came back to him. But he saw no dogs, only bony cats, sitting on doorsteps or padding purposefully nowhere.

He'd passed a silent queue of women outside a baker's shop. They'd stared at him meaninglessly. He caught a gust of smell from them as he went by. It was sharp, acrid, almost vinegary. It was the smell of the town. Every city has its own peculiar smell compounded of food, refuse and sweat. An easy city smells of food; a frightened city smells of sweat. Paris reeked of sweat.

He had reached the bank with profound relief . . .

'The exchange rate at the moment, I'm afraid,' murmured M. Paré, stacking Mr Boston's assignats in a neat pile on the counter, 'is thirty-seven per cent of face value. I'm sorry, monsieur. Politics, you know, have their effect. I take it you still wish to convert?'

Lewis nodded and M. Paré snapped his fingers at a clerk who brought over a black metal box. He began to unlock it, then, sensing an interested scrutiny, looked up past Lewis. He saw the red of a cockade fixed to the window like a clot of blood. Below it was a hat, and below that were the fiery eyes of the greasy little corporal. A hand came up in a sketchy salute, and the cockade bobbed away.

M. Paré moistened his lips and frowned. He opened the box and, pulling on a pair of snow-white gloves, began to count out English bank-notes. Fascinated, Lewis watched the incredibly rapid white fingers and was reminded of the man he'd met in the snuff-shop in the Haymarket. He had the strange sensation that what was going on had happened before, and that he knew the course of the future if only he could remember it.

'There, M. Boston! I wish you a very good day and a safe journey . . .'

Lewis took the English notes and stowed them away in a purse as if he had done it all before. He shook his head and thought suddenly how curious it was to have come so far to exchange one bundle of paper for another . . .

'You are going back directly, monsieur?'

Lewis nodded.

'Ah! How I envy you! Grosvenor Square! The Strand! Piccadilly! Dear, dear London!'

M. Paré looked up through his cage with the melancholy smile of the cosmopolitan whose heart is never where his person is.

Lewis left the bank clutching the purse. As he stepped outside, the short, greasy corporal stared at him with interest. Lewis had the feeling that his entire transaction had been closely observed. His feelings of apprehension increased. He remembered the rumour of thieves and murderers escaped from the city's prisons. The corporal shouldered his musket and made as if to approach, when another man in a grey topcoat hurried between them and knocked against Lewis in his haste to enter the bank.

'Pardon—'began the stranger, when his eyes widened and his mouth fell open. He laughed aloud in amazement and delight.

'Lewis! Lewis Boston!'

It was Richard Mortimer! Once more the extraordinary sensation of repeating a dream swept through Lewis; and then he remembered the Haymarket meeting and the feeling vanished.

'I – I was coming to see you!' Lewis stammered excitedly . . . and then felt a little uncomfortable at having been caught out putting business before friendship. He tried to hide his fat purse, but Mortimer, absolutely astonished to see Lewis, didn't seem to notice. He overwhelmed Lewis with questions as to where he was staying, how long had he been in Paris, what was he doing that day, was he alone . . . ?

Lewis answered as best he could, when Mortimer begged him to wait while he went into Drummond and Coutts. He had an appointment. He wouldn't be a moment . . .

As Mortimer pushed open the door of the bank, Lewis heard a voice exclaim:

'M. Paré! *L'Anglais est ici!*'

Then the door swung shut and Lewis waited.

The corporal, with his musket firmly shouldered, was now marching to and fro. He caught Lewis's eye and offered his curious salute, which was more in the nature of a London cabman's acknowledgement of a fare – consisting of a single finger raised to eye-level – than anything military.

In a few moments, Mortimer emerged. He was looking flushed and intensely excited; Lewis put it down to the unexpectedness of their meeting.

Seeing Mortimer again, after the initial surprise was over, Lewis was struck by the change three years had wrought. Always lean, Mortimer was now quite thin – the bones of his face were very prominent, giving him a passionate austerity, as if all nourishment went to feed his spirit alone. His eyes were singularly bright and tended to fix themselves burningly on whatever chanced to meet them.

He was clutching a linen bag which emitted the unmistakable clink of coins. Catching Lewis's look, he laughed awkwardly and explained that even here one still needed money to live; fortunately (here he cast his burning look through the windows of Drummond and Coutts) he had friends who still helped him.

But it had not been the bag of money that had surprised Lewis; it had been the hand that grasped it. Fastidious, well-bred Mortimer's hand was filthy.

'Please, Lewis – can we meet later?' He'd broken off abruptly. Plainly his thoughts had been elsewhere. He stared at Lewis penetratingly and then added: 'In, say, two hours? For God's sake don't think me rude or anything like that! But . . . but I have urgent business. I must go to the Faubourg. People are waiting for me. I *must* go. But in two hours – or maybe less – at – at the Café de Foix. It's in the Palais-Royal. That's quite near here. Anybody will show you. We can talk then. But I must go now! I must, really!'

A little resentfully Lewis watched the tall, grey-coated figure almost run away. It was hard not to feel slighted, to feel that Mortimer had outgrown him and regarded him as unimportant beside his present concerns.

The corporal, having reached the limit of his self-appointed sentry-go, turned and approached. He halted, lowered his musket and gave his cabman's salute again.

'Good day,' he said affably. 'Nice weather we're having, don't you think?'

Startled at being addressed in English, Lewis uneasily agreed. He wondered what might be coming next.

'You are, p'raps, acquainted with Mister 'oskins of 'umpshire?'

The corporal's fiery little eyes examined Lewis greedily.

'N–no. I am sorry. I don't know him.'

'Very rich gentleman,' offered the corporal as an added inducement.

The bizarre thought struck Lewis that 'Mr 'oskins of 'umpshire' might be the password to some dark conspiracy. Henrietta would have known. He shook his head vigorously. He wondered how he could get rid of the corporal who was rapidly putting the fear of God into him.

'I – I must go to the Café de Foix. Can you tell me the way?'

The corporal frowned, scratched his moustache and examined the result as if for the required information. It was very complicated, he said, for a foreigner to find. But he himself would be happy to conduct Lewis thither.

'I must be there in—'

'Two hours,' supplied the corporal, looking remarkably unabashed by this admission of eavesdropping. 'Plenty of time.' He slid his musket from his shoulder, caught it between his knees and fumbled inside his coat, producing a large pewter watch.

'Plenty of time,' he repeated, studying the dial. 'Nice

watch. Mr 'oskins give it to me.' He pressed a catch and an engraved disc sprang up on which Lewis was urged to read: 'To Marcel Bouvet. Not so much a servant as a loyal companion; from E. Hoskins Esquire of Hampshire.'

The loyal companion replaced the watch and stared pointedly at Lewis's dangling fobs. Convinced now that the soldier intended to rob him and hoping that he'd be satisfied with that, Lewis eagerly produced his own elegant timepiece. Corporal Bouvet examined it, returned it and remarked that Mr Hoskins had possessed a similar one, but with diamonds.

'You like to meet charming French lady?' suggested the corporal helpfully. 'Very pretty.'

His moustache expanded in what was probably a smile, but in the absence of a mouth, it was hard to be sure.

'Very cheap,' pursued the not-so-much-a-servant, breathing mixed fumes into Lewis's face. 'Clean as a whistle. Mr 'oskins said so.'

'N-no. Thank you!'

'See Notre-Dame, p'raps? Mr 'oskins very fond of Notre-Dame when Madame 'oskins come to Paris. Very interesting. And save your money, what-ho?'

Once more Lewis declined, now not knowing whether to laugh or run for his life. He was certain that somewhere beneath the greasy, affable manner was a very sharp brain working to an unknown purpose.

Corporal Bouvet shrugged his shoulders, and, lifting up his musket, suggested a stroll through the city with, maybe, a glass of brandy until it was time to meet his friend.

There did not seem to be any chance of getting rid of Corporal Bouvet and as they set off together Lewis had the highly uncomfortable sensation that the corporal had tactfully placed him under a very mysterious form of arrest.

CHAPTER TWELVE

'MR 'OSKINS WOULD 'ave sent that pig's piss back,' said Corporal Bouvet sternly. 'Pretty damn quick!'

They were seated in a little café where Lewis had ordered brandy. Corporal Bouvet, who occupied the adjoining table (there had been empty chairs at Lewis's, but he'd saluted and chosen his own), had leaned over and sniffed the glass.

'*Patron!*' he called; and when the proprietor came, the corporal sent him off with, as he explained, a flea in his ear, bidding him fetch liquor fit for an English gentleman.

'These peasants,' he confided, 'don't know their arse from their elbow. That's what Mr 'oskins say.'

Lewis, who had been unable to rid himself of the National Guardsman, reddened slightly. Mr Hoskins of Hampshire didn't seem to have been a credit to his country. The corporal, on the other hand, plainly regarded Mr Hoskins as the last word in elegance, refinement and taste.

'You go back soon, M. Boston?'

'On Monday.'

'I fix it,' said the corporal. 'No trouble. Cost you nothing.'

Lewis wondered politely if, perhaps, the corporal's military duties might not have a prior claim? But no; the corporal's duties were unusually elastic. As he explained this, his fiery little eyes flickered over Lewis's face so that once again Lewis felt there were schemes in Corporal Bouvet's head of which he had helplessly become a part.

'Nice shoes,' remarked the corporal, gazing down at Lewis's glittering feet as they left the establishment for the Café de Foix. 'Mr 'oskins get 'is shoes made in 'olborn. Cost five pound a pair.'

'These cost six,' said Lewis, unable to restrain a note of triumph.

Mortimer arrived at dusk and joined Lewis in the crowded, noisy coffee-room. Corporal Bouvet had stayed outside. The evening being warm, he'd chosen to stroll in the gardens among the shadowy lovers and the lantern-lit trees. He'd promised he wouldn't be far away, and Lewis had kept glimpsing him through the windows, affably saluting pretty girls and offering them his company.

'Everything happens here, you know,' said Mortimer knowledgeably, seating himself and glancing round. 'It's *the* place!'

Mortimer was still wearing his grey topcoat, the pockets of which were pulled out of shape and greasy with constant use. He was full of news, full of talk, full of excited pride. In vain Lewis attempted to gain some share in the conversation, to fill in his own three years; but Mortimer was obsessed with the life he was leading and seemed unaware of any other world than his own. He kept pointing out famous politicians – great men all of them. Fate of the world in their bristling red hands. Repeatedly he leaned forward and seized Lewis by the wrist, as Lewis remembered Mr Archer had often seized him, to gain his wandering attention . . .

'Your mother is very ill,' Lewis managed to squeeze in at last.

'I know . . . I know . . .' said Mortimer, fixing his eyes on his coffee-cup with precisely the same degree of burning intensity that he'd accorded to Lewis. 'But there's nothing I can do there . . .'

Then he saw someone he knew – a wretched, shabby, devilish-looking man. He waved; his whole face lit up. Lewis felt a sharp pang of jealousy; he wished with all his heart that he hadn't met Mortimer.

His face must have betrayed this, for Mortimer

seemed to make a gigantic effort to put aside whatever was occupying his thoughts. He smiled at Lewis almost pleadingly, as if to say: Very well, I'll give you some attention . . . but it's at a great cost!

'How long are you staying here? You didn't say. You didn't, did you?'

'I'm going back on Monday.'

'Good – good!'

Lewis felt like hurling his coffee-cup in Mortimer's face. Suddenly he remembered the dream he'd had about his father on the night before he'd left Lancing. Now it was Mortimer in the coffee-house and Lewis was sitting there, longing to strike him again and again.

'Why should it be good?'

'I – I didn't mean it like that, Lewis,' muttered Mortimer, realizing how offensive his words must have sounded. 'I swear I didn't. Only – only something might be happening soon. There could be danger—'

He broke off and actually had to wipe some sweat from his forehead. His hands were still filthy.

'Is it the war?'

Yes; it was the war . . . but not the war altogether. The real enemy was in Paris. There was a terrible conspiracy afoot. Everyone knew of it but was powerless to stop it happening. This enemy was the aristocracy – the filthy leeches who were still bleeding the people white!

Someone in the Assembly had already called for the destruction of all of them. There'd be no peace, he'd said, till a hundred thousand aristocrats' heads were off. What a day that would be!

'And yet,' he broke off, musingly, 'I'm an aristocrat myself: how strange! But I suppose it always takes a scoundrel to know a scoundrel?'

For a moment the intense, burning look left him and was replaced by a hint of his former weariness. But only for a moment, and he was off again. The conspiracy. The political prisoners – the aristocrats who had been imprisoned – had planned a monstrous revenge. They had bribed certain gaolers—

'I've heard that!' put in Lewis eagerly. Mortimer had left him far behind so that he was particularly pleased to come upon common ground . . . even if only a rumour.

'Can you imagine such a thing?' Mortimer had again seized him by the wrist. 'Such a horrible thing? They mean to let all the murderers and thieves loose to terrorize the city!'

'And it's certain?'

'Yes – yes!'

'How do you know?'

'Friends . . . one hears these things . . .'

'In the bank?' Lewis didn't know why he said this, but he'd felt that Mortimer's connection with Drummond and Coutts was curious. Besides, he'd mentioned friends when he'd come out with the bag of money.

Mortimer grew very pale. 'I said I had friends. I didn't say any more than that!' He looked genuinely frightened . . .

'Is there anything wrong, Dick?'

'What do you mean? Why should there be anything wrong?'

He paused to acknowledge another acquaintance, even seedier than the last. A man with a boiled face and a threadbare cloak. He had been an actor; but now he was 'one of us'. A man of immense powers of speech. A man who could rouse a crowd from lethargy in no time. A man who touched the springs of the people's heart. There were many such as him . . . workers for liberty . . . real people.

He left Lewis for a moment and went to speak to this man. When he returned, he seemed calmer.

'Oh yes. Is there anything wrong. No . . . no. I'm alive, that's all. Today in Paris, suddenly in the Café de Foix, Richard Mortimer, dearly beloved son . . . alive!'

'I'm going, Dick.'

'Why? We've hardly talked yet! Please, Lewis . . . stay with me!'

'What for?'

'Because . . . because . . .' Mortimer hesitated. Lewis

saw that his anxiety was quite real. He wished with all his heart he could reach him and understand him.

'Lewis, dear Lewis! I've been a pig! Tell me your news . . . tell me all about home! How is Mr Archer, and Dr Stump? Still arguing – still setting the world to rights? And how are all your family? I miss them. I miss having breakfast in "the office"! Did you know, Lewis, that that was my favourite room in all England? Perhaps even in the world. And tell me, how is my favourite young lady in all England? How is Henrietta, Lewis?'

There was absolutely no mistaking the sincerity of Mortimer's feeling. His affection for the Bostons was as real as anything about him. The seedy actor passed close by the table as if wanting to speak to Mortimer again. Lewis felt intensely happy as the man was ignored.

Impulsively he put his hand in his pocket where it encountered a twist of silk. He drew it out and, rather shyly, offered it to Mortimer.

'What is it?'

'Nothing very grand, really. But I was asked to give it to you . . .'

Mortimer undid the silk. Within was a coil of brown hair.

'It's from – from your favourite young lady in all England, Dick.'

'Henrietta's?'

Lewis nodded, feeling acutely vulnerable on his sister's behalf. Mortimer touched the hair, picked it up, studied it.

'It's darker than it was,' he murmured. Lewis heaved a sigh of relief. He'd been terrified that Mortimer would have treated it with his old mocking contempt.

'She must be . . . grown up, now.'

'She's seventeen.'

'Is she—?'

'Yes. She's very handsome indeed. I think she's much prettier than Eliza . . .'

'I wish I could see her.'

'Then why don't you come back?'

Lewis spoke with sudden hope. He knew that Mortimer would undoubtedly have been the finest 'anything' he could have brought back for Henrietta.

'No, Lewis. It's impossible. But listen to me, Lewis. If you're in Paris tomorrow, please stay indoors. Don't go outside in the streets.'

'Why not?'

'The plot I was telling you of . . . the prison plot . . .'

'But what will you do?'

'Me? Oh, we have our own plans. We know what to do. Don't worry about me.'

'Can't I help? Isn't it possible?' A vision of being at Mortimer's side in some fiercely heroic undertaking had come into Lewis's mind. God knew why, but he imagined banners, plunging horses and whirling swords. Above all, he imagined rescues.

'What? You, Lewis? Oh my God! What a thought!'

Mortimer's words were not uttered contemptuously. They were incredulous. Lewis glared at him. He was bitterly offended ... perhaps more by this out-of-hand rejection of assistance than by anything else.

'I must go now,' said Mortimer, standing up. Lewis looked away. The actor was still hanging about by the door. Mortimer nodded to him, then turned once more to the angry Lewis.

'If we don't see each other again,' he said, without apparently even noticing the mortified expression on his friend's face, 'before you go back, give my love to ... to everyone.'

He picked up the lock of hair and stuffed it into his greasy, misshapen pocket. He left Lewis without another word.

Lewis remained seated at his table for about another quarter of an hour. He felt bitterly disappointed. He'd said none of the things he'd meant to say. Mortimer had scarcely troubled to conceal the fact that his friend was an embarrassment, an encumbrance to him. He had outgrown Lewis as surely as a child outgrows its clothes. He stared blindly at the great politicians overflowing their tables and waving their red hands. He saw himself for what he was: an overdressed schoolboy in a world of men. He got up to go; his eyes were stinging with tears of humiliation.

Outside the café a figure detached itself from the shadows and from a pretty, feathery girl. It was Corporal Bouvet. He approached and saluted.

'If you stay in Paris tomorrow,' he said, 'p'raps you like to meet charming French lady for company? Very cheap. I fix it.'

CHAPTER THIRTEEN

WHERE DO CORPORALS go in the night-time? A hard question – almost unanswerable. Corporal Bouvet had accompanied Lewis to his lodgings – an inn near the Porte Saint-Denis – inspected his bedroom and then vanished as if off the face of the earth.

On the Sunday morning Lewis descended into the parlour – and there was Corporal Bouvet, comfortably seated, his hat on the table before him with its bright cockade and blood-red tuft looking oddly festive. This was the first time Lewis had seen the corporal's head and hat parted; he observed that his principal stock of hair had been laid out on his upper lip, leaving very little to be disposed on his head. What there was seemed to be glued down and varnished, as if to prevent theft. Lewis had the distinct impression that Corporal Bouvet had smartened himself up.

'Nice day,' said the corporal, rising and saluting. 'Real 'umpshire weather, what?'

Following on the warm evening, the morning had

turned out hot and bright; neither cloud nor wind ruffled a royal sky. Lewis, looking out, reflected that Mrs Hoskins had certainly misrepresented the weather in Hampshire.

It was a lazy, smiling day, a sunbaked, stirless day; not a day for plots, not a day for conspiracies, not a day for Mortimer . . .

Danton, the establishment's fat, mottled cat, slept on the window-sill while parties of flies picnicked on the meadows of its fur. Previously Danton had been known as Petion (the Mayor of Paris); then Roland, then LaFayette, in honour of yet another hero. All in all the placid animal represented the whole course of the turbulent times, and did credit to the patriotism of its owners; Danton was undoubtedly the man of the present hour.

Madame, the proprietor's wife, came in with coffee. She hoped monsieur had slept well and that the soldiers hadn't disturbed him.

'What soldiers?' Lewis's thoughts flew to Mortimer and the conspiracy.

'Always soldiers coming and going. I've complained and complained, but it does no good. They say it's necessary. We live in troubled times, monsieur.'

'It will blow over,' said Corporal Bouvet, receiving a cup of coffee and saluting madame.

The proprietor himself entered, absently thrust Danton from the window-sill and planted his own large bottom in the animal's place. Danton went morosely towards its mistress. The proprietor bade Lewis good morning and asked the corporal if there was any news?

Corporal Bouvet shrugged his shoulders. He was not in the government's confidence. Madame explained to Lewis that it was their wedding anniversary. They were going to the theatre; they hoped nothing would spoil it for them. In the last scare all the shops had been shut . . .

'It's always the same,' said Corporal Bouvet. 'Whatever government it's the same.'

The corporal did not like governments – any governments. They oppressed him; they were consistently rude to him. As an example: he had ruptured himself during the troubles at the Bastille. Right? So he'd gone to the official and applied for a disablement pension, like it said you could do. Right? The official had looked down his nose and then what do you think? He'd told Bouvet that there must have been a weakness before. There were no grounds for a pension. That was governments for you! Change and change about and it's always the same bad-tempered official between a man and his benefits . . .

'But in 'umpshire, England,' said the corporal hopefully, 'of course it is different?'

'Oh yes, yes,' answered Lewis abstractedly. He had been watching passers-by, seeing in each a conspirator hurrying to some secret gathering. He longed to follow . . .

'You can't make an omelet without breaking a few eggs,' remarked the proprietor, examining Corporal Bouvet's hat, on the cockade of which were embroidered the words *Liberté, Egalité, Fraternité*.

'That's true,' agreed the hat's owner. 'But what if you and me are the eggs?'

The proprietor sighed indifferently and tried the hat on.

'Bravo!' exclaimed madame, coming in from her kitchen. '*Vive la nation!*'

The passers-by seemed more frequent. Lewis began to fancy he could read uneasiness, expectancy in their faces. Mortimer had warned him to stay within doors that day. He had no intention of doing so. He would never have forgiven himself if he'd missed whatever it was that might happen.

Shortly after twelve o'clock a man in dark clothes ran past the window. Lewis caught a glimpse of his face; it was excited, eager . . . A few moments later a whole group of perhaps a dozen men hastened by, chattering anxiously. Corporal Bouvet, perhaps catching a few words, frowned. He stood up as the clatter of more feet on the cobbles approached. He put on his hat, picked up his musket and went outside. Another group came by; he stopped and spoke with them. He saluted and returned to the parlour.

'Well?'

'Danton's done something,' he announced.

'Dirty beast!' cried madame, who had just come in again. She picked up her startled cat and smacked it soundly. 'Where? Where has he done it?'

'No, no! Not the cat. Danton in the Assembly. He's made a big speech. Everybody must defend Paris. That's what he says. To arms.'

Silence. The corporal, the proprietor and his wife stared at one another. They looked dismayed. Lewis felt embarrassed. A great moment had plainly come, and all he could feel was an awkwardness and pity for a couple whose anniversary was about to be spoiled.

Madame began to clear the table. Suddenly there was a terrific roar. A cannon had gone off nearby. The Austrians already? No; it was the alarm cannon. One could always tell the sound of a blank charge.

A church bell began to peal; then another, and another, in no sort of sequence. The air was full of bells, banging, cascading, deafening . . . Good God! What next?

Soldiers were running past – children were trying to

keep up with them, waving bits of red, white and blue rags; children pursued by angry, shouting mothers.

Lewis, his heart beating with excitement, went outside into the street. The uproar of the bells in the still, warm air almost knocked him flat. Corporal Bouvet was at his side; he felt his arm grasped.

'Better inside.'

'No, no! What's happening?'

Obligingly the corporal held up his hand to stop a citizen.

There was to be a great proclamation. Where? At the Hôtel de Ville, one supposed. Where else? What proclamation? God knew – but everybody was running to hear it. Something important about the war. The corporal let the man go and endeavoured to pass on the news above the racket of the bells. They clamoured and pealed and boomed; one in particular had a throat like hell and crashed monstrously every few seconds so that Lewis flinched in expectancy of the assault. With no movement of wind, there was no natural defence against the brazen uproar; the metallic notes rolled and lingered till they were hammered flat by those that followed, over and over again.

Although the majority of people seemed to be hastening in one direction, there were numbers who broke off knowledgeably at various corners for other destinations. There were many public places in the city: the Bastille, the National Assembly, the Place Louis XV. Thus small crowds gathered in each, and, finding themselves to no purpose, ran off to the next, pursued now by the fear that they'd be too late and miss the proclamation altogether.

Then mysteriously, as if it had been carried by invisible airborne seeds, the news began to lodge here and there until it became common knowledge.

The worst had happened! The army had been shattered. Verdun had really fallen and the enemy was almost at the gates. Everyone must really take up arms and defend Paris! Men, women and children must be prepared to lay down their lives in the streets to defend liberty!

Liberty! Equality! Fraternity! The huge, crashing bell seemed to be beating out the great watchwords on the very anvil of the sky. It was the bells more than anything that created the universal motion of the crowd; their continual uproar, which had become rhythmic, seemed to have pulverized all separate spirits into identical grains; in places it poured down the streets like a metallic flood.

'Where are they all going?'

'To Saint-Antoine. They're going to defend the gate.'

'And you?'

'Ah! Mister Boston . . . I have a rupture.'

Lewis stared at his companion with undeniable contempt. Even women were running by – women with fierce eyes and pitchforks to slaughter their attackers. Although he himself was but an onlooker, it was impossible not to feel the tremendous enthusiasm of the moment . . . and consequently to condemn Corporal Bouvet for not being swept away by it. His thoughts momentarily reached back to his own home. My God! What a tale he'd have to tell! And when the Austrians came? What sights he'd see: savage soldiers riding madly through the streets, slashing at heads and arms – then dragged from their horses by the brave defenders! Mortimer with a banner, streaming blood and courage . . .

Curiously, even in the heat of his imaginings, Lewis did not feel himself to be in any danger; he was unable to rid himself of a deep sensation of detachment. He knew Mortimer would have despised him for this. Their meeting in the Café de Foix now revealed that Mortimer knew Lewis better than he knew himself. . .

Suddenly Lewis thought he'd glimpsed Mortimer's companion, the seedy actor from the previous evening. He made to follow; but the corporal moved to hold him back. Angrily Lewis pushed him aside. He'd seen it *was* the same man. He was rushing down a narrow alleyway across the road, his cloak swirling out like a black cloud. Lewis ran, anxious not to lose sight of him. He hoped he might be led to Mortimer.

The actor halted on a corner where the alleyway gave onto another street. He looked about him and began to shout and wave to people passing. He possessed an exceptionally powerful voice and his gestures were large and striking. In no time at all he succeeded in capturing attention. Perhaps thirty or more men and women, pathetically armed with broomsticks, choppers and kitchen knives, gathered to listen; and children, fidgeting, excited children . . .

Rapidly his words painted fear and anger on every face. There was a new terror. Worse than anything yet. It was the old rumour again – the evil prison plot. But no longer a rumour. It was about to happen. Traitors feed on panic; murderers drink disaster. Now – at this very worst of all times – with the enemy at the gates – the gaols were about to erupt and discharge their terrible contents! Murder in the parlours; murder in the beds; murder on the sunshine doorsteps where the children played! The monsters in the prisons were ready; the keys were even now in their hands!

'He ask all men who hate wickedness to follow. In the name of Liberty, Equality, Fraternity. In the name of the people.'

Corporal Bouvet, who seemed as firmly fixed to Lewis as another limb, laboriously conveyed the orator's words. 'Some brave men, there.'

There was no hint of irony in the corporal's voice. He was not capable of that. He spoke seriously, as if stating a well-known fact.

The actor had darted off, followed by two or three men from his audience. The rest watched them, shivered and hastened away. Lewis, his thoughts full of Mortimer, kept the actor in sight. Again he halted; again he harangued and then rushed on, with a following now of some four or five. He picked on corners remote from the main thoroughfares where he might have been hard put to attract an audience. He never played to more than small crowds; it was as if he knew his own limitations and the range of his burning eyes.

Nor was he alone in this curious enterprise. Once he passed another such as himself. They exchanged glances across a street. Their faces were cold and grim. In all likelihood there must have been more of them, darting here and there, pausing to terrify and inspire . . . then off with their little knots of followers. Perhaps there were as many as a dozen, twisting and turning through prearranged streets and winding their way to some common place known only to these inspirers, the gatherers, the saviours of the city . . . the Septemberers.

* * *

Nightfall. The city gates were shut and massively guarded; lanterns glinted on set faces and trembling hands. Pikes and muskets made little forests in the night . . . and horses, dragged from carts and coaches to be imprisoned in the shafts of gun-carriages, pulled restlessly so that the black cannon barrels shifted and seemed to be searching of their own accord for the enemy by night.

The bells had long since ceased, and the narrow streets, so recently the passageway of multitudes, were now dark, quiet seams or clefts in a stone landscape.

From time to time a burst of flickering light and a confused sound of shouting and even singing would erupt, and then be extinguished in some covered alley-way . . . only to reappear and be cut off again.

This eerie phenomenon − this fiery worm of the night − was steadily traversing the city; it had moved eastwards from the Palais-Royal towards the Hôtel de Ville, and then beyond.

'It is the way to the prison of La Force,' murmured Corporal Bouvet. 'They keep important prisoners there. Real enemies of the people.'

Lewis, exhausted, battered by the crowd and altogether dazed by the huge excitement of the day, had refused to abandon his search for Mortimer. All bitterness was forgotten. He was in a mood to plead with

Mortimer to let him play some small, humble part in the great enterprise.

He had scoured every street, forced his way back and forth across the river, but he had seen neither Mortimer nor any of the strange little army that had been gathering throughout the day.

Again the shouting erupted, and this time it was not extinguished. A little way ahead, firelight was reflected in the sky. The shouting grew wild and joyous. Lewis began to run towards it, praying that he'd be in time.

Someone was screaming. Weird sound. High-pitched, regular screams. Ah – ah – ah – ah! Hard to say whether it was of terror or excitement. Ah – ah – ah – ah!

It stopped and the shouting rose into cheers and laughter. Lewis turned a corner. Before him loomed the solemn bulk of the prison. Torches were everywhere; and there was a terrific smell of wine and spirits. A real celebration! Figures – impossible to say how many, so black were they against the torchlight – were pushing and laughing and shouting round something in their midst.

What was it? A woman's dress! A really tremendous cheer and a pole went up in the air. A pole with a woman's head on it. She had fair hair and it floated down as if surprised to find no shoulders to rest upon. Where were her shoulders? Oh, down there among the crowd.

Still in her dress. The pole dipped and she looked down curiously, weeping tears of blood from her neck.

Her dress, her fine silk dress, was being ripped in pieces. Now it was quite off. The pole swung drunkenly; the hair swirled as if to mask the staring eyes from watching a man fumbling for her heart.

'And dogs shall inherit the land, biting legs and running through the streets with the private parts of princesses in their jaws.'

A young fellow – no more than sixteen – had made himself a moustache with fine downy hair stained with red. Now he was a man! But it was thirsty work.

'Monsieur! Monsieur l'Anglais!'

There was a movement and torchlight fell full on a figure in a grey topcoat. Mortimer. He was holding a flagon of wine or spirits. He kept pouring it out, pouring it out as the saviours of the city came for necessary refreshment. His thin face was extraordinary. It looked almost saintly.

'You're mad!' screamed Lewis suddenly. 'Mad! Mad! Mad!'

Chapter Fourteen

IT WAS DOUBTFUL if Mortimer saw or even heard his friend. He was in a state of considerable exaltation. He had had a great deal to drink (on previous occasions he had found it to be helpful); but this elevated his spirits rather than confused them. He was able to see over and beyond the immediate action to its ultimate purpose and consequence.

The executed young woman was no more than a symbol; and yet, when one said *no more than a symbol*, one underestimated the importance of symbols. One should have said the executed and dismembered young woman was, in herself, in her flesh, no more than a creature of sex and appetite. It was *because* she was a symbol that her death served a purpose . . .

The conspiracy – of which he had been given positive proof by M. Paré – had to be destroyed, root and branch. It was the knowledge, the consciousness of this great aim that made him realize that no degradation was too foul . . . and indeed, that such degradation lent a superb satisfaction to it.

Had Mortimer seen Lewis in those moments, he would, most likely, not have recognized him, nor raised a finger to stop him being murdered by the extreme patriots with whom he was involved.

By now two groups of men had formed on either side of one of the prison's gates. Pikes, choppers and even carpenters' hammers were lifted in readiness to execute judgement on the enemies of the people as they were forced outside.

'Mr Boston – Mr Boston! It is me – Marcel Bouvet! You must stand up, sir. You must come away!'

Lewis was half lying, half crouching by a wall against which he had been jostled by a gathering crowd.

Wave after wave of shouting and laughter seemed to be beating in his mind, accompanied by the curiously homely sound of cutlery being clashed as if some gigantic table was being hastily cleared.

With difficulty he remembered he'd seen a young man who'd looked exactly like Richard Mortimer. But of course, that was impossible! He had really seen nothing at all. He had fainted. The appalling vision that still haunted him had been the natural consequence of his thoughts suddenly sliding all of a heap. Extreme weariness and lack of food during the hectic day had been his downfall. That was why he now felt so sick. Perhaps he had been sick? Guiltily he peered down among the cobbles. There was a very nauseous smell in the air . . .

'Please, please, Mr Boston . . .'

Corporal Bouvet struggled to drag him upright; his rupture had begun to ache abysmally.

'Please, Mr Boston! Come this way!'

The streets about the front of the prison were rapidly becoming choked with onlookers – whole families from the surrounding tenements who had crept out in terrified curiosity.

At last the corporal succeeded in dragging Lewis to his feet. Sternly – with all the authority of his fierce military aspect – he brushed aside casual offers of assistance.

'This way – I order you, sir, to come this way!'

But Lewis was maddeningly reluctant. He kept stumbling to a halt and staring back at the massive bulk of the crowd. Irritably he shook himself free of the corporal; he was determined to force his way back. It was absolutely necessary for him to convince himself, not of what he'd seen but of what he *hadn't* seen. He wanted to see the figure in the grey topcoat who'd so closely resembled his friend. He wanted to destroy the likeness utterly. The scene drew him horribly; he blundered towards it as one magnetized.

Another joyous shout of triumph burst out. The crowd pressed forward, black against the torchlight, like a wall of stones. Pushed, elbowed and buffeted, Lewis was forced to fall back. As he did so, the pole with the lonely head of the slaughtered young woman upon it soared upward again. Someone had tied a tricolour ribbon round a pole, just below where it entered her neck. Her hair, now become a little muddy and tangled, brushed against her open mouth and caught in her teeth. Strange sight. A little human ball shining in the firelight like a painted balloon . . .

A host of memories came rushing back upon Lewis.

'Mortimer!' he howled, in incredulous dismay. 'It *was* you! I know! I know!'

Really frightened now for the young man's safety – God knew what the patriots might have done! – Corporal Bouvet, regardless of the fearful dropping sensations he felt, pulled Lewis away from the crowd and towards the rear of the prison.

'That woman – that woman! What was it for? Why – why?'

'They were saying . . . ah! Pardon me, Mr Boston. I have a little discomfort. They were saying she was an aristocrat – a princess . . . a friend of the queen. It had to be so . . . believe me. The people are angry . . .'

'Her face! You saw her face? And her hair . . .'

The corporal nodded. He looked down so that his hat with its enormous cockade and embroidered *Liberté,*

Egalité, Fraternité obscured his countenance entirely. For a moment he became no more than an empty suit of clothes.

The shouting had momentarily died down; someone coughed or cleared his throat; a voice began to talk, to argue, to plead, to cry out! Lewis did not understand the words but the bleakness and fearful loneliness were unmistakable. Then steel clashed and the voice was drowned under an avalanche of cheers.

'Can – can nobody save them?'

'They are enemies of the people,' answered the suit of clothes dully. 'Everyone says so.'

'So many?'

A face appeared from under the hat. A hand grappled with the huge moustache. Fierce eyes examined Lewis.

'It will be over soon.'

'It will never be over.'

'In England, Mr Boston, you will forget.'

Lewis shook his head violently. He would not forget. He would never forget. Until his dying day he would remember that he had stood by and watched and listened.

There was another burst of cheering; Lewis scowled and thrust his hands in his pockets, as if to pretend he had none, so useless did they seem. His scowl became intense as he wrestled with a problem that had just beset him. His eyes began to glitter almost feverishly. He breathed rapidly as a new excitement rose within him. His heart was beating painfully.

'Listen! Listen to me! I have money – a great deal of money! Surely to God I've got enough to unlock a door? Look, look! Here it is!'

He dragged out the bulging purse he'd got from the bank. Such was his haste that he tore his coat.

'It's good money! I promise you! Please, please! Now – while there's still time! Think of it – we can save someone! Even one!'

As he uttered the words the uproar in front of the prison swelled out again; the crowd sighed, murmured and shifted. A mother and two children, who seemed to have been squeezed out, came stumbling by. One of the children was crying and the woman dragged it unmercifully. The scene, of no particular significance and open to many interpretations, appeared to affect Corporal Bouvet. He stared after the little group until it disappeared.

'Every minute – every second there might be one we could have saved! There *must* be a way!'

Corporal Bouvet, tearing his eyes with difficulty from the shadows into which the mother and children had vanished, now seemed transfixed by the sight of the purse with its fortune in English banknotes. He was a sensible man, an experienced man, a man not given to hasty enterprise.

He began to argue, still staring at the purse, that the notes could not realize a fraction of their value, that the money would be thrown away, that there was too little time, that it was probable that no guard or turnkey would risk his own neck even for a bribe . . .

'One human being,' cried Lewis, furiously thrusting out his father's purse, 'for this!'

But the corporal continued to argue, using every wile he knew, even though his very reasons seemed to add fuel to the young man's ardent nature. They swayed back and forth like drunkards, scraping and stumbling on the cobbles; they appeared to rage at one another while the relentless waves of noise battered their ears and the steadily increasing stench of the massacre slowly engulfed them.

At last, partly out of self-interest, partly out of compassion and partly out of the weariness of an older man before a younger, the corporal capitulated.

Even as he'd been arguing, denying the very possibility of the enterprise, many thoughts, many schemes had been busy in his mind. It was difficult, but he had to admit to himself that it was not impossible. Nothing was impossible. Corporal Bouvet was a born obliger. He had obliged Mr Hoskins in many a doubtful undertaking ... and found a craftsman's pleasure in the exercise of his skill. He knew he could oblige this English gentleman. Under no circumstances would he willingly fail him. The mysterious arrest under which he'd placed him must not be broken.

Everything had a back door. There was always a way in. The corporal was peculiarly experienced in back doors. All his life had been spent in approaching them. He was confident that, when the time came, he would enter Heaven by a back door.

Such a door, obscure, furtive, mean and filthy, had the prison. It was set in the wall that encompassed the rear of the building and was liberally daubed with expressions of liberty, amorous messages and childish drawings of people who were all heads and no bodies.

Two soldiers stood on guard – or, rather, leaned against the wall and, from time to time, as inspiration struck them, added to the complex decoration on the door. Already several frightened officials had left by way of this door and the soldiers, interrupted in their artistry, had merely grunted and stepped aside. Now they stared sullenly at the corporal and his companion. They were unshaven, weary and generally distrustful. A brief conversation ensued. The soldiers frowned, looked doubtful, then half smiled and stood aside.

'What did you say to them?'

'I tell them that we want to go in and we want to come out. I tell them that we will be no more than five minutes. Also I promise them that when we come out you give them some money. They are poor men, Mr Boston. They have to live. It is the way of the world, what?'

In a great stone room where torches flame and cast coffin shadows on floor and walls, stands a table, thick enough for a butcher. On this table lies the prison register. At first one by one, but now in pairs, prison-filthy enemies of the people are dragged before the table to hear their crimes read out by a lanky stick of a man with an idiot's shock of hair. It matters to no one that he cannot read and therefore does not know who is before him; he has a good strong voice and can shout as well as anyone: 'Enemy of the People! Condemned!'

Then a door opens and a flickering vision of distant faces appears through a hole in the shadows. There seems to be nothing between the opening and the watchers beyond. It is a clear walk, or even a run. Quite suddenly a nearer face appears, giving the game away. An eager, grinning face, and above it peeps something like a workman's hammer.

'This way – this way! Hurry now! We've not got all night!'

He, she or they – the condemned – hesitate. But not for long. Hands push them, feet kick them. They begin to run; they are in the air! Then the sky opens and a rain of iron and steel falls down . . .

Five minutes! I have only five minutes! Lewis Boston is obsessed with time and the shortness thereof. Corporal Bouvet has found a turnkey – a desperately frightened man who wants only to escape. He has pleaded with him – bargained with him – ordered him. Now the turnkey, dazed and bewildered, thinks only of the fat purse of money which has been repeatedly waved under his nose. Already he dreams of running away with it – to the far south, of buying a farm, maybe, and living to forget this horrible night.

'Quickly! Quickly! Here – here is a cell! Take one! Any one! I don't care! But quickly – they're coming.'

Already the turnkey hears footsteps. He will hear footsteps for the rest of his life. He grasps his ring of keys, but his hand shakes so much that he has difficulty in picking the right one.

The prisoners in the huge dark cell shrink back. They dread that it is now time for them.

'Quickly! Choose one!'

Lewis stares through the black bars into the deeper blackness beyond. At first he sees nothing but heaps of filthy clothing; then he sees faces turning towards him

. . . faces made horrible by fear. Take one. Which one? All that money . . . for one. Pick a good one. Get value for money at least. Pick some benefactor of mankind – a doctor or a poet, perhaps. The various bundles of clothing are trembling, shrinking back, back as if to press their way through the very stones of the wall.

Is there nothing else? he longs to ask. Perhaps I can find something that suits me better elsewhere? But that's impossible. Three of his five minutes must have passed already.

A woman! That's it! He'll choose a woman. A mother, perhaps . . . There's a woman! Ah! She's so old . . . That would be a waste.

Who is that? Standing up there in the corner? In blue, is it? Yes, in a blue dress. For a moment Lewis is reminded of someone. But she is dead. Smashed on a pavement long ago.

The woman in blue moves and catches a stray flicker of the turnkey's torch. Eagerly Lewis points. The turnkey nods; he beckons. The woman extends her hand to someone behind her. She comes forward. Lewis catches his breath. He was right. She is beautiful. Suddenly he blushes in shame at what he is contemplating. He only intends to save her *because* she is beautiful. Fiercely he tries to persuade himself that this is not so, that he has seen great qualities in her: wisdom, virtue – generosity. She has a great soul; he has seen it!

Her eyes meet his; his own fill with tears of humiliation as he knows the shallowness of his lies. But it is too late. The turnkey has already whispered to her. Her eyes widen incredulously. She reaches out through the bars as if to grasp freedom before it is given. Her hands, foul with prison slime, catch Lewis by the wrist. She is pleading. Her mother and father are in the cell with her.

'Quickly! Quickly!' mumbles the turnkey. He hears footsteps so loudly now that they cannot be in his head alone.

The mother and father approach. Is there – is there enough money for all three?

'For God's sake hurry!'

With hands that shake so wildly that Corporal Bouvet has to guide them, the turnkey unlocks the gate. First the daughter then the mother and father step out. The gate closes; faces from the darkness watch bitterly, sullenly. But no time for that. The turnkey seizes the purse and vanishes; perhaps he will not stop running till he reaches the far south, buys his farm and then at last sinks into his bed.

'Three!' breathes Lewis triumphantly. 'Three for the price of one!'

* * *

The great stone room was quiet; the prison register was shut. The lanky giant with the idiot's hair had gone to exercise his scholarly zeal elsewhere. Outside, in front of the prison, the crowd also had withered away; some had gone in the wake of the Septemberers, others had drifted home. No more than half a dozen souls remained, trapped like flies in the compulsive web of ruin.

The street was thick with bodies. Arms, legs, heads stuck out everywhere in casual disarray. The smell was monstrous and the dark ground, where it could be seen, shone with blood.

Lewis and his three purchases, who had waited till the fury had passed on, began now to creep away. Corporal Bouvet remained a little apart. The fierce, sturdy little man, proud under his guardsman's hat, lingered to stare down at the slaughtered enemies of the people. Many eyes were still open; and many mouths gaped blackly. There was a buzzing in his ears; he felt he was being deafened by an enormous silent scream.

One of the half-dozen who had remained approached the corporal timorously.

'It was done for the people,' he murmured.

Corporal Bouvet stared at him. The man retreated.

Corporal Bouvet looked up. His face was screwed into an almost comical ferocity.

Suddenly he shouted out so loudly that his voice cracked with the strain:

'*Le peuple? Le peuple? Moi! Je suis le peuple! Moi! Moi!*'

Chapter Fifteen

SINCE MAN HIMSELF is a prison from which his soul or spirit is eternally dedicated to the proposition of escape, it follows that all his creations are but variations on the same image. The very street is a prison, barred by tenements, watched by windows; the public square, wide and desolate, is a prison, guarded by immense, threatening statues, patrolled by shadows and scoured by moon or starlight; the city itself is a gaol, walled, obstructed, frightening at every turn . . .

Nor are these dark, dirty, stony places the limits of imprisonment; even sound is confined so that the very footsteps cannot escape but must return and return, echoing till they die.

Liberté, Egalité, Fraternité, says Corporal Bouvet's hat. Liberty is a dream – a chimera. What of equality and fraternity? See: five figures moving through the night. One walks faster, panting with effort but sustained by the consciousness of his magnificent act. The others, two men and two women, having no such strength, cannot

176

keep pace. Strike out equality. Fraternity alone remains.

'*Monsieur! Monsieur!*'

Reluctantly Lewis slackens his pace. He shrinks from the very idea of stopping – not because he is frightened that he might be caught, but because he longs to reach his lodgings and collapse in sleep. He feels that were he to halt he would never be able to stir his limbs into motion again; they seem to move by force of gravity alone; he is falling rather than walking.

'*Monsieur!*'

The young woman, smelling powerfully of the prison, taps and rustles after him. He hears her breath catching in her throat. He frowns. He has set her free; why hasn't she vanished into the night? Why are the three of them still at his heels? He dislikes the idea of turning and seeing once more the three faces looming after him. They are too like ghosts . . .

'*Monsieur* – please!'

He does turn, and notes that she is not so beautiful as he'd first supposed. Her features are big and strongly formed. Her chief attraction is undoubtedly her eyes, which are long, dark and of great brilliancy. He is thankful, in a way, that she is not so beautiful; it makes his rescue seem less influenced by unworthy motives. One might say she is attractive rather than pretty. . .

'You have saved our lives! How can we thank you?'

He shakes his head, and longs with all his heart to disappear and leave no more behind than an enigma – a mysterious rescuer in the night who has bestowed freedom and wants nothing for his gift.

'Your name – at least tell us your name?'

Her voice is low and husky with privation. Her English is good, though it is heavily accented – thus lending her words a piquancy and originality not wholly deserved.

'Boston. Lewis Boston.'

'Lewis? Ah! Like the poor king!'

He falters. The curious sensation that he'd had outside Drummond and Coutts – of his life repeating itself – returns bewilderingly. The brief exchange, so like a previous one on the Brighton road, brings back a whole segment of time, as if to offer it for use all over again. He struggles to order his thoughts and escape from the suffocating web of memory.

The mother and father, taking advantage of Lewis's slackened pace, approach. They are an oddly assorted couple, he very tall and she frail and slight; sadly they attempt dignity in disastrously soiled clothes. Wave after wave of gaol stench comes off them. They smile hesitantly, gratefully, but do not speak. Their daughter seems their ambassadress. Perhaps she alone speaks English?

He returns the smile, even though his face seems to

crack with the effort. He longs to cry out: why didn't you run – run for your lives? That's the way it should have been! A salute, a deep look from brimming eyes – and then a breathless whirling away . . .

He sees Corporal Bouvet bringing up the rear like a grim shepherd with a musket instead of a crook. Silently he offers his cab-driver's salute. Lewis shivers, turns away and quickens his pace. But it is no use; he hears the multiplicity of footsteps behind him, the haunting rustling of gowns, the panting of breath; and at every turn where the air blows differently, there floods across him the soft, pervasive stink of the gaol.

Of course! Now it dawns on him. They are with him because there is nowhere else for them to go. All holes are stopped; all holes but one, that is . . . With a rush of alarm he realizes the full extent of his unconsidered act. By freeing them from one prison, he himself has walked inside another, locked the door and thrown away the key. He is shackled by gratitude. The family following on his heels, relentless and interminable in their thanks, are henceforth his responsibility and care. In more ways than one he has purchased a freehold . . .

On Monday, September 3rd, the confusion already existing at the Porte Sainte-Denis was immeasurably increased. The tragedies of the night and the continuing tragedies of the day – for the Septemberers were now hacking and stabbing their way through the seven crowded prisons of Paris – produced an awed terror before which authority, in any shape or form, stood paralysed.

The banking-houses, particularly those of Harley and Cameron and Drummond and Coutts, experienced the most extraordinary fluctuations of fortune; the effect of government inaction in the face of such unrest was to increase the value of foreign currency to such an extent that it might fairly have been said that every litre of blood that spurted onto the cobbles added a nought to the exchange value of foreign banknotes. In such circumstances it was hard to say where the greater degradation lay: with those who dealt in blood or with those who dealt in paper. M. Paré, in his little brass cage, was overwhelmed with work, but managed to find time to render a satisfactory account of the recent events to his good friend Mr Dignam-Browne.

Although he disliked bloodshed, it had been M. Paré's duty as a banker to take advantage of it – even as it had been Mr Dignam-Browne's duty as a servant of His Majesty's Government to provoke it by whatever means he could. Whether or not there had ever been a prison plot or whether it had been an ingenious fabrication of Mr Dignam-Browne and his masters now no longer mattered. Either way, the outcome had been a success. The bank had benefited and so, doubtless, would Mr Dignam-Browne and his colleagues. Momentarily M. Paré's thoughts flickered towards the young man – *l'Anglais* – through whose lips had passed the necessary rumours and through whose honourable hands had passed the necessary money . . . and who knew no more than the man in the moon of the forces that directed him. An enthusiast. Without doubt, there had been many more. Without such men, where would we be? M. Paré smiled ruefully as he sealed his letter to London. A courier left with it at midday . . .

During that day and for several following, many passed through the city gates who otherwise might have been prevented. The scrutiny of papers was reduced to the merest formality – often neglected altogether; in most cases the wearing of a national cockade sufficed as a passport and safe conduct.

Among those who left on that Monday morning were a corporal of the National Guard and four civilians, all of whom wore the tricolour very prominently. They boarded the Boulogne coach and were on their way to the coast by nine o'clock that night.

It was only at the post-house at Ecouen that they experienced any alarm. Here, while changing horses, a ragged, confused group of men and women armed with pikes and farm implements approached and demanded to see passports. Most likely none of them knew what a passport was, but regarded the activity as a pleasant amusement for a hot day. A huge female, her face all burning carbuncles, poked her head inside the coach where it hung like a hideous Chinese lantern, smoking sweat. Corporal Bouvet frowned at her and let loose such a stream of invective that she instantly retired in blushing confusion. Last seen she was leading a fresh assault on another carriage in order to bolster up her wounded authority.

It was during the four days of the journey and the subsequent two days waiting at Boulogne for a passage on a vessel to Dover that Lewis really made the acquaintance of the family he had rescued.

Their name was Latour. They had been in La Force for nearly two weeks awaiting trial. They knew nothing of any prison plot; they themselves had been arrested without any warning and for no reason they could imagine. They supposed a servant had denounced them from motives of spite or personal gain.

Before the Revolution they had lived peacefully in their château on the Loire; unwisely they'd come to Paris to present their daughter, Gilberte, at court. Then, like so many of their friends, they had been overwhelmed by events. They were bewildered by it all; they had no idea what was expected of them. If it was for the good of the people – of France – that they should give up their lands and their title, then they would willingly do so. Although they were a very old family, they did not oppose the principles of the Revolution. They were not plotters, they were not tyrants. All they asked was to be able to live their lives in peace and see Gilberte well and happily married.

All this was confided to Lewis by the Count de Latour, assisted occasionally by Gilberte, who leaned over to supply the word or phrase lacking from her father's indifferent English.

The count, a large, stoutly built man, occupied a corner seat in the coach beside his wife and daughter. The countess, who had borne up wonderfully during the first hours of their flight, had succumbed to the tremendous strain of their experiences; she alternated between sleep and silent weeping, covering her face with a handkerchief gallantly provided by Lewis.

Corporal Bouvet travelled outside. The corporal's presence plainly intrigued the count, and perhaps worried him, too. The family had good reason to distrust the National Guard. The count murmured something to his daughter; she compressed her lips and leaned towards Lewis.

'My father wonders if, perhaps, you have known this Bouvet before? He seems so – so attached to you, M. Boston . . .'

'I met him only the day before I—'

'Please, M. Boston – I cannot hear! So much noise!'

Lewis moved closer to the young woman and couldn't help noticing how fine and delicate was her neck. He recounted the whole of his acquaintance with Bouvet, without particularly drawing attention to the undoubted mystery of the corporal's continuing presence.

The count listened intently – his proud, heavy, Roman-featured face jerking back and forth with the motion of the coach. His eyes were dark and brilliant, like his daughter's; only they protruded slightly, giving him the curious appearance of a prince in a fairy-tale who was to have been transformed from a frog but had been interrupted at the very last moment.

The countess also possessed the same dark eyes; most likely theirs had been a marriage between cousins. When she removed the handkerchief, the effect of the three pairs of black, shining eyes steadfastly regarding Lewis tended to unnerve him.

'My father wishes to put you on your guard, M. Boston. He knows these soldiers of the people perhaps a little better than you do. They can be very devious – and very cruel. Is it possible your corporal is a spy? Is it perhaps his intention to trap you, M. Boston?'

The possibility had not occurred to Lewis; he found it very disturbing. He stared at the count's coin-like profile. Gilberte leaned so close to him that the jogging of the vehicle caused their faces to brush together.

'Beware, monsieur! We already know what it is to be trapped and declared enemies of the people. I beg of you, remember where you found us. In La Force!'

'Ah! La Force!'

It was the countess who cried out. Her eyes widened in terror, and the terror spread till the family's eyes seemed to bore their way into Lewis's brain.

Once sown, the seeds of mistrust and fear grew in Lewis's mind. The days in Boulogne were days of terrible anxiety, through which the unknown – in the person of Corporal Bouvet – stalked him through the narrow streets and through the shadows of his dreams. Whenever he went down to the quay, the corporal watched him; whenever he approached a ship's captain, the corporal was there listening. There was no escape from this cockaded little man with his fierce eyes and huge moustache.

At last Lewis was promised a passage on a vessel leaving on Sunday's tide. To the best of his knowledge, Corporal Bouvet knew nothing of this arrangement. He congratulated himself on his skill and confided the good news to the Latours.

That night he lay down, trembling with excitement. Sleep was out of the question; only a very few hours remained. Just before midnight there came a sharp, arresting knock on the door. It was Bouvet.

'Mr Boston?'

'Yes?'

The corporal entered, carrying a candle and his inseparable musket. He did not remove his hat or salute. He put the candle on the table.

'I find out you 'ave a passage for tomorrow.'

Lewis felt his heart contract. He said nothing but watched the corporal's newly polished boots which shone like the cobblestones of Paris by night.

'Mr Boston.'

'Yes?'

'Since I see you outside the bank, I 'ave taken you to the Café de Foix where you meet your friend. What?'

'Yes . . . yes.'

'You leave your friend and I take you back to your lodgings. What?'

Lewis nodded. The history of his activities was relentlessly unfolding.

'On the next day, Mr Boston, I accompany you

everywhere. I watch what you do. I go with you to the prison of La Force.'

'We – we both know that. I – I don't deny it.'

Corporal Bouvet's eyes glittered in the candlelight.

'You see certain things it is better not to 'ave seen. It cannot be 'elped. You ask to save someone from the prison. I argue. Remember that. I try to stop you. But you are fixed on it. So – so I am forced into 'elping. It is against my will. I arrange and you bribe. You spend your money. It is you who choose the prisoners. I 'ave no part in that. But together it is that we take them out. Together – what?'

'Together.'

'Next you want to leave the city. I 'elp. Remember that. People want to drag you all back again. I stop them. And now, now in' – here he thrust his musket between his knees and drew out his enormous pewter watch – 'in six hours you 'ope to leave for England with M. le Comte, Mme la Comtesse and Mlle de Latour. What?'

'Yes . . . yes. What is it you want with us?'

Lewis's mind was in a turmoil; he was contemplating killing the meticulous corporal and hiding his body under the bed.

'I want to come with you, Mr Boston. I 'ave often 'ad it in mind. I 'ave obliged you, as you must see. Now I ask you to oblige me. What?'

'To – to come with us? I don't understand! You – you would be a – a deserter!'

Corporal Bouvet replaced his watch and looked very seriously at Lewis.

'I join the army to eat, Mr Boston. Now, like Mr 'oskins say, I 'ave 'ad a bellyful. Mr 'oskins of 'umpshire promised me that if I should come to England, I should look 'im up and I would be welcome. Marcel! 'e say; just look me up anytime! Now Mr Boston – you are an English gentleman like Mr 'oskins. I ask you to oblige me like I 'ave obliged you.'

Corporal Bouvet briefly removed his hat and polished his head on his sleeve. The conversation had been a great strain on him. At last his secret was out.

'I want to go to 'umpshire, Mr Boston.'

Lewis stared at the National Guardsman, and marvelled. A chance remark made many years ago had so lodged in this man's mind that, in all the turbulent times that had followed, Mr Hoskins of Hampshire alone had stood for peace and paradise. It was perhaps the one thing that had sustained Corporal Bouvet and kept him the man he was; his greatest hope must have been to find such an English gentleman as Lewis, whom he could gladly oblige, and ask no other reward for his services than to be taken to England, home of Mr Hoskins.

'I will oblige you, Corporal Bouvet. I will indeed.'

The corporal picked up his candle, saluted and vanished into the night. Next day, on the early tide, Lewis and his four companions left France for England.

CHAPTER SIXTEEN

IT WAS IMPOSSIBLE for Lewis to arrive that day. With the aid of a road-book, a map and a table of tides, Henrietta had calculated it all exactly. Even supposing there had been no upsets, broken wheels, impassable roads or variable winds – some of which must have occurred – no reasonable person could have expected Lewis home before Thursday. Therefore there was no point in flying to the window every time the wind in the trees made a noise like carriage wheels. Besides, today was Tuesday and it was raining. Nothing ever happened on Tuesday; it was scarcely a day at all; it was just something to stop Monday from running straight into Wednesday.

Henrietta, high in her tower, surveyed the glum, damp landscape and returned to the desultory letter she was writing to her sister in London. Her boredom with the depleted mansion had sunk her to this last resort of an active mind.

'Everything here,' she wrote, 'is as dull as—' She bit

her pen. 'Ditchwater' was feeble. Besides, ditchwater was not necessarily dull. Forsaken maidens had been known to have been drowned in ditchwater and their ghastly faces had been come upon, glaring up through reeds, like crossed-out nymphs. 'Dull as Ma and Pa,' she longed to write; or, better, 'dull as you, Eliza.'

What was the dullest thing she knew? Dull as Dr Stump. Dull as church. Dull as Tuesday . . .

She dropped her pen and went once more to the window embrasure from which the ill-fated architect had peered his last peer. There had been some argument as to who was to have this melancholy room, and Henrietta, being the youngest, had lost. She gazed forth in search of an image that would be the very crystallization of dullness.

Dull as an empty drive . . . She stared above the high-growing shrubs and the roof of the gate-keeper's lodge. Dull as life. What was the use of her beauty that ravished the senses, her dazzling wit, her learning, her poise, her cupboard of rustling gowns – in stinking Lancing?

Dull as a land without Richard Mortimer! The knowledge that he must, at this very moment in time, have her lock of hair, be holding it, perhaps kissing it, made her head tingle as if that short article was still attached.

A carriage had appeared. In spite of the undeniable

impossibility of its containing Lewis, her heart quickened. It turned out to be the ugly carriage belonging to The Ship in Shoreham. A caller for Pa; some beery sea-captain . . .

She went back to her letter, crossed out the last sentence and wrote: 'A carriage is coming. I'm sure it's as good as empty but—'

She rushed back to the window. The carriage had come to a halt. Henrietta leaned out as far as she dared. The driver was climbing to the ground. He was letting down the steps with maddening slowness. He was opening the door.

A soldier came out; a stubby French soldier with a blue tunic and a hat with a red, white and blue cockade. Next came Lewis.

Before all other emotions, an instinctive dread seized Henrietta. Something terrible had happened to Mortimer. The French soldier was bringing news of it. Her agitated thoughts flew directly to battlefields and blood. She dared not move. Why was Lewis standing there? Why wasn't he rushing inside?

Careless of the rain, he was handing someone else out of the carriage: a young woman . . . and then two other people. Her mother had rushed out and was embracing Lewis with impulsive violence. *Now* he must come up and see her . . . and tell her what had to be told.

Why was he bothering with introductions? They could wait. If it was all about Richard Mortimer, then *she* ought to be the first to know!

At last she overcame the paralysis of excitement; she flew from her room and down the stairs . . .

'Lewis!'

'Henrietta!'

Brother and sister embraced. Lewis smelled strangely; he smelled of the sea and there was another, slightly disagreeable smell clinging to him.

'My sister Henrietta—' He attempted to disengage her and present her.

'Did you see him?'

'Later – later!'

'Did you *see* him?'

'I – I—'

'Please!'

'My sister Henrietta!' interposed Lewis, furious and ashamed of Henrietta's behaviour. 'The Count and Countess de Latour and their daughter, Gilberte! This is my sister, Henrietta, Corporal Bouvet. Corporal—'

'He's dead, isn't he?'

'No – no!'

'Then what is it? Who *are* these people?'

Henrietta's agonized questions were put in undertones; she was scarcely capable of attending to anything

that was said to her and made only the most perfunc-
tory attempts to welcome the guests. God knew what
they were thinking of her . . .

'Your brother, Mlle Boston,' said Mlle de Latour,
who had tremendous dark eyes that Henrietta felt could
not be real, 'has saved our lives. Perhaps he is too modest
to tell you all; but I promise you he is a hero.'

There was no doubt that Gilberte, seeing Henrietta's
obvious agitation, meant well. Unfortunately Henrietta
took an instant dislike to her. The Frenchwoman seemed
to extend some sort of ownership over Lewis and
Henrietta resented fiercely any idea that she might
already have received her brother's confidences. She
wondered if Gilberte was Lewis's mistress? She compressed her lips and resolved to be aloof.

The house is full, wrote Henrietta, who had retired to
her tower at the first opportunity to continue with her
letter to Elizabeth, *of French aristocrats. You would think my
brother had had enough of countesses; but no! He's fetched back
a complete* set *from Paris. Picked them up in a prison, it seems,
just like we might get hats in the Strand. They have* suffered,
*of course. Why is it everyone is allowed to suffer except you and
me? My brother is a fool, Eliza; and so is our ma. She has
been falling over herself so that you would imagine she was
selling them the house instead of entertaining them. Most
likely, when you come back they will have gone, so I will tell*

you what they are like. Their family is so old that you would think the babies were born wrinkled! He, the Count de Latour, is a great pompous man with popping black eyes like grapes. The countess is small and quite elegant, but as she doesn't speak English, one can't really make up one's mind about her. The worst of the three is their daughter, Gilberte. She's about my size and wears a dress so low in front that nothing is left to the imagination except why. She has staring black eyes, a big nose and a big mouth which she never keeps shut. I think she fancies herself a beauty. Of course, my fool of a brother is besotted with her. There is also a French corporal, complete with musket and moustache. As you can imagine from the foregoing, the whole house stinks of France. I don't know what Pa will say when he comes home. But I do know, really. He'll want to give a function. I can just hear him: 'We must send out cards! Henrietta! Make a list—'

At this point there came a knock on the door. Hurriedly Henrietta thrust the somewhat incriminating letter into a drawer.

'Come in—'

It turned out to be Lewis. He came in and shut the door behind him. She waited for him to speak. He made some unnecessary remark about having been unable to bring her back a present. She watched him closely. She knew him well enough to sense that something was troubling him deeply. He could never conceal anything really. Compared with her, he was quite transparent . . .

'You did see him, didn't you!'

Lewis looked momentarily nonplussed by the sudden interruption – almost as though he hadn't expected it. He had long debated with himself whether or not to tell Henrietta what he *had* seen. At first he'd thought of pretending he hadn't seen Mortimer at all. But then he realized Henrietta might well demand back her lock of hair. He could, of course, say he'd lost it, but did not think she'd believe him. No; he'd have to admit he'd seen Mortimer and presented the precious token. At once, the image of Mortimer stuffing Henrietta's hair into his greasy, misshapen pocket rose up in his mind. He recalled, with sickening clarity, the murdered woman's hair floating round her butchered neck; he saw again the obscene youth with that other downy hair plastered on his upper lip with blood. And there was Mortimer, looking on . . .

'Yes. I saw him.'

'How was he?'

'He – he was thinner. Quite skinny, really.'

'Not ill?'

'Oh no. He was quite well.'

'What did he say? Did he ask about – me?'

'He said . . . he said you were his favourite young lady in all England.'

'He didn't! You made that up!'

'On my honour. My word as a Boston!'

'Worthless! Did he really say that?'

'Really.'

'Did you give him—'

'The lock of hair? Yes.'

'What did he say to that?'

'Thank you, of course.'

'Be serious.'

'I am. He said it had grown darker; then he – he put it in his pocket.'

'Which pocket?'

'Next to his heart.'

Henrietta sensed the lie but was content to let it go.

'Did you tell him that I've grown up now?'

'I told him you were much prettier than Eliza.'

'What did he say to that?'

'He – he smiled.'

'How?' Henrietta couldn't rid herself of the mortifying fear that her gift of a lock of hair had been sneered at. She felt sure that Mortimer still thought of her as a fat, vulgar fourteen-year-old.

'He just – smiled,' said Lewis, with irritating vagueness.

'Did he say anything else? Did he send anything? A letter?'

'He . . . he was going to. We were to have met again. But then there was so much confusion . . . and there was the – the prison and the Latours—'

'Damn the Latours! I detest them!'

'Henrietta!'

'How could you think of *them* when – when your best friend was in the same town? Richard Mortimer is worth a thousand like them!'

'Richard Mortimer is—' began Lewis, stung into indignation by his sister's unreasonable attitude. He was trying, as hard as he knew how, to preserve Richard Mortimer for her. Under no circumstances must he allow himself to be goaded into telling her the truth. He shrugged his shoulders and turned to the window.

Henrietta stared at him angrily. She knew there was something else. She could only suppose they'd quarrelled again. Lewis was jealous of Mortimer. He always had been!

'Well? What *is* Richard Mortimer? Don't just stand there, looking out of the window! Tell me! No? All right then – I'll tell you! Richard Mortimer is a great idealist. He's not a money-grubbing wine importer's son who thinks of nothing but profit! Richard Mortimer went to Paris to fight for humanity – not to get his hands on a few dirty banknotes. I suppose you feel very proud of yourself, Lewis. I suppose . . . I suppose . . .'

Here the last vestiges of Henrietta's composure vanished. Her whole being seemed to explode with the force of neglected passion. She flung herself on her bed and wept furiously, bitterly. For a moment, Lewis watched her; he felt wretched. Then he sat beside her and touched her shaking shoulders.

'Go away!'

'Henrietta—'

'Go back to your bloody French bitch!'

'Henrietta . . . he – he said he wished he could see you again. I swear he said that!'

'Then why didn't he come back with you?'

'He – he couldn't. He had . . . things to do . . .'

'What things?'

'I – I don't know. He wouldn't say.'

'He's not married, is he?'

Henrietta sat bolt upright. There was a look of terror on her face.

'No. There's no one else. I'm sure of that.'

'Then what is it, Lewis? What's wrong?'

Lewis sighed hopelessly. The closeness between brother and sister made any complete deception impossible. Henrietta was staring at him with piercing anxiety. He knew he'd failed to reassure her. He tried to think of something – anything to account for his own troubled manner. Mercifully there was something else. It was perfectly true that a certain matter had been troubling him, on and off, for several days. It was a matter not remotely connected with Mortimer . . .

'It's the money,' he said, after a substantial pause.

'What money? Can't this family think of anything but money?'

'The money I was sent for—'

'What about it?' She was wavering, but far from convinced.

'It – it's gone.'

'What do you mean, gone? Where has it gone?'

'I spent it.'

'Good God! All of it?'

'Every penny.'

'What on?' (Could he have given it to Mortimer? Could he have been talked into giving it to Mortimer's cause?)

'The Latours. To get them out . . .'

'You – you idiot!' (Damn him – damn him!)

'What else could I do?'

'Ask Pa. It was his money.'

'I know.'

'When will you tell him?'

'When he asks.'

'Poor Lewis!'

'Worse; much worse. Penniless Lewis!'

Brother and sister smiled mournfully at each other. As of old, all doubts and differences between them and all private passions were sunk before the prospect of parental wrath.

Chapter Seventeen

THE STORM HAD not yet broken; obstinately, wilfully it remained suspended over Lewis's head. The distinguished guests had long since retired and Mr Boston had taken Lewis into his study for yet another and uninterrupted account of his adventures in France. He wanted to hear everything – everything!

Henrietta, divided between keyhole and the incessant demands of her exhausted mother, still could hear only affability drifting through the closed door. More and more she neglected Mrs Boston; the suspense was intolerable ...

'Henrietta!'

'Coming, Ma!'

Reluctantly, she crept away ...

On either side of the fireplace in the study sat father and son. The one regarded the other with the utmost complacency; he knew of no reason why he shouldn't. The other couldn't help pitying him for this, knowing, as he did, every reason why he shouldn't.

'I am proud of you, Lewis,' said Mr Boston, for perhaps the sixth time. 'Here! Have some more wine. Don't stint yourself, my boy!'

He leaned forward and refilled his son's glass. Lewis smiled feebly. He had not been stinting himself; he had been drinking rather freely – and for medicinal purposes. But his uneasiness had not gone away; if anything, it had become worse. Even the most expensive wine cannot supply calmness and courage where those qualities are lacking . . .

'Humanitarian,' said Mr Boston. 'A wonderful gesture. That a son of mine should be so – so—' He snapped his fingers, being at a loss for the precise word that would describe his son. (Later, a word would occur to him, but at the moment he couldn't think of it.)

'That count, I must say, is really quite the nobleman. Did you notice how he bowed to your mother? Effortless. He certain makes some of our local families look poor fish, eh?'

Mr Boston's eyes glistened thoughtfully.

'Of course, we must have a function. Perhaps another garden party, if the weather holds? One forgets, it's still September. And the young lady – Mlle de Latour – would be a real flower in our garden, eh? A lovely creature, Lewis. I really congratulate you. I wouldn't mind if . . . but we mustn't think of such things, eh?

All I hope is that they can manage to stay with us long enough for a function. That's all I ask.'

So Mr Boston prattled on, leaning back in his chair and regarding his handsome son with the greatest warmth. Lewis really was turning out remarkably well. There was no doubt that, when the time came, he'd be able to manage the business capitally. Such charm and capability . . .

'By the bye, my boy – how went it at Drummond and Coutts? Did you have any difficulties? After you went, we were a little worried, you know. In London they were only offering twenty-eight per cent. But I imagine you were shrewd enough to do better than that.'

Lewis poured himself some more wine. His hand shook.

'Thirty-seven per cent, Pa.'

Mr Boston chuckled delightedly. 'I knew you had it in you, Lewis! I always knew it! Time and again I've told your mother – that boy will make a first-class business-man! You cannot imagine how pleased I am with you! In days to come, my boy,' he went on moistly, 'when your father is – is no more, your mother, thank God, will be left in capable hands. That's all I've ever asked. You are a good son . . . a credit to me . . .'

Lewis drained his glass of wine and, watched

indulgently by his father, refilled it. By this time his hand was shaking quite noticeably.

'You took English notes, of course?'

'English notes, Pa.'

'You have them on you?'

'No, Pa.'

'Upstairs, then?'

'No, Pa.'

'You gave them to your mother?'

'No, Pa.'

'Then where are they, Lewis? Where is the money, my son?'

'It's gone, Pa.'

'It — it's *what*?'

'Gone, Pa.'

'Now don't joke with me, Lewis. It's too late at night. Don't joke with me. I don't like jokes about money. Tell me at once, where is it?'

'Gone, sir,' said Lewis. 'I swear it. I gave it to the turnkey in the prison to let out the Latours.'

'You what? You *what*? You WHAT?'

Mr Boston's voice rose in a steady crescendo. He leaped from his chair and overturned the decanter of wine which ran over the carpet like blood. Outside the door, Lewis fancied he heard a sharp intake of breath. He actually saw the door handle tremble.

The thought of the unseen witness gave him a spurious courage.

'What could I do, Pa?' he burst out desperately. 'There they were! You – you said it was humanitarian. And they're a very good family—'

'Don't talk to me about humanity!' raged the betrayed father. 'You went there on business! Business! Do you know what you've done? You – you idiot!' (Mr Boston had found the word that had eluded him earlier.) 'You've thrown away a fortune! A fortune! Do you think it grows on trees?'

'But you said—'

'Don't dare to argue!'

'You did say you were proud—'

'Proud? Proud of what? Of having a fool for a son? Not even that dolt of a brother of mine would have done such a thing!' He began to pace the room in the utmost agitation.

'I don't know – I really don't know how to break it to his mother,' he said, as if suddenly entering into a rational conversation with some invisible third party. 'How can I tell her that her son has ruined his family? How can I tell her children that their brother has given away – *given away* – their marriage portion?' (Here, Lewis was sure he heard a muffled cry from the other side of the door.) 'Given it to a prison turnkey! A fine thing!'

'It wasn't a gift, sir! It was to save lives!'

'What's that got to do with it?' Mr Boston had blazed up again, but almost immediately relented a fraction. 'All right . . . a few pounds I wouldn't have begrudged. I'm not unfeeling. But *everything*? No.'

'You said that the count was—'

'Ah yes. The count.' Mr Boston's voice dropped to a terrible calm. 'And the countess. And the daughter. And, one must suppose, the corporal. As God is my witness, I don't know how I can look anyone in the face after this. I send my son to Paris on business. And what does he do? Buys himself a whole family with his father's money. Brings them back to his father's house. And I'll tell you another thing. They have mouths, you know. They have stomachs. They won't live on air. Ha! Had you thought of that?'

Mr Boston's face twisted in a bitter smile; but there was no doubt his wrath was diminishing. Lewis waited patiently.

'And here's something else. That money, you know. I was going to give it to you. Yes, I was going to make you a present of it because I thought you had come of age and deserved it. Now – now you have robbed yourself, my boy! Yes, Lewis, that's what you've done. I hope you are pleased with yourself.'

This ingenious method of making Lewis the chief

sufferer mollified Mr Boston considerably.

'Now that's understood, we will say no more about it. The subject is closed.'

He repeated this for about another ten minutes until he detected signs of relief in Lewis's face, when he felt it necessary to add to his son's guilt. He declared that he didn't see how they could afford even a small function in the circumstances. There would have to be economies. In the morning he would have to let a footman and the gatekeeper go. Lewis might blame himself for causing two innocent people to lose their employment. And now the matter was closed . . .

The matter was absolutely, definitely closed. Mr Boston could not have been more emphatic. He'd had his say and not another word of reproach would pass his lips. However, it was beyond human nature to prevent certain unspoken words passing by way of his eyes. The injured father couldn't help watching every mouthful of food the Latours ate and every chair they sat in without turning to Lewis with a profound expression that plainly said: 'Ha!'

Yet it was equally beyond human nature for Mr Boston to remain unmoved, for any length of time, by the thought of entertaining the nobility. He couldn't find it in his heart to blame them. They were entirely innocent in the matter; the last thing he wanted was to make them feel embarrassed. Quarrels between father and son were of a private nature. Guests must be made to feel welcome. One did not wish to appear boorish before one of the oldest families in Europe. He made great efforts to control himself, frequently glancing at them with fond admiration – to which they responded with pleasantly natural smiles.

It was this naturalness that finally captivated Mr Boston . . . the surprising fact that they *were* natural – the count had even belched—

'They are quite like ourselves,' he confided to Mrs Boston. 'One cannot help admiring them.'

Inevitably, the plans for a function were revived and, as a mark of courtesy, a certain indefinable refinement invaded the Bostons' way of life. Anything strictly English tended to be apologized for, and Mrs Boston conversed as if she were laboriously translating from the French for the benefit of less cultured members of her family. Stairs were negotiated with dignity, rooms were entered calmly; all flouncing and shouting about the house was banished, together with any carelessness of dress and raging hair.

We are behaving, wrote Henrietta to Eliza, *like guests in our own house. The Latours are the only ones who seem at home. Ma and Pa are so refined that no one could imagine them unbending enough – even in bed – to produce us!*

Sometimes I long to burst out at table and say something really outrageous — anything to break the spell! As it is, I have to go and sit in the office every morning to make sure I am really in our house and not in a bloody French château!

The office — the Bostons' informal breakfast parlour, so long the sentimental heart of the mansion — had fallen into disuse since the coming of the Latours. Its gaily papered walls and clumsy, chipped furniture were suddenly felt to be things outgrown. There was even talk of having the room 'done up' and improved. This was inexpressibly painful to Henrietta. Lately the room had become peculiarly intimate for her, even more so than her high, romantic tower; it was in the office that she had seen Richard Mortimer for the last time. She did everything she could to preserve it, even undertaking the dusting and cleaning herself. Had the key not been long since lost she would have kept the room locked; as it was she went there early in the mornings and stayed, in sole possession, for as long as she dared. Hence her feelings were considerably disturbed when she approached one morning and heard voices coming from within.

Angrily she opened the door and found Lewis and Gilberte seated at the table laughing together. Lewis reddened slightly, but Gilberte rose to greet Henrietta with perfect composure.

'Such an enchanting room!' she exclaimed. 'I had no

idea! It is a room one might dream of! It is a home!'

Henrietta turned away and frowned. The privacy and intimacy of the office had been spoiled. Now it was no more than a showplace for Mlle de Latour to gush over with all her irritating graciousness and style. The sooner it was 'done up', the better.

'Your brother has been telling me of your childhood games. See, he is in the royal chair! *Voilà! Louis le Roi!*'

'Not a very good name for a king,' said Henrietta, almost venomously. She was furious that Lewis had so readily betrayed *everything*.

'Henrietta!' began Lewis, redder in the face than ever.

'No, no!' said Gilberte calmly. 'Your sister is right. Alas, our Louis is not a wise king.'

'He is a fool,' pursued Henrietta, determined to sting Gilberte into anger. 'And his wife is beneath contempt.'

'It may be as you say, Miss Boston. It is often so with pretty women; and the men who marry them are often fools. But surely one should pity them now?'

'Pity a king and queen?'

'Pity anyone who has fallen from a high estate.'

'I pity no one who's lost what they never had to work for!'

This last retort of Henrietta's was delivered so pointedly and with so resentful a look that the impoverished Mlle de Latour went quite pale and turned away. Lewis glared at his sister in fury. He did not quite know how to intervene; he felt like leaping up and hitting Henrietta.

'Your sister is a great revolutionary,' said Gilberte at length. Henrietta noted with satisfaction that her voice shook slightly and her long, thin hands were clenched.

'It is a luxury I myself would like to afford.' She tried to smile, but her lower lip was trembling. 'What a pretty plate!' she exclaimed abruptly, changing the subject and rustling hastily to the old pine dresser to avoid Henrietta's relentless eyes. She reached to take down one of the Bostons' nursery plates that had somehow survived the holocaust of childhood.

Henrietta observed that her sleeve was torn and stained under the arm. In spite of herself she felt a pang of distress and pity for the young woman she had wounded. Gilberte caught her expression – perhaps divined it – and looked down. It was impossible for the younger girl – always violent in her changes of mood – not to feel bitterly ashamed and, consequently, try to make amends.

'I – I came,' she said with difficulty, 'to ask you, Mademoiselle – Gilberte – if you had need of any clothes. I – I realize you could bring nothing with you … so – so I thought, as we are the same size—'

'I *wish* we were the same size!' murmured Gilberte,

casting a quick, admiring glance at Henrietta's well-rounded figure.

Henrietta, taken completely by surprise by the neatness of the compliment, beamed helplessly.

'Miss Boston – Henriette – I am so grateful to accept your offer! It is most generous . . . and most truly kind!'

Lewis heaved a sigh of relief. He could have kissed Henrietta; he could have kissed Gilberte as well.

It must be admitted that the thought crossed Henrietta's mind, as she led the way to her tower, of offering Gilberte a gown that would not suit her. It was probable also that the same thought occurred to Gilberte as she rustled in Henrietta's wake. What should she do under such circumstances? She would have no choice but to accept, and then do her utmost to make it a reproach.

'Have you a favourite colour, Gilberte?' asked Henrietta, opening the doors of her wardrobe.

'I – I would rather you chose,' said Gilberte softly; and her voice trembled again.

Henrietta hesitated; she frowned. Gilberte smiled painfully, feeling herself at the younger girl's mercy.

'Do you still care for blue? Or have you become tired of it?'

'No. Not at all. I like it very much indeed.'

Henrietta lifted out a gown of flowered blue silk embroidered with silver lace.

'But it is magnificent!'

'I – I don't wear it.'

'But you should – you should! You must look lovely in it!'

'My brother likes it.'

'Then all the more reason—'

'For you to wear it! It's ridiculous for a sister to please her brother, Gilberte!'

Henrietta held out the gown, almost thrusting it into Gilberte's hands.

'Your brother is a wonderful young man, Henriette,' said Gilberte, holding the gown as if still reluctant to take it. 'You should be very proud of him.'

'Is he in love with you, Gilberte?'

It was as if the gift, now in Gilberte's hands, gave Henrietta the right to ask so searching a question. Gilberte, at first startled, sensed this and looked down at the gift before answering.

'Henriette . . . we – we hardly know each other . . .'

'Have you had many lovers, Gilberte?'

Henrietta's voice took on an edge of excitement. Once having plunged into such a subject, she was disinclined to abandon it until she had plumbed its depths.

'You are very inquisitive, Henriette.'

'Surely it's a natural enough question – between women?'

'Between *women*? How old are you, Henriette?'

'Seventeen. And you, Gilberte?'

'Very old. Twenty.'

'We are both women, then! Old enough to be mothers . . . certainly old enough to be in love.'

'You are very outspoken.'

'Do I embarrass you?'

'A little.'

'I'm sorry. I won't ask you again about your lovers.'

'It doesn't matter. There have been none. My life has been perhaps more sheltered than yours. I was taken to Paris to find a husband. But that was not to be. Now you know all. Now tell me about your lover?'

'I have none.'

'That is not true.'

'How do you know? Did my brother—'

'No. He said nothing. I know. That is enough. After all, as you have said, we are women.'

'All right, then. He – he is in Paris.'

'A Frenchman?'

'No. He is English. He went there to – to help the Revolution. You see, Gilberte, we are on opposite sides.'

215

Gilberte crossed the room and looked out of the window. She answered without turning.

'I see nothing of the kind, Henriette. We are on the same side. We are both victims.'

After Gilberte had left the room, Henrietta went to her wardrobe and sighed. The dress she had given Gilberte had been her best one. She tried hard not to regret it.

CHAPTER EIGHTEEN

CORPORAL BOUVET WAS persuaded to remain in
Lancing until after the twenty-seventh of the month,
when Mr Boston was to give a small function in honour
of the visitors from France. He was particularly anxious
for the corporal, in his bright uniform and cockaded hat,
to grace it.

The corporal had not yet located Mr Hoskins of
Hampshire. To his surprise there turned out to be no less
than five gentlemen of that name residing in the county,
all of whom had seats blessed with fine prospects; all, in
short, Hoskinses of undoubted substance. But which of
them was *the* Mr Hoskins baffled the mind and puzzled
the will. From the descriptions published in the road-
book and gazetteer, none of them quite answered to the
Oriental splendour of the Mr Hoskins of Corporal
Bouvet's acquaintance.

The corporal, who had conceived of Hampshire as
being an immense park with Mr Hoskins's mansion in
the middle of it, was dismayed. He looked disconsolately

at the alien sky and seemed to shrink inside his uniform. He declared his intention of setting off into Hampshire to search for himself, and it was only after Mr Boston had promised to write to each of the Mr Hoskinses to discover which of them had invited Marcel Bouvet of Paris to 'look him up', that the National Guardsman had agreed to stay in Lancing.

He had shrugged his shoulders, offered his curious salute and had proceeded to make himself useful about the house in an astonishing variety of ways.

He turned out to be adept at cleaning and repairing clothes, at polishing furniture and restoring the shine to gilt – in which the Boston mansion was prodigiously rich. He even tuned the harpsichord and played on it a pretty Breton folk song he'd learned as a child.

In the mornings he liked to go down to the village and visit The Plough where he quickly acquired a taste for English ale. In fine weather he would sit on the bench outside, with his musket beside him and his hat, with its enormous revolutionary cockade, perched on his knee. Truly, in the quiet little village he presented a most curious sight. At first the local children were terrified of him; then they began to make fun of his moustache, and finally they plucked up courage to approach and ask what it was like to be a Frenchman and live on the other side of the sea. While he told them, frowning and glittering and gesticulating with his tankard of ale, they would slyly play with his musket and extinguish each other under his hat.

It was here that he met Mr Archer and struck up a cautious relationship with that one-time friend of Tom Paine. At the beginning, the tutor tended to regard the National Guardsman with awe – as might a mythographer confronted with a unicorn. Here was your actual people – or, rather, your actual person – straight from the very volcano of liberty. Was it not written in his eyes, in his powerful hands? Why, it was even written on his hat! Respectfully the tutor sat beside the fierce, cockaded little man who had taken part in events that were still shaking the world.

'Let us hope, eh? that your Revolution succeeds better than ours did!'

Uneasily Corporal Bouvet nodded. He was not familiar with English history or politics but did not want to give offence by admitting it.

'Were you – were you *there* on the glorious fourteenth of July? At the Bastille?'

Corporal Bouvet nodded again and explained about his rupture and his subsequent failure to qualify for a pension.

Mr Archer smiled sympathetically and listened while the corporal expanded on his unfortunate condition and the limitation it placed on his activity. When he paused for breath, Mr Archer plunged in eagerly with:

'What a moment it must have been! When the privileges of the aristocracy were finally abolished! What a moment, eh? That was in August, wasn't it?'

The corporal believed that it was; in fact he was almost certain he'd heard it mentioned when he'd been queueing to see different officials about his pension. One after another! And you had to tell them all the same story over and over again. You'd have thought they could have written it down and passed it on. God alone knew there was enough paper about! In the Palais-Royal it used to blow about like a snowstorm. Leaflets, pamphlets, government forms—

'Ah! The Palais-Royal!' broke in Mr Archer. 'That's where it all happens, eh? How I wish I could have been there! The orators, the pamphlets, the excitement! What a place – what a place! They say it's the real heart of the Revolution! The middle of the exploding world!'

Corporal Bouvet tugged at his moustache and twisted his hat round on his knee. It was certainly a pretty place, he agreed. He used to go there quite often. Nice walks and seats . . . But now the cafés were too expensive for him, and the girls were so young – would you believe it, fourteen and fifteen, some of them! – that it made him feel too old. One could certainly do better elsewhere . . .

The corporal paused and glanced at Mr Archer, half knowingly, half uncertainly.

'I – I am a sympathizer, you know,' said Mr Archer, feeling that the National Guardsman needed reassurance on that point. After all, he must have been feeling uneasy in this land of dukes and earls and scandalous inequality. 'I was once a friend of Tom Paine, you know. I assure you, that were I a younger man nothing would have prevented me—'

He stopped, realizing awkwardly that he was possibly talking to a man as old, if not older, than himself.

'That is,' he went on, feeling himself going red, 'I too might have been more – more . . .'

He stopped again. He had been intending to bring the conversation round to his pupil, Mortimer, who, at this very moment, was fighting the good fight in the streets of Paris; but he felt a *presence* at his elbow that inhibited his speech. He looked round and saw, to his intense annoyance, that Mrs Coker was standing in the doorway of The Plough and regarding him with glassy intensity. For a moment he thought she was drunk; but she remained perfectly upright and swayed neither to the right nor the left. She was resplendent in a tightly fitting black gown that had been bequeathed to her by a lady of significantly lesser dimensions. Her hair appeared to have been newly dyed and emerged all round her white cap like glazed piecrust.

'Ah! Mrs Coker!' muttered Mr Archer savagely.

Mrs Coker smiled maternally but did not move. To Mr Archer's further annoyance, he observed that Corporal Bouvet had risen to his feet and was plainly awaiting an introduction. Mr Archer had no alternative but to oblige and observe the corporal combine his curious salute with a briskly gallant bow. At the same time he ran his hand over his polished head as if to smooth down a suddenly youthful lock. Mrs Coker responded by sinking and rising in a mysterious curtsey. The corporal and the seasoned widow regarded each other keenly and warily.

Mr Archer, who could think of no way of avoiding it, granted an invitation to Mrs Coker to join them. Had he not done so, he felt that she might have remained standing where she was for the rest of the day. Mrs Coker beamed and seated herself on the furthest edge of the bench so that three-quarters of her amplest part remained suspended in air. Corporal Bouvet resumed his own place and leaned forward with a smile of vintage charm. Mrs Coker also leaned forward and contrived to look demure. Mr Archer, seated in the middle, felt horribly uncomfortable.

He attempted to resume the conversation where it

had been interrupted, but was unable to remember what he'd meant to say; he was put off by sensing Mrs Coker's cow-like gaze transfixing him in order to get to the other side. At length defeated, he sank back. He noted that Corporal Bouvet had replaced his hat at a singularly saucy angle and was tugging at his moustache while Mrs Coker quivered gently. He could feel the bench vibrating.

'If you will excuse me,' muttered Mr Archer in a panic, 'I – I have work to do ...'

As he fled, he heard the widow and corporal begin their acquaintance. At first hesitantly and then with increasing animation they set about urging the rival merits of the households of Mortimer and Mr Hoskins of Hampshire. Although it was evident that neither was listening to the other, it was equally evident that each had found a vein of deep mutual interest.

'Such people,' muttered Mr Archer bitterly, 'don't deserve a Revolution!'

On the twenty-seventh of the month everyone came; they always did. Though there were certain elements in the neighbourhood who liked to look down on the Bostons' functions, they never missed them.

Mr Boston himself, standing on his terrace between the Bastille stones, looked over his cheerfully crowded lawn with the utmost pleasure. He knew – he could hardly fail to have known – that his functions excited a measure of good-natured contempt among his social superiors. He knew, even, that his own family tended to smirk over them and make jokes; but it no longer seemed to matter. There had been times, in the past, when he'd wondered if his functions had really been worth-while. Once he had almost not given one, but the general disappointment over its possible absence had so strongly moved him that he came to realize, with a glow of surprised pride, that the Boston functions had become an agreeable part of the neighbourhood's life. Not to have had one would have been unthinkable.

He watched his guests fluttering and milling about one another, drinking his wine, eating his food and enjoying his home, and reflected wonderingly on his own achievement. Where else would lowly Mr Coles of Worthing exchange smiles and words with proud Lady Bullock? Where else would the scruffy landlord of The Plough wish Mr Mortimer of Salvington a very good day – and be answered for his pains?

He, Alexander Boston, from the humblest beginnings, had brought all this about. He had created a democracy ...

Where else would one of the best families in Europe be found associating with some of the least distinguished?

Here Mr Boston's democracy wilted a little as he contemplated the glory of having acquired the Latours. What splendid people they were! Everyone admired them. Even the little French corporal – who had spruced himself up and was looking a picture of military deportment – seemed unable to tear himself away from them.

At times, Mr Boston thought wryly that Corporal Bouvet was overdoing his concern for his distinguished compatriots. He seemed to be plying the count with wine almost to the exclusion of everyone else. He kept returning and returning and standing stiffly in the count's shadow.

Mr Boston wasn't the only one who noticed this; the count himself remarked with a smile to Mr Mortimer that he suspected the good Bouvet was angling for a situation in the Latour's château in the Loire when the present troubles should be over. Nevertheless, he thanked God that there were still such loyal and attentive Frenchmen as Bouvet!

Mr Mortimer graciously inclined his head. He rather liked the count, who was the only really tall man he had ever met. For some time he had been occupying himself with trying to determine whether he was taller than the count or not. He had noted the count's shadow on the grass and had then attempted to stand in the same position to see if his own shadow exceeded it. It was an amusing thing to do . . .

The count, on the other hand, did not seem unduly worried about rival statures. He was altogether livelier than Mr Mortimer and necessarily more concerned with politics. The news, that had been in the *London Chronicle* only the day before, that the French monarchy had been abolished, had come as quite a blow; but he explained that his own extensive domain in the Loire was likely to remain loyal to the family. He had always treated his tenants well and had no reason to suppose that they would turn against him now.

Mr Mortimer smiled. He had discovered he was almost certainly half an inch taller than the count. The thought pleased him; irrationally he felt even better disposed towards the Frenchman.

'Ah, Bouvet! Encore?'

The corporal had again presented the wine tray.

'Maybe I call you *buvette*, eh?' The count laughed good-humouredly and explained to Mr Mortimer that *buvette* was a room in which one drank.

Although there had been the merest hint of a reproof in the count's little joke with Bouvet, he was content to take another glass.

'It is a very good wine, M. Mortimer. Very good indeed. M. Boston is an expert, yes?'

'Mr Boston is a – a wine dealer, my dear count. I

myself obtain my wines from a House in London. At the moment I have a particularly fine claret. If you would care to visit . . . ?'

'Charming! Madame la Comtesse and I would be delighted to— Ah! Where has that Bouvet gone?'

The count, who had finished his wine, looked about for the corporal to relieve him of his empty glass. But Bouvet, perhaps feeling the count's reproof, had vanished.

'I think I see him,' said Mr Mortimer, taking advantage of his height. 'He is over there, by those people with your daughter. Can you see him, count? Perhaps you are not quite tall enough . . .?'

'What is it, Corporal Bouvet?'

The corporal, who had been trying to attract Lewis's attention, had at last succeeded. As it happened Lewis was not sorry to be called from the conversation in which he'd become involved. Gilberte de Latour, resplendent in Henrietta's gown and quite hauntingly lovely, had moved away to join her mother. Lewis had meant to follow her but Mr Archer had approached and had begun to question him closely about Mortimer.

Despite his usually cynical exterior, it was plain that the tutor was pathetically eager to learn about his favourite pupil's activities and achievements. Mortimer, to him, was his other, better self – heroic, idealistic, leaping forward into the future of mankind. Lewis had felt himself flushing and even sweating as he evaded Mr Archer's questions, knowing at the same time that such evasions must have made him seem an ignorant fool in everyone's eyes. Then, as luck would have it, Dr Stump had joined them and had begun by denouncing the horrible prison massacres that had so recently revolted the civilized world.

'These were the actions of something worse than the beasts of the jungle,' the doctor had wholesomely declared. 'The most savage of nature's creatures only destroys out of need. These were the acts of devils and madmen! Now you see what your Revolution really is!'

'Violence, sir,' Mr Archer had retorted with dignity, '– and I don't deny there has been violence – is not action. It is re-action. You, as a man of so-called science, should know that. It does not come of its own accord. Violence is *provoked*, sir. And the provocation here was immense.'

'There are other ways, Archer, such as—'

'Dying?' put in Mr Archer neatly.

'Better than killing!'

'What? Do you draw no distinction between innocence and guilt, sir? Is it your opinion that the innocent should die rather than the guilty be destroyed?'

'If the innocent do the destroying, then they become guilty. Besides, we differ in our notions of guilt. Any rebellion carries a measure of guilt, Mr Archer. The revolt of a pupil against his master, the revolt of a son against his father, the revolt of a people against the state; all disturb that unwritten contract that even your Rousseau acknowledged.'

'What do you know about Rousseau, Stump? You can't even read French!'

'I don't have to read French, Archer, to understand that what has been happening in that misguided land is an affront to humanity. I don't have to read French, sir, to know that your ideas are pernicious rubbish—'

'The language of the oppressors! Servile nonsense!' Mr Archer was losing his temper.

'The trouble with people like you, Archer,' replied Dr Stump, who was no less angry, having resented the remark about being unable to read French, 'is that you don't know the difference between servility and ordinary courtesy.'

'And the trouble with you, Stump, is that you don't know the difference between the violence of the jungle and the righteous wrath of a suffering people! It's people like you, sir, who discredit everything! You pass on lies, sir! You turn a few executions of villains into a massacre of the innocents!'

Trembling with indignation, the tutor applied to Lewis, who had been an eye-witness to the events in question.

'Tell him, young man! Tell him what you actually saw!'

It was at this point that Corporal Bouvet had interrupted and gained Lewis's attention.

'What is it, Corporal Bouvet?' said Lewis with immense relief.

'A little talk, Mr Boston, yes?'

Gratefully, Lewis left the argument unresolved and followed the corporal into the shrubbery. Evidently whatever the corporal had to communicate was of a highly private nature.

'Well, Corporal Bouvet?'

The corporal had halted and was peering about him as if for eavesdroppers.

'It is a 'ard thing to talk about, Mr Boston.'

'For whom?'

'For many. For all.'

'What is it, then?'

The corporal scratched the side of his face and rearranged the glasses on the tray he was still carrying. He frowned as if over a difficult problem in chess. How should he begin?

'I 'ave a friend, Mr Boston.'

'So?' Lewis was beginning to be impatient.

'She is a fine lady. My age, you understand. A widow. English.'

'Are you getting married, corporal?' Lewis's impatience turned to mystification.

'As Mr 'oskins say, that is in the lap of the gods. But I am worried. It is Mrs Coker.'

'I'm delighted, Corporal Bouvet! There's no need to be worried. She's a very respectable person. I can promise you—'

'She is a very foolish person. She 'as bought – these!'

Corporal Bouvet bent to put the wine tray down on the path; he stood up and fumbled inside his tunic.

'Look, Mr Boston.'

He held out a small bundle of banknotes. They were French assignats.

'Look close, Mr Boston.'

A weird uneasiness had begun to take possession of Lewis. He held the notes and stared at them.

'Well?'

'They are forgeries, Mr Boston. I know them well. There are many such forgeries in Paris.'

'Where – where did she . . . buy them?'

The corporal looked deeply unhappy.

'I think first it was a honest mistake . . . that there were no more. But soon I discover that my friend, the landlord of The Plough, 'as bought some. Also a friend of 'is. Maybe more, also. I don't know.'

'*Where did she buy them?*'

'Alas, Mr Boston – she buy them from the Count de Latour. It seems 'e do 'er a favour and let 'er 'ave them cheap. She, foolish lady, was so honoured to be spoke with by a French count, that she straightway give 'im 'er savings. She told me yesterday.'

Lewis felt sick. Throughout the corporal's recital, the black eyes and the smiles of the Latours seemed to have been circling round him. He really thought he was going to faint.

'I 'ave said nothing,' went on the corporal quietly, 'till I see the count making friends with so many people 'ere today. And I know what that means. I tell you this now, Mr Boston, so you may look to things before it is too late.'

'The count . . . the count . . . I don't believe . . . I – I—'

He wanted to sit down, to lean against something. He reached out to support himself against a wall of green. Like everything else he turned to, it gave way. He collapsed stupidly among branches and leaves and made no effort to rise. Much concerned, the corporal observed that Lewis had gone desperately white. He knelt to the tray for a glass of wine and almost had to force it between

Lewis's lips. It seemed to restore him a little.

'You *must* believe, Mr Boston. What I tell you is true. Please remember what I say to you in Boulogne. I tell you then *I* did not choose the prisoners to save from La Force. I 'ad suspicions. You understand, they were not in a part of the prison for politicals, but for criminals. Yes. Even such old families can 'ave bad ones. Oh my poor young man! What a shame! All your money, all your goodness, all your bravery – and all you come 'ome with is a family of – of forgers! Criminals! That is why they were in prison, Mr Boston!'

Dully Lewis nodded. He had been far too happy for it to last. He put his hand to his head as if wondering why it weighed so much to so little purpose. What else should Lewis Boston have rescued but a family of thieves? Suddenly his whole life seemed to have been a succession of calamities of which this was undoubtedly the worst. He climbed to his feet and mechanically began brushing the leaves and twigs from his clothing. In passing he observed that he had substantially damaged the bush . . .

'Do you know what, Bouvet?' he muttered, giving a singularly ghastly smile. 'I've done it again. Yes. I've done it again.'

His eyes filled with tears; his lips trembled. Corporal Bouvet feared he was about to break down completely.

He put out his hand. Lewis shook his head.

'No, no. It's all right. It's just that I was thinking of – of those others . . . the ones we didn't take . . . of ones we passed over in – in the prison . . . of the ones I turned away from, for – for—'

A spasm of hatred passed across his face as he thought of the ones he *had* saved. His heart was filled with an almost murderous loathing for them; it was like the loathing of spiders, snakes or scorpions. He remembered the bloody street with all the bodies in it – and experienced the most appalling sense of guilt for his own blindness and stupidity, and worse.

'He was right, you know, Bouvet. He was right and I was wrong.'

'Who was right, Mr Boston?'

'The madman, Bouvet. My friend Mortimer. Yes. Mortimer was right. Such – such people ought not to be allowed to live. Mortimer knew it all.'

PART THREE

Fraternité

CHAPTER NINETEEN

MR DIGNAM-BROWNE was uneasy. He lay back in his bath and studied the memorandum that had reached him that morning. He held it delicately to avoid wetting it in the thick yellow stew in which he was almost totally submerged. The recipe for this – which was largely sulphur – he had been given by M. Paré who, in turn, had got it from M. Marat's secretary in Paris.

There was no doubt it was soothing, though the smell was disagreeable. He would like to have remained in it for hours; he dreaded the prospect of emerging and drying himself. He had a painful and rather horrible affliction of the skin. He was covered with pustules that irritated intensely. The only parts of his body that were free of them were his face, neck and the soles of his feet. It was for this reason that he always wore gloves. His hands were as gross as old potatoes.

But it was not his condition that made him uneasy; he had learned to live with that. It was the memorandum. It had originated with an Under-Secretary at the

237

Ministry and had been initialled by so many hands that it seemed to have contracted a special disease of its own.

The memorandum referred to an exchange of letters between His Majesty's Minister and the French Minister in London. The Frenchman had accused His Majesty's Government of interfering in the internal affairs of France. He blamed the fearful prison massacres in September on agitators who had been paid with English gold. There were witnesses, ready to testify on oath that they had seen an Englishman in a drab greatcoat taking part in the murders outside La Force and actually encouraging them.

His Majesty's Minister had of course indignantly repudiated the suggestion that his Government had been in any way concerned. Like the rest of the civilized world he was appalled by the bestiality to which France had sunk. The responsibility for the horrors of September were not to be so readily shifted.

The word 'repudiated' and the word 'responsibility' had been underlined. Mr Browne studied them and sighed, thereby creating a yellow tidal wave that slopped dangerously about the rim of the bath. The implication of the underlinings was very plain. Being the last recipient of the memorandum he felt the full weight of them. The paper was like lead in his hands. Dearly he would have liked to have dropped it into the yellow stew and obliterated it altogether. But that was not to be. Every initialling betrayed the memorandum's course and pointed infallibly to its present destination: Dignam-Browne. It was like a children's game in which an object is passed from hand to hand until the music stops; and then woe betide the holder. Unless he continued the game he would be left to bear the consequences, which might well be grim. Well, well, the music was still playing ...

He rose from his bath in a sulphurous rush. It was to be noted that he lacked bodily hair entirely; the naked Dignam-Browne resembled a monstrous baby, apparently still covered with the membrane of birth.

He dressed rapidly but carefully, finally pulling on his snow-white gloves. He glanced at himself in a mirror. He really looked quite wholesome; there was a pleasant flush of health in his cheeks that had been imparted by the warmth of his bath. No one would have suspected that from the neck down he was a mass of fearful corruption.

He left his rooms and made his way briskly to the House of Drummond and Coutts in Lombard Street. Here he cancelled certain arrangements that had been in operation with the Paris branch. He regretted that he had been unable to let M. Paré know in advance, but he trusted that the shrewd Frenchman would draw his own conclusions and understand that Mr Browne was not his own master.

However, there was good news for him at the bank as well. His own personal account had benefited considerably. During the week of the massacres when French currency had fallen to its lowest level, M. Paré had cleverly bought. Then, when the news had come in of French military successes against the Austrians, the currency had risen and become almost stable. M. Paré – who always worked closely with Mr Browne, hand in glove, one might have said – had sold his holdings and trebled the original investment. Mr Browne now found himself to be quite comfortably off.

Yet – and here was an interesting side to Mr Browne – he could not help feeling a divided satisfaction in this outcome. He was a man who was loyal to his masters; he had always served them industriously, and, he prided himself, with some success. The arrangements he had been instrumental in making in Paris had been more than satisfactory. The massacres had so shocked the world that the Revolution had been universally discredited and its principles brought into contempt. Whatever sympathy there had been in England for a movement that had threatened property and speculation was at an end. Yet in spite of this, the Revolutionary government had somehow survived; its army had been victorious and Mr Browne's masters – the Under-Secretaries, the Secretaries, even the Minister himself – were plainly disappointed.

In these circumstances Mr Browne couldn't help feeling mildly guilty about his personal prosperity, which had proceeded from a state of affairs he ought to have deplored. It made him feel underhanded ...

He smiled ruefully. It was all as a consequence of being partly Irish; he was inclined to see too many sides to every question. He envied M. Paré his single-mindedness ... and his unblemished skin.

As Mr Browne had hoped, his friend M. Paré understood perfectly the reason for the cancellation of the arrangements with London. An object had been proposed; an object had been achieved. There was no more need ...

It happened also that the yellow little Frenchman in his brass cage in the bank on the Rue Saint-Honoré was personally relieved by the news.

In the wake of the terrible massacres, many questions had been asked. Who were the Septemberers? Where had they come from – and where had they gone? In the streets of Paris, some fifteen hundred human beings had lain, hacked to pieces by hands unknown. The

Septemberers seemed to have come out of the bowels of the earth, and then vanished back there again.

Perhaps that cabinet-maker had been one – or that joiner – or even that young baker's apprentice with the cunning, sidelong smile? No man would admit to it – not even to his mother or wife. To have been a Septemberer was to have been a soul damned and cast out of mankind. If they recognized one another in the street, they paled and hastened away.

One or two met sometimes, near the Café de Foix: ghastly, haunted creatures with strained grins that served only to forecast their final state. It was here that Richard Mortimer came, in his misshapen greatcoat, to talk of the Revolution and what still remained to be done. There was always injustice, there were always enemies of the people ... The others grinned at him, nodded – and held out their hands for English gold.

It must have been in the first week of October when he went back to Drummond and Coutts and half ran to the yellow man in the brass cage.

'Is there – is there anything for me?'

M. Paré turned a pair of parrot eyes up through the polished bars.

'Monsieur?'

'I need some money!'

'Ah! So do we all, monsieur.'

'Then – then there's nothing today?'

'Nor any other day, monsieur.'

'What do you mean?'

Mortimer's eyes blazed in a feverish panic.

'I'm sorry, monsieur, but I do not have the honour of knowing you.'

'Not know me? But – but that's impossible! You *must* know me! Are you ill or something? I've been here many, many times! You know that! I've always had money from . . . from you! In gold. Stop joking with me! Don't joke about such things, for God's sake! Look at me! I'm *l'Anglais!*'

'Undoubtedly you are English, monsieur. I envy you. I am very fond of your country. But alas! I do not know you. You have never been here before. I have never given you money.'

M. Paré put his head on one side, looking more parrot-like than ever. Mortimer had the sudden feeling that he was about to bite the bars.

'Why are you lying to me?'

'Lying, monsieur? *I* am not lying. Perhaps it is you? I advise you to go away, monsieur, and try to earn some money. Banks do not give it away for the asking.'

'What is the reason for this? Why – why?'

M. Paré shrugged his shoulders.

'Is it Mr Browne? Has *he* said anything? Surely to

God the work was well done? We stopped the – the prison plot!'

'What prison plot, monsieur? I know nothing of such matters. Nor do I know a Mr Browne. I advise you, monsieur, to go elsewhere. Perhaps you are mistaken in the bank?'

'You're keeping the money for yourself!' shouted Mortimer, flying into a terrified rage. He had actually seized hold of the bars and was beginning to shake them, when M. Paré picked up a heavy, metal-edged ruler and rapped his fingertips with it. Mortimer gave a cry of pain and released his hold.

'You fool – you fool!' he cried out. 'There's got to be money – or nothing more can be done! Don't you see that?'

'I'm afraid, monsieur, that I do not understand. I am a simple banker. I know nothing of plots and plans. I wish you a good day, monsieur.'

Scarcely knowing what was happening to him, Mortimer found himself seized by servants of the bank who seemed to have appeared from nowhere, like wolves in a forest. Firmly they ushered him outside into the street. The door of Drummond and Coutts shut behind him; it sounded like a cannon in his ears.

He staggered away. Passers-by supposed him to be drunk; perhaps, in a way, he *was* drunk, but not with

wine. Tears were streaming down his face; he was unable
to see clearly and he had the curious sensation that
the streets were passing *him* by instead of he them.

He was filled with a murderous hatred for the yellow
little Frenchman who had treated him with such bland
contempt. He felt outraged and humiliated to the very
depths of his soul.

Someone knocked accidentally against him;
instinctively he lashed out with his clenched fist – and
almost overbalanced. The woman, whom he'd nearly
struck, looked at him in terror, as if he were mad.

The yellow little banker would have to be destroyed
– like an unwanted animal. He must be hacked to pieces.
He was a traitor to the Revolution. He was an enemy of
the people.

There would have to be meetings again, of course. It
would have to be discussed . . . arranged.

Mortimer was now walking swiftly, purposefully; he
felt a little calmed by having an object in view, and
particularly by the thought of the necessary meetings.

The truth of the matter was that he had a desperate
need of company – of the company of his fellow
conspirators. They were the only human beings in whose
presence he could immerse himself utterly and be lost.
He had reached the uttermost limits of human rage and
ferocity . . . and it was only the consciousness – the

ever-present consciousness, most important, that! – of the high purpose behind it all that kept him sane. His companions in blood were the only ones who understood this.

Presently he reached the dingy room in the Faubourg Saint-Antoine where he lodged. He had never been much concerned with animal comfort and lately it had mattered not at all. He flung himself on the filthy, unmade bed and glared at the wall which was scribbled all over with important dates, long since passed. His loneliness actually produced an aching feeling within him – a dryness of the mouth, a shortness of breath. He could hear himself panting.

He sat up and tried to put his thoughts into some sort of reasonable order. He must have money – English money. Nothing could be achieved without it; not even a single meeting. (Mortimer never thought of anything being *done*, but *achieved*.)

He stripped off his coat and searched the pockets; he found four coins that had become lodged between scraps of soiled paper – proclamations torn off walls, pamphlets, scurrilous poems cut from the daily press. Much encouraged, he continued to search, scattering the papers on the floor and on the bed. To his intense delight he came upon a further three coins that had slipped through a hole in one of the pockets and had become matted in the greasy fluff of his coat's hem. He cleaned them up with his fingernail and added them to his capital.

He found no more; the only unexpected thing that came to light was the twist of silk Lewis Boston had given him and which still contained the lock of his sister's hair. Almost without realizing what it was, he undid it and stared blankly at the hair. A spasm of repugnance overcame him. Lately he'd noticed that the very thought of a young woman – any young woman – caused him to shrink within himself. He was sure in his own mind that this sensation dated from the murdering and dismembering of the young princess outside the gates of La Force. He assumed it was the price he had had to pay for his passionate idealism. He had always known that some sort of spiritual sacrifice would have been necessary; there was nothing unusual about the one he had made – many of the most violent revolutionaries were famous for the austerity of their private lives ...

He wrapped up the lock of hair and thrust it back into his pocket, feeling, at the same time, an angry affection for Lewis in his great warm noisy mansion. Almost at once the memory of his own early years came flooding back to him and it was only by resolutely fixing his mind on his present problem that he was able to escape yet another fit of profound and useless misery.

He began gathering up his papers, studying each

carefully, as if it were a document of great value, before thrusting it back into his coat.

Suddenly he heard a commotion, an argument coming from somewhere downstairs. He could hear his landlord's voice raised. He grew terribly pale and finished his stowing away with trembling hands. He was three weeks behind with his rent and was forced to enter and leave the tenement like a thief for fear of being caught by the landlord. He pressed his ear to the door and waited till the argument had ceased; then, his fortune clutched firmly in his hand, he slipped downstairs and managed to gain the street unobserved.

He was not aware that his landlord was equally anxious to avoid *him*. The bleak, haggard figure in the filthy, bulging greatcoat had the air of a damned soul about it. Mortimer stank like a slaughterhouse . . .

At first he began to walk quickly towards the Palais-Royal; but as that way took him past La Force, he frowned and turned northward, intending to skirt the prison as widely as possible. After about half an hour he realized he'd missed his way and was at the Porte Saint-Denis. He paused to recover his sense of direction. A man was showing his papers to two soldiers at the gateway. They were scrutinizing them by the light of a lantern. The man looked anxious and uneasy. At length the papers were handed back and the man allowed to proceed on his way. Mortimer couldn't help seeing the look of overwhelming relief on the man's face as he took back his papers and hastened out of the city. It was a story in itself, apparently with a happy ending. Mortimer stood for several minutes staring at the cobbled street beyond the gateway. He could hear quite distinctly the sound of harness and of coach doors opening and closing.

A tremendous longing to go through the gateway welled up irresistibly within Mortimer. Even as it did so, a precise pattern of thought arranged itself in his mind. If he were to get through the gateway, there would be nothing to stop him making his way to Boulogne or Dieppe. From there he could get a ship to England.

Already his heart was beating with excitement. Once in England he could go to London – to The Cock in Fleet Street, or to the house in the Haymarket. He would be able to see Mr Browne himself and denounce the treacherous little banker who had humiliated and cheated him. The formidable Mr Browne and his mysterious associates would not take such a thing lightly. Doubtless arrangements would be made that would be more effective than anything he, Mortimer, could have achieved unaided. Then the money would start again and all problems would be solved. It would be like the old days . . .

All that stood in his way were the soldiers on the

gate. All that mattered in the world was to get past them without papers. Everything suddenly came down to this one necessity. He approached the gate. The soldiers watched him. He drew near, intending, at the last moment, to make a run for it. His courage failed him. He thought they'd shoot him in the back . . .

'I want to go through,' he muttered piteously, like a child. 'I *must* go through . . .'

The soldiers did not answer. Instead they drew back at Mortimer's approach. They made no effort to stand in his way or even to interfere with his progress. Their dim faces, like pale smudges among the shadows, neither flickered nor moved as the gaunt figure in the drab, misshapen coat crept abjectly past them. They seemed devoid of expression or interest. Mortimer began to run; the two soldiers, with mingled revulsion and relief, watched the Septemberer as he rushed wildly into the engulfing night.

CHAPTER TWENTY

LEWIS BOSTON HAD a terrible dream – or, rather, a half-dream, for he was not in a natural sleep. He had taken a small quantity of laudanum in order to subdue his distracted state of mind following on Corporal Bouvet's revelation concerning the Latours. He was still horribly shaken and supposed that the deep sleep induced by the drug would leave him sufficiently refreshed to deal with the appalling problem that had sprung out upon him.

Unfortunately, owing to ignorance of the drug's curious properties, he erred on the side of caution and took too little; consequently, no sooner had he lain on his bed than he became prey – at first to a feeling of nausea, and then to a brilliantly clear hallucination.

Opposite him was a tall religious casement through which the moonlight streamed onto his bed. He felt he was encased in a silver lozenge that appeared to be afloat. His nausea returned but was instantly dispelled by the sight of a face at the window. To his surprise, it turned out to be Mortimer's.

'Brought you a present,' mouthed Mortimer, climbing into the room and standing by the bed. 'A present from Paris.'

He thrust his hand into his swollen greatcoat pocket and brought out a head. It was Gilberte's. He put it on the pillow next to Lewis. Its black eyes were dimly, seductively open.

'Some more here somewhere,' mouthed Mortimer, fumbling again.

He pulled out several tufts of hair and then took off his coat and laid it on the bed. Lewis stared at the huge, misshapen pockets. Several thin black snakes came out.

'Stop them!' shouted Lewis; but Mortimer took no notice. The snakes dropped off the bed and wriggled towards the door. Lewis jumped up and tried to stamp on them; but they had already crawled into the passage. He could hear them slithering away. He ran out and began rushing from room to room – his father's, his mother's, Henrietta's – in an effort to prevent the poisonous creatures stinging his family. He stuffed up keyholes – only to catch sight of scaly inches vanishing under doors. He reached down and grasped at a writhing tail. He actually felt the muscular vigour of it twist and turn in his grip. He squeezed – and his hand was full of moisture ... then a little malignant head whipped round and bit his finger till he screamed and awoke.

The moonlight had shrivelled to a dim, tinselly glimmer. His head ached, his mouth felt sour and dry; the problem that had beset him had neither diminished nor gone away. The only result of the laudanum had been to increase his feeling of urgency and panic. He had to act at once.

He got out of bed, staggering slightly, for the effects of the drug had by no means worn off. With curious difficulty he lit a candle and left his room. As he passed along the arched corridors and up the queer romantic staircases, he had the sensation that he might still be dreaming. He walked carefully, for fear of snakes.

He reached his sister Elizabeth's room. She was still in London and her room was occupied by Gilberte. He knocked on the door. There was no answer. He knocked again . . .

'Yes?' The voice was low and startled.

He opened the door and went inside.

'Mon Dieu! What is it?'

Lewis, holding his candle fantastically high, scowled savagely at the tousled, black-eyed daughter of criminals. Gilberte gazed at him in amazement.

'What are you thinking of? To come here – now!'

What was he thinking of? A good question; and an even better answer. He must turn her and her vicious family out of his father's house. He had brought them there; he must flush them out.

'Get out!' His voice shook as he spoke. He was surprised at how harsh it sounded. The girl was now staring at him in terror. He did not like inspiring such an emotion; but there was no other way.

'Get out of this house. You and your – your family.'

'Why? What is it? What have I – what have we done to you?'

'You are criminals – forgers. All of you.'

'How dare you!' Gilberte looked furious, outraged. Nevertheless, she kept her voice low.

'Today I found out,' pursued Lewis, wondering for an uneasy moment if a terrible mistake had been made; Gilberte's indignation undeniably impressed him. 'Your father has already robbed – cheated people here. Poor people who never did anyone any harm . . .'

'It's not true!' burst out Gilberte. 'We are an honourable family. You – you have insulted me. You have insulted me horribly! Who told you such a thing?'

'Corporal Bouvet. He knows. He knew from the first.'

'And you take his word? The word of a man like that – a soldier of the Revolution? Perhaps a murderer, even – like those in the street?'

'He's not a man like that!' Lewis's thoughts touched fleetingly on Mortimer. He felt confused.

'If – if he knew at first,' went on Gilberte, racking her

brains for what to say, 'why didn't he say so? Why did he not – not inform you?'

'He . . . did not want to interfere. He said the choice was mine.' He paused, and then went on with a rush of bitterness that was all too apparent: 'And what a choice I made!'

Gilberte clenched her fists among the bedclothes. She knew it was absolutely necessary to maintain her indignation. Everything depended on it. Her father and mother would have had no difficulty; she knew that. Her father would have frightened the wits out of this pale, unhappy-looking young man in his absurdly embroidered nightgown. Her mother would have sent him abjectly packing.

But Gilberte lacked the count and countess's long experience. She had not quite outgrown gratitude and remorse. She was still too easily shamed. Also she had been taken off-guard . . .

'And – and now you think, monsieur, that you have made a – a bad choice?'

As she spoke it was impossible for her not to remember the dark and terrible prison and the stranger who, like a miracle, had come and extended his hand and set them all free. Her eyes prickled with tears.

'I – I admit nothing,' she said, almost inaudibly. 'I – I am crying because – because you have wounded me, monsieur. That is all, I promise you.'

'I didn't mean to,' murmured Lewis, his sternness somewhat abating. Unlike Mortimer he was rarely capable of keeping to a fixed resolve. Too many things distracted him. He was always too conscious of multitudinous emotions – his own and those of others – to succeed in anything without considerable luck. If ever he set the world on fire it would have been by accident.

He relaxed his doom-like attitude and approached the bed. The spectacle of Gilberte in tears moved him deeply.

'But please understand, Gilberte, what a – a shock it was. I didn't know what to do . . .'

Gilberte carefully blotted her eyes on a fold of the sheet. Instinctively she divined that her immediate danger was over. She did not plan or calculate, but she couldn't help being aware that there was no need for further indignation and that her best course was to abandon denial. A feeling of great relief came over her. The angry, almost violent young man was already faltering. A certain submissiveness on her part might well bring about even more. Again, this was not calculation, but instinct.

'I understand. Really, I understand. I am sorry. Do you . . . do you want us to go . . . directly?'

'No, no!' said Lewis impulsively. 'Not at once,

that is. Oh Gilberte, what a horrible world this is!'

The sudden and unexpected despair of the young man's outburst affected Gilberte strongly; she realized how deeply he must have felt for her. She'd had no idea, really. Inevitably the thought crossed her mind that it would be very easy to take advantage of this. She bit her lip.

'We will make arrangements tomorrow. I swear it.'

'Please! Not so soon! I didn't mean that.'

'But your family? What will your papa say?'

'He doesn't know.'

'You – you have not told him?'

'No.'

'Why not?'

Even as she asked, she felt she knew the answer; it was because of his attachment to her. She had already begun to arrange her reply to the expected confession—

'I daren't,' said Lewis. 'You see . . . I have a – a history.'

Gilberte suppressed a feeling of disappointment and possibly anger.

'A history, monsieur?'

Lewis, catching an edge to her voice, was aware he'd made a blunder, but couldn't imagine what. He was unused to young women like Gilberte de Latour; he felt himself to be clumsy and insensitive. With barmaids or casual ladies of the town, he could be quite masterful; indeed, he believed he had quite a reputation for dash and finesse . . . but with Gilberte de Latour, as with Jeanne de la Motte-Valois, he was out of his depth. He smiled as if apologizing for his offence, whatever it might have been.

'Come,' said Gilberte, relenting a little. She extended her hand for him to sit beside her. 'Tell me this history of yours, monsieur. Tell me what it is that has made you . . . spare me? Truly, I want to know.'

Obediently Lewis sat down and told her. He told her of his rescue of the Countess de la Motte-Valois and the calamity that had followed it. He told her of the huge sum of money he had been entrusted with and had failed to bring back from Paris. He dwelt lengthily on his father's response to that misfortune.

'And now there's – there's *this*,' he finished up miserably. 'It's really too much. I daren't tell him. Oh God, what's wrong with me? Everything I set my hand to – maybe it's some sort of disease? Or a curse. It's as if I have a Midas touch in reverse!'

He paused and glanced at his listener. Her elbows were propped on her knees and her head was resting in her hands so that he could not see her face. Her shoulders were shaking; she was laughing. Angrily he made to get up. She put out a hand to prevent him; the other remained covering her face. Tears were running down over her thin fingers.

'You are laughing at me!'

'I – I am not laughing now. Can't you see I am crying, Lewis? I am crying . . . a little for you, and a great deal for . . . myself. I don't know why, but – but I cannot stop. The tears keep coming and coming. Perhaps it is because I have not cried for a long time? God knew I had cause . . . but one got into the way, you know, of crying within, so that one's eyes were always bright and dry. One must not show too much, you understand! So these tears are many years old. Never mind – never mind! Let us think of you! Oh my dear friend – what have I brought on you? Now please listen to me and do not speak. We will leave tomorrow. I promise you that. There will be no more . . . robbing your friends. I swear it. Besides,' she looked up and smiled with sudden brilliance, 'there is no more of that horrible money left! Thank God Papa was not able to bring much. Now it is all gone. How fortunate! We are honest now. We have no choice . . .'

She hid her face again. 'I feel so ashamed . . .'

Inexpressibly disturbed, Lewis put his arm gently round her rather angular shoulders. He felt her shudder so that he was alarmed. The spiced warmth of her bed rose up all round him.

'You must stay,' he muttered. 'Please, you must stay.'

'No, no! It is impossible!'

'Why? No one knows . . .'

'Do you not understand? We have betrayed you . . .'

'But that's done with! You said yourself that there was no more of that money . . .'

'That is true, but—'

'I'll repay everything myself! Yes! That's it! I'll buy back the forgeries! They can't amount to much?'

'I think it was forty pounds . . . I think I heard my father say that. But Lewis, Lewis! Why should you save us yet again?'

'Don't you know?'

She stared at him. He marvelled that he could ever have imagined that her eyes were like her father's; they were so rich and warm.

'Please go now. I don't want to cry any more.'

Lewis stood up. 'You've given your word that you won't leave?'

'Yes.'

'Again. Promise.'

'I promise.'

He went to the door.

'Lewis—'

'What is it, Gilberte?'

'Put out the candle. Someone may see you.'

He pinched out the flame; the room was plunged into darkness. He fancied he could still smell the spiced perfume from the bed.

'Lewis?'

'What is it?'

'Do you know what?' The voice from the bed sounded curiously melancholy, like one might have supposed the voice of a phantom.

'Tell me.'

'When you came in – at first – I really thought . . . I was frightened that you had come to make love to me. I thought you had been drinking . . .'

'You were frightened of that? Of my making love to you?'

'In such a mood, yes!'

'And instead I came to throw you out! To call you a forger and a thief! Was that better, then?'

'Much, much better, dear Lewis! Believe me—'

'I love you, Gilberte.'

Silence. Lewis waited, but the silence remained unbroken. He opened the door and crept outside. He felt excited and happy; at the same time he couldn't subdue a feeling that he would have to pay for his happiness. He shrugged his shoulders: it was the human condition – no pleasure without pain. He smiled cheerfully and hoped that this time he had paid, well and truly, in advance.

Next day Lewis went up to town. He took with him several of his most valuable trinkets, intending to sell them and thereby obtain enough money to reimburse the cheated Mrs Coker, the landlord of The Plough, and any other hapless victims of the Count de Latour he could discover.

His spirits remained wonderfully high; he was not unduly depressed, even, by the inevitable discovery that he was selling his goods at the wrong time, that he had overvalued everything and that objects the jeweller had sworn would double in value had most uncannily halved. This was to be expected; it was the way of the world. In all he received, for some four hundred pounds' worth of property, seventy-five pounds and a few shillings. He was not dissatisfied.

He stayed the night near Charing Cross, intending to get a coach early on the following morning. Then on an impulse he went to the Haymarket. He strolled several times past number eighty, savouring many memories of Mortimer and the countess who was dead. He smiled as he recalled his scuffle with Mortimer on the stairs. He had been very young in those days.

He paused outside the snuff-shop, remembering the gilt box he'd bought for Henrietta. He had a few pounds to spare. He went inside and chose another box – a gold one that cost him twenty pounds – and had a 'G' engraved on it while he waited.

After this he could scarcely contain himself; he was filled with joyous expectation. The coach journey back to Lancing seemed intolerably slow. He believed he could have walked more quickly. He got back to his home soon after seven o'clock that night. He had been absent for less than two days.

During that time, Dr Stump – ever ready to oblige an aristocrat – had parted with fifty hard-earned pounds in exchange for some assignats the Count de Latour had chanced to bring out of France with him. It seemed that the nobleman was temporarily embarrassed for want of English funds. Nor was this all. The landlord of The Ship – a royalist to his heart's core – had obliged the huge, affable aristocrat by changing a further thirty pounds of the same currency at a very reasonable twenty-eight per cent of its face value.

Mrs Coles, the wife of the Worthing printer, immensely flattered to have been asked, had given the gracious countess ten pounds in exchange for a bundle of the same ubiquitous currency; and God knew how many others there were besides. If Lewis had sold every item he possessed, he could not have kept pace with the rapacity of the Latours.

CHAPTER TWENTY-ONE

'I SWEAR I did not know!'

'Liar!'

'No – no! I told you the truth!'

'Liar – liar!'

'My father *had* – no more! It was my mother! I did not know *she* had brought some! That is true. As there is a God above—'

'*Atheist!* I suppose you'll swear *she* has none left now?'

'Yes, yes! I swear she has no more! I looked – I searched!'

'That only leaves you. How many have *you*?'

'For pity's sake—'

The above conversation, conducted in passionate whispers and with burning looks, took place on the stairs, in the hall and outside the front door of the Boston mansion. Before this Lewis had maintained a terrible silence towards Gilberte. He had avoided her with fanatical care. She, in her turn, had attempted to waylay him, to confront him – anything, in short, to regain what had been lost. Now on the Monday following the disastrous discovery of her family's further activities (faithfully reported by Corporal Bouvet), she took the wildest chances as the two families were assembling to drive to Salvington to visit the Mortimers.

'Please believe me!'

'No!'

'I never knew—'

Further exchanges were put an end to by the arrival of Henrietta. The two young women were being driven by Lewis while their parents travelled in the family coach.

Lewis's righteous anger on behalf of the people who had been swindled was now entirely overshadowed by feelings of the bitterest humiliation. *He* had been cheated; *he* had been deceived . . . These crimes against himself affected him ten times more deeply than the misfortunes of Dr Stump, Mrs Coles and any others who had been stupid enough to trust the Latours. He was not unaware of this and could only put it down to an unworthy nature.

He had convinced himself that she had told her father about his night-time visit. The very idea frightened and sickened him. Over and over again he imagined her describing the ease with which she'd twisted him from anger to abject pleading, and then, finally, with her maddening smile, repeating his damaging words: 'I love you.'

The thought of the three of them – eyes like black stones – nodding and sneering, drove him into a hectic rage. He lashed at the horses and the frail carriage fairly bounced into the air. He was grimly pleased to hear the desultory conversation behind him die away with every sign of alarm.

He tried to be just; he tried to remember Gilberte's exact words; he tried to remember anything, however slight, that might have been used in her defence. But such was his present, breathless state that he could see only duplicity and measureless contempt in her every look and gesture. He became aware of what *she* must have been aware of all the time: the gulf between an aristocrat and an upstart merchant's son. The Latours, swindlers though they were, were immeasurably superior to the Bostons. Let the Bostons pay and pay and pay, they could never buy that cold assurance of blood rooted in time – that awareness, that confidence, that absolute *certainty* that stations itself outside the laws, loves and moralities of lesser men.

For this reason his love was merely homage, and must be treated as such. Had she *really* told her father of his declaration?

'For God's sake drive carefully, Lewis!' cried Henrietta.

'Oh – I think he is really very safe,' said Gilberte.

Her words released a new flood of anger. He felt himself trapped into being a mute accomplice . . . He became obsessed with the idea that Gilberte, at this very moment, was smiling contemptuously at the back of his neck. The road ahead was straight. He would catch her at it. He would turn round unexpectedly—

He did so; both she and Henrietta were sitting rigidly, clinging to the sides of the carriage. Both of them looked terrified.

'Watch the road!' screamed Henrietta. 'Can't you keep your eyes off Gilberte for a moment?'

When they reached the Mortimers', Lewis dismounted and waited for the arrival of the family carriage. He had made up his mind to confront the count – not with words, but with looks. He *must* know if Gilberte had betrayed him. Life had suddenly become intolerable with uncertainty. He hadn't the slightest doubt that he'd be able to tell if the count knew.

The carriage arrived; stiffly Lewis handed out the occupants.

'*Merci, merci*, my dear boy,' said the count, turning his large, bland face down upon Lewis. Lewis stared fiercely into the black, toad-like eyes. He gave a quick, confidential smile. His lips all but framed the words: 'You *know*, don't you!' The nobleman returned his smile with a look of polite enquiry.

'Is there — is there a black on my face, perhaps?'

Baffled, Lewis fell back. He felt like a naked savage who had just cast a stone against a fortress. The count shrugged his shoulders and Lewis could have sworn that his expression declared: 'We have survived the wrath of a whole people, child. What do you suppose you — little you — can do where a Revolution has failed?'

They walked past him into the house, leaving him standing by the carriage, more tormented than ever. Presently he followed them, imbued now with a new resolve; whatever the cost he would free himself from this family of vampires.

There was no doubt that the Bostons brought a touch of the Eastern bazaar wherever they went; in the Mortimers' quietly refined drawing-room they had an indefinable air of being for sale — they contrived to look so bright and *new*. Mrs Mortimer, who had come downstairs in honour of the visit, kept staring at them almost fearfully and turning to Dr Stump as if for protection.

As it was a Monday and Mrs Coker was absent, the doctor himself was in attendance and had supervised the exhumation of his distinguished patient from her bed and her reinterment in a sepulchre of shawls and cushions on a sofa by the fire. He had stationed himself behind her, from where he kept tightly bending forward and offering himself as an intermediary between her and her guests.

She spoke very little except of her health and how distressed she was that she was able to entertain so rarely.

'We are not feeling our best today,' murmured Dr Stump, leaning forward with a loud creaking of his breeches. 'It was touch and go whether we would come down or not. But then the weather brightened and we felt that we really must make the effort . . .'

Mrs Mortimer smiled wistfully and, finding her eyes fixed on the other side of the room, remarked on how well the Count de Latour looked, and that Mr Boston was also looking in good health. However, she went on with a spark of interest, she fancied Lewis was a shade *drawn* and *pale*. Didn't Dr Stump think so – or was it the light? She noticed particularly about Lewis as she'd always thought how *healthy* and *ruddy* he looked beside her own son whose complexion, she recalled, was more sallow. However, she thought now that Lewis had quite Richard's pallor. Mr Mortimer, on the other hand, never seemed to suffer; thank God, she added as an afterthought. His family had always enjoyed good health . . .

'*Qu'est-ce que c'est?*' muttered the countess to Gilberte. 'She speak so soft.'

'We were saying,' said Dr Stump before Gilberte could answer, 'that Mr Mortimer's family has always enjoyed good health.'

Mr Mortimer, hearing his name mentioned in connection with family, looked round with amused unconcern.

'How odd,' he said. 'The count and I were just discussing families. It is most interesting. It turns out that the Latours originated in the time of Henry I, who, you may remember, was the *youngest* brother of William II. He married a Scottish girl: Edith-Matilda. The Mortimers, as you know, date from William II himself, so it seems we are scarcely a generation older than our guests, my dear. Is not that a remarkable coincidence?'

He smiled with genuine pleasure, when the count, with an affable chuckle, interrupted him:

'Ah! You mistake, monsieur! I mean Henri I, not your 'enery I. Henri I of *France,* you understand! 'E marry a Princess Maud.' The count pronounced it 'Mowd'. 'But 'e 'ave no children with 'er. It 'appens sometimes, eh? 'E was the overlord, I think you say, of William of Normandy 'oo was the *papa* of your William II. The papa, M. Mortimer, not the youngest brother. But still, I agree, it is quite a coincidence.'

'How amusing,' said Mr Mortimer remotely, but was unable to keep a slight tremor out of his voice.

'For you and me, yes; but not for the young ones, eh?' said the count indulgently. 'I think they 'ave more interest in nowadays than in such old times! I think my young friend 'ere' – he glanced warmly at Lewis who grew very red – ''as more interest in 'oo will marry 'oo tomorrow than 'oo married 'oo so many years ago!'

'Papa!' exclaimed Gilberte involuntarily – and went as red as Lewis.

He knows – he knows! thought Lewis with absolute terror. She *did* tell him! Oh my God, what a bitch she must be! He glared at Gilberte with hatred; she looked away. Henrietta surreptitiously pressed her hand . . .

Mrs Mortimer, sensing a sudden change in the atmosphere of the room, looked vaguely frightened and mutely appealed to Dr Stump. The doctor, glancing rapidly at the red-faced protagonists, bent over his patient and murmured something to her. She sank back, appeased. Dr Stump straightened up and smiled knowingly at Mrs Boston. On the other side of the room Mr Boston looked at the count in pleased surprise; then he turned to Lewis. He saw his son's trembling confusion and, at the same time, couldn't help observing Gilberte's similar condition. He felt very tender and happy. He laid his hand on Lewis's shoulder. Lewis felt his father's fingers vibrating musically.

'My own son is in Paris,' said Mr Mortimer coolly; he was totally oblivious – perhaps deliberately so – of the mysterious current of feeling that had swept through the room. 'He is perfecting himself in the language, I understand. I consider foreign travel is peculiarly necessary for a gentleman, these days . . .'

As Mr Mortimer droned on in praise of the heir to his name, Lewis looked at his mother. Mrs Boston's eyes were moist with affection. She nodded imperceptibly and inclined her head towards Gilberte. He looked at Dr Stump who bowed slightly and offered wordless congratulations. In bewilderment he turned to the Countess de Latour. She frowned critically, then smiled in a resigned fashion as if to say she could not find it in her heart to oppose the lovers and the general will.

He did not look at Gilberte. He felt utterly terrified and trapped. Had he at that moment been condemned to death instead of to marriage, he could scarcely have felt himself more the victim of a conspiracy, or more bitter towards a world that had betrayed him.

'I've been telling Gilberte,' whispered Henrietta to her brother as they left the Mortimers, 'that you must get married before Christmas.'

'What did she say?'

'Oh – she agreed.'

* * *

Night, deep and moonless, enfolds the Boston mansion. Starlight wrinkles its battlements so that they seem to be crumbling away . . .

Henrietta, in her high lonely tower, looks out across the night and sees a double wedding. Herself and Richard Mortimer; her brother and the fair daughter of the Latours. Blessed by the Archbishop of Canterbury . . . But stay! The lady is a Catholic. Weddings in Rome, gondolas in Venice, honeymoons on the silvery Loire . . .

Mrs Boston, alone in her empress-sized bed, ponders sleepily. As usual her thoughts go first to her eldest daughter Elizabeth who had made a wholly unwelcome conquest of one Lieutenant Philips, a half-pay officer in the Royal Navy. She ought never to have gone to London. She sighs and then smiles indulgently. She turns to the still empty pillow beside her, and murmurs intimately: 'My son Lewis, you know. Our eldest. Yes . . . it rather looks like it. She's their only child. The count and countess . . . such a *fine* family . . .'

Robed for the night in their rich and lofty bedchamber, the Count and Countess de Latour resemble, in their attitudes, poet and muse. The count is at the dressing-table, writing; the countess leans over him, watching the progress of his skilful pen.

'Ah! *Notre chère Gilberte! Notre fille!*'

The count interrupts his labours to look up and smile.

'*Trés chère! Trés, trés chère! N'est-ce pas?*'

The countess examines the written work. She frowns, purses her lips, then laughs, and tenderly wipes an ink stain from her husband's cheek.

Downstairs, the Boston clock – which marks the quarters of the moon, the months of the year, the days of the week, the tides, and even condescends to denominate the hours of the day – begins to chime midnight.

Gilberte de Latour lies perfectly still and strains her ears for the sound of a footfall she feels *must* come. Does she want it? Yes . . . no! What will he say to her? What can she say to him? Is there anything still possible between them? She trembles; she thinks she hears him, but it turns out that it is only the mechanism of the clock, subsiding after its principal effort of the day.

'It's twelve o'clock,' said Lewis. Mr Boston nodded. He had been talking with the count until quite a late hour. He had particularly asked his son to wait up for him.

'I wanted to have a little talk with you,' he said, playing small arpeggios on the arm of his chair, 'seriously. I thought it better that we should be alone. I felt we should be able to discuss freely, you understand. Both the young lady's father and I have guessed – for some time – how things stood. We are not blind, you know, my boy!'

Mr Boston smiled.

I must tell him! thought Lewis. I can't let this horrible charade go any further! He's got to know the type of people he's dealing with. Oh my God – how to begin?

Lewis licked his lips and stared round the great drawing-room. His eyes fell haplessly on the monstrous urn decorated with the arms of Schleswig-Holstein. Mr Boston, observing the fixity of his son's gaze, turned slightly to follow its direction. A chain of association was at once set up that caused him to drift away, momentarily, until he was recalled by seeing Lewis's anxious expression.

'I have no material objection, you understand,' he said carefully. 'Far from it! The young lady is everything a father could wish for his son. Charming, well-mannered, accomplished, I have no doubt – and of a really first-rate family. *First-rate!*'

He repeated the expression and accompanied it with a veritable diapason on the arm of the chair.

Now! thought Lewis, with a sudden access of courage. The way to begin! I can tell him now! The first-rate family—

'I looked them up, of course,' went on Mr Boston,

ignoring Lewis's somewhat desperate leaning forward, 'in the court almanacks. I felt it to be only right. And you'd be amazed, Lewis, at their connections. From the point of view of breeding, you couldn't have done better. Even the count himself agreed . . . but we both felt that a little fresh blood was no bad thing for an ancient dynasty. One of his ancestors, he told me, actually married the daughter of a tanner . . . A *tanner*,' he repeated, playing a single note as if to underline the unsupported nature of that alliance.

Lewis, the moment gone, sank back in his chair and transferred his gaze to the gilt candelabra that stood on the table between them. He saw Mr Boston through the dancing flames; how like a moth his father was! Dazzled. That scoundrel of a count is making a fool of him! How is it possible to tell him now? He'll go mad! He'll have a seizure! Oh Pa! What a fatal weakness you have!

'All I ask,' said Mr Boston, having concluded his survey of the Latours' lofty state, 'is that you should be sure in your own mind. Don't be dazzled,' he went on somewhat incredibly, 'by a great name. Remember, a wife is a companion for every day of your life. There must be affection – deep affection. There must be mutual respect. Marriage is a serious matter. Ask yourself, my boy, do you really love her?'

He hated her! He loathed her! And, if he was

completely honest, he was a little frightened of her. He thought of her upstairs in her bed, her black hair streaming and her thin shoulders gleaming through her shift. He could even smell the disturbing warmth that had risen from her bed as he'd sat beside her . . .

'I – I don't know,' he stammered. 'I – I'm not sure, Pa . . .'

'Not sure?' said Mr Boston, a shade irritably. He had made every effort to speak seriously – to treat Lewis as a grown man. He had the feeling that his words had been thrown away. 'That is certainly not the impression you have conveyed to me – to the young lady's parents, to your mother . . . and to the young lady herself. Really, Lewis,' he went on with increased irritation, 'you are not a child any more. You must understand that when you give every indication of affection – of the very deepest affection – in public, so to speak, you raise hopes, you raise expectations that you have no right to ignore. There are other people involved. I will not be made a fool of in this matter, Lewis. I don't want to bring up previous occasions when you have made the family look ridiculous; I am talking about now. Matters have already been gone into. I demand to know, Lewis, are you about to make fools of us all again, or not? Surely the young lady herself has some claims on your consideration?

'Now! I don't want to hear any more from you

tonight. Think over what I've said. Try to clear your mind of nonsense. Then come to me tomorrow. I promise you you won't regret your decision. She's a lovely girl, Lewis,' he said sternly. 'Your mother and I would be very happy . . . very proud.'

His eyes flickered momentarily round the room. 'And then, as soon as you've made up your mind, I think we might arrange a little function to announce the engagement, eh?'

Chapter Twenty-Two

HE HAD SCARCELY opened his mouth; as usual every single one of his resolutions had vanished as soon as it had been put to the test. He went heavily upstairs and lay on his bed. He was the most contemptible of cowards. What in God's name was he afraid of? His father's anger? Did he really suppose his father would – would *attack* him? He could have restrained him easily. So what was it?

He glared up at the ceiling, imprisoned by thoughts and feelings that seemed to have nothing to do with him. Circumstances that existed entirely in other people's minds were forcing his life out of his hands. Absurd, ridiculous considerations confronted him at every turn – considerations that any philosopher would have dismissed with contempt. Yet where was the philosophy that was capable of persuading *him* to dismiss them? All he could think of was escape. With all his heart he longed for a solitary, anonymous life . . . an existence in some remote land where, preferably, he might pass his days in monastic penury, performing good works for perfect strangers.

From this notion into which he'd drifted, it was no great leap to dream of slipping away from his father's house and making his way to Paris where he might bury himself in Mortimer's Revolution, assist ailing humanity and live off crusts and sour wine. He smiled ruefully; he might even go down in history instead of just going down.

Sooner or later, in the very nature of things, the Latours would grow over-confident and be caught. It had happened to them before and it would happen again, and they would be returned to their rightful habitation: prison. And in the very nature of things he would be dragged down with them. He was an accessory; he knew of their crimes and had done nothing. Already he could hear himself being publicly castigated for moral cowardice and criminal neglect. The very least he supposed he could expect from a court of law would be seven years' transportation.

He would go to Botany Bay, in chains. There would be no respite from his labours under the burning sun; there would be no mercy for – for at least a year. Then, perhaps, some Christian gentleman might take pity on him – attracted, possibly, by his gentle demeanour. He would hear his story, be moved by it (having a long-lost son of whom Lewis inexplicably reminded him) and offer him a position of trust in his own household.

Oh dear God! How he'd repay that saintly gentleman! He'd work for him, protect him, advise him, beat off attackers in the night ... In time, maybe in six months (Lewis saw no way of accomplishing it in less), he would have earned the old man's respect and trust to such an extent that he'd be made his treasurer, his chief minister. He would become justly celebrated for his probity and when the old man died (he had been almost dying from the beginning and had only survived through Lewis's devotion and knowledge of herbs) he would be made Governor of the Colony to dispense justice with unequalled wisdom and mercy.

Here, certain parallels with the tale of Joseph in Egypt entered Lewis's reverie, and lo! Gilberte was brought before him to be examined. Naturally she did not recognize him in his exalted state which, by the happiest of chances, included a coat of many colours. She had last known him in abject misery, a figure of nearly naked scorn. He smiled in his heart. He caused her baggage to be searched by his servants and lo! a silver beaker was discovered. It belonged to his household; of course, he himself had secreted it among her possessions. She wept, she pleaded, she protested her innocence. But the stern judge remained unmoved. 'Go thou, woman, and let thy head be struck from thy body.'

Then, as the chopper was poised above her fair neck, did the rich-robed judge reveal himself as the spurned convict of long ago. Amazed, she flung herself at his feet and, sobbing with remorse, declared her boundless love.

Lewis, lying on his bed and gazing at the ceiling, frowned. Having drifted imperceptibly to Egypt, he found himself suddenly beset by a totally new and unexpected problem. For no clearly understandable reason, he was trying to recall the names of Joseph's brothers.

At length, sleep being out of the question, he got up, took a candle and went quietly to 'the office' where there was a battered schoolroom Bible. He opened it and had begun to immerse himself in the Book of Genesis when Gilberte came in.

Lying awake and waiting for his visit, she'd heard him bid his father goodnight and then go to his room. Some time after, she'd heard his door open and close again. She'd waited, waited, but he had not come . . .

'What are you doing here?' Lewis shut the book, feeling obscurely sheepish.

'I – I could not sleep. I heard something . . . I saw the light from under the door—' She broke off, observing his confusion and then the book he had been consulting.

She stared at it, bewildered, and wondered fleetingly if he'd been seeking divine guidance?

'I couldn't sleep,' said Lewis defensively.

'Nor I.' She continued to stare at the Bible.

'There . . . there was nothing else to read.'

Lewis felt the utter impossibility of explaining that he'd come to find out the names of Joseph's brothers. In all probability he couldn't have remembered by what stages he'd come to be curious about them.

'It – it is a very interesting book,' said Gilberte, feeling, at the same time, a certain inadequacy in her remark. 'When I was – was a child I used to read it; I used to read about the Garden of Eden . . . and how woman was made out of a sleeping man. It seemed to me even then that we were but dreams . . . not real, you understand?'

As always, Gilberte's instinct led her to seize upon anything to hand and extract from it what she most needed. She approached the table and rested lightly against the back of one of the throne-like chairs. Her perfume seemed to fill the lively little room.

'It was a happy fancy for a child,' she went on, glancing from time to time at Lewis and then about the room with evident affection, 'but it is hard now. I learned, too quickly, that dreams can be terrible, even nightmares . . .'

'You should have remained a dream,' muttered Lewis, following her imagery but avoiding her looks; 'and not listened to the serpent . . .'

'You mean my papa?' interrupted Gilberte quickly. Her eyes glittered in the candlelight. 'That is easy to say, Monsieur Lewis. But you do not know what it has been like. Do you suppose I feel nothing? Do you suppose I am not . . . ashamed? And – and frightened, too!'

'Frightened? Of what?' Lewis was surprised by how contemptuous his voice sounded.

'Of prison, Monsieur Lewis. Do you think I want to go back there? Do you know what it was like there – *really* like? If you knew that you would understand why I would do anything to avoid it!'

'Even – marry?'

'Oh! Mon Dieu! *Marry?* You cannot imagine what a – a sanctuary that could be for someone like me! At a stroke to be free of this – this *pretence* at living!' Her breast was heaving with agitation and her fingers tightened over the back of the chair. 'Do you know, there were times – in Paris – when everything seemed settled . . . I was so happy! There were two – no, three young men . . . we moved about a great deal, as you can imagine! . . . I didn't dislike them, you understand, but I never loved them (what a luxury *that* would have been!). But with each one – each time – a *discovery* was made . . . and it was only because they pitied me that we escaped prison! I was not heartbroken, only humiliated. They say, in time, one gets used to it and it no longer matters very much. But I am still young . . . Now you ask me if I would *even marry*! Every night, monsieur, I go down on my knees and ask *le bon Dieu* for just such a fate! Please, may I sit down?'

Lewis nodded; he felt like a judge, striving against impossible odds to administer a stern law. Gilberte sank into the chair, modestly holding her dressing gown about her.

'So . . . so that is why you told your father . . . that I'd come to you . . . that night—'

'No! No! I said nothing! Why should you think that?'

'The way he spoke . . . the way he looked – today. He and my father have been talking . . .'

'Oh mon Dieu, mon Dieu! I swear I said nothing to him! Here – here! On this book I swear it!'

She reached forward and put her hand on the Bible; her fingers were widely stretched so that they resembled the bones of an ivory fan.

'Then how—?'

'Oh, he has ideas. They come to him from anywhere! He gets these ideas . . . He is a man of great force . . . I have nothing to do with them—'

'But you agree to them! You don't reject them!'

'I have told you, I long only for escape. If they offer me that, why should I say no?'

'Even to marrying . . . the – the son of a wine importer?'

'Why not? You said, Monsieur Lewis, that . . . that you loved me. Believe me, that was a wonderful thing to hear! And for me – to marry a man who loved me? When you had gone that night – and that is why I asked you to blow out your candle – in case you took it into your head to look back – when you had gone, I say, I knelt and thanked God for what He let me hear from your lips!'

'And you? And you, Gilberte . . . do you . . . love me?'

Seized with a feeling that his whole life was suddenly poised in this moment, Lewis stretched his hand and laid it over Gilberte's. For a moment she smiled gratefully, then a flicker of fear crossed her face. Lewis was holding her hand fiercely down upon the Bible as if to commit her to a holy truth.

'Do – do you not think, then, that I will make you a good wife?'

'That wasn't what I asked you.'

'You – you will not regret your choice.'

'I would regret it if you did not love me.'

'I – I will be properly . . . affectionate. I swear to that! See! My hand is still on the Bible!'

'Why won't you answer my question? Do you love me?'

'With my hand on this book, Lewis, I do not know. That is the truth. I am trying, very hard, to be honest. I do not want to lie now, even though the truth is difficult for me to say. I want very much to be married with you.' (Her command of English – which was unusually good – tended to weaken under stress.) 'That is true. But how is it for me to say, with my hand on the Word of God, that my feeling is love or only the hope of a better life? I do not know . . . I do not know! Have pity on me, please!'

Enormous tears filled her eyes; she lowered her head to hide them. Lewis released her hand and saw with shame that his fingers had left red marks on her flesh.

'I – I cry too easily nowadays! There – there . . . it is finishing. I have stopped now and will be sensible with you. We will be sensible with each other, Monsieur Lewis Boston.

'You will not lose by this marriage. Again I swear it. There will be no cheating, no forged money. I, at least, am real; I am what you see. If I am what you wish, that is what you will obtain. If it pleases you, Monsieur Lewis Boston of Lancing, think of me as a – a purchase such as you might make in a market. Feel for yourself my arm, my hand, my hair; touch my eyes, my mouth . . .' She laughed to conceal the painful humiliation to which she was subjecting herself. 'Compare them, if you will, elsewhere . . . All will be yours in exchange for – for your name. It is a good bargain. No fraud, no deceiving. As I believe in God above, there will be no forgery . . . Please, monsieur, will you buy?'

'You leave me no choice, mademoiselle. Do we shake hands?'

Next morning, in his father's presence, Lewis gave Gilberte the little gold box with her initial on it that he had bought in the Haymarket. Inside he had put an onyx and diamond cravat-pin in the shape of a heart that his sisters had given him for his eighteenth birthday.

The count and Mr Boston exchanged glances, and Lewis felt a sense of enormous relief. It was over. The only thing that still troubled him was Corporal Bouvet.

Lewis had already given the corporal money to buy back as many of the forgeries as he could, and Bouvet had obliged. He had taken the money, shaken his head, tugged at his moustache and called Lewis – as nearly as was compatible with his invariable respectfulness – a fool. It worried Lewis absurdly to think of what the little Frenchman would say when he learned that he was proposing to marry the daughter of the family that had robbed him. He felt ashamed to face Bouvet and did his best to avoid him. However he could not quite succeed.

He met Bouvet one morning as the Frenchman was marching down towards The Plough. Bouvet halted and saluted.

'I 'ear you get married soon, Mr Boston?'

Lewis nodded guiltily. He felt he ought to have told Bouvet himself. The corporal shrugged his shoulders.

'I think, maybe, you take a chance, eh? Well, as Mr 'oskins say, you make a honest woman of 'er, per'aps? I 'ope also you make a honest mama and papa, too!'

Mr Boston had gone up to London where he stayed for something over a week. Among other matters, he had been to see his lawyer. When he returned he was looking exceedingly thoughtful and on the same evening he invited the Count de Latour to join him in his study. The count, with a glance towards his wife, declared he would join Mr Boston shortly; he wished first to fetch something from his room. Mr Boston bowed slightly and then, putting his hand on Lewis's shoulder, murmured: 'My boy – my boy.' He followed the count out of the room.

After about an hour and a half, during which conversation seemed congealed, both gentlemen emerged from the study and rejoined the company in the drawing-room. They were both smiling. Everyone looked relieved.

'Your papa,' said the count to Lewis, 'drive a 'ard bargain. Not even with our best French families 'ave I met with such – such strongness.'

Mr Boston beamed. 'Come, sir – you are quite my equal in matters of business. I respect you. You are certainly a difficult man to get the better of!'

'Ah! But you manage, eh?'

'Not at all! I think honour has been satisfied on both sides!'

Here the countess interrupted.

'Honour? Honour? I do not compre'end? Is it a duel? You talk so *mystérieux*!'

'*Ah, ma chère! C'est les contrats.*'

'*Les contrats?*'

'*Oui! Pour Louis et notre pauvre Gilberte!*'

'*Ah! Sa dot?*'

The countess dabbed her eyes and turned away. At this point Mr Boston felt it incumbent on himself to enlighten the company as to what had been arranged.

His own idea had been that a house should be bought for Lewis on his marriage and his allowance handsomely increased. But the count had felt, quite understandably, that this was scarcely enough security for his daughter who, after all, would be bringing a valuable connection. Not only this, but, being an only child, she would inherit considerable property which, by French law, would pass into Lewis's possession.

Mr Boston had seen the force of this argument, but, in view of the present uncertainty in France, had not been able to see his own way clear to increasing his offer over and above a sixth part of his own estate to be given to Lewis and Gilberte on the birth of the first issue of their union. Mr Boston had come out with this rather proudly and had assured the count that his lawyer had found precedents in the marriage articles of some of our best families.

But the count had shrewdly pointed out that this might entail several years' delay. Such things happened. On the other hand, he was prepared to make concessions, but only if Mr Boston also moved towards a compromise. If Mr Boston was willing to waive the birth of the issue clause, and increase Lewis's proportion of his father's estate to one third, payable on the marriage, then he, Count de Latour, would immediately make over to his daughter the freehold of a valuable property in the heart of Paris. This property, which had originally been a convent, was in the Rue Saint-Honoré. At the present moment it was let, at a rental of three hundred and fifty pounds a year (in English money), to a very substantial body. In point of fact it was the Jacobin Club.

By the greatest good fortune the count had been able to bring out of France with him both the title deeds and the lease which was signed, on behalf of the club, by one of its most prominent officials: a M. Robespierre ...

Mr Boston held the documents up for the company to see. Lewis, his mouth as dry as sand, stared at them. The signature of M. Robespierre looked scarcely dry ...

'*Non! Non! Non! Non!*'

It was Gilberte who had suddenly screamed. She was staring at Lewis. Her face was contorted with terror and grief. She fled from the room as if she could no longer bear the sight or sound of anyone present again.

A moment later Henrietta followed her, amazed and frantically curious. The countess had gone quite white and made as if to go after her daughter; but the count, equally pale, had shaken his head. It was better to leave her to someone nearer her own age ...

CHAPTER TWENTY-THREE

THE SEPTEMBERER IN October: cold, cold . . . Mortimer in Dieppe, the sea winds going through his coat like knives. Vessels cramming the harbour till it seems like another street. Ships for Folkestone, ships for Dover . . . full up, always full up. Refugees streaming out of the land, flying from the wrath of the Revolution, filling the boats to overflowing.

No room anywhere for the gaunt, filthy fellow in the stinking greatcoat. Mortimer grins like a death's-head at the irony of it. The very exodus he has helped to provoke now chokes his path and so stands in the way of its own continuance. He runs from vessel to vessel with the utmost urgency; but there is no place for him.

In order to keep himself in mental health, he begs news of Paris from every coach that rattles in. Nothing but rumours; every rumour reflecting only the fears and hates of the rumourer. Paris is burning to the ground; the king has been killed; the king has escaped. Mortimer nods and makes notes on scraps of paper from his pocket.

It is necessary to be busy; it serves to fix certain moments in his mind ... as landmarks in time. Lately he has noticed that he has acquired the trick of existing only in important instants which are illuminated with incredible detail; the rest is nothing ... The last man he'd spoken to, for instance; Mortimer recollected he had a half-healed cut on his forefinger with a scab that resembled flowers. The man's face has vanished – even his other fingers. It is as if all superfluous fat has been stripped from Mortimer's memory, rendering it as lean and shapely as the bone that contains it.

At last! A passage. A battered fishing vessel limping low in the black water; a crazy boat like that which ferried the ancient dead. By an unlucky chance she is bound not for Dover but for Shoreham.

Mortimer is terrified he will be recognized in Shoreham before he has had time to get to the London coach. Nevertheless he boards the vessel, even though the very thought of being seen, approached, talked to, fills him with impatient rage. He cannot endure the idea of anyone imagining he is going home. There is only one reason for his journey: vengeance. He stares into the misty gloom into which the harbour of Dieppe has slunk away. He will be back soon ...

The thought of recognition still preys horribly on his mind. He speaks to a woman on the deck near him and asks her for a mirror. She stares at him in revulsion and shakes her head. He moves away, looking for some polished surface in order to examine his face. He has a sparse beard now, but yet he feels his eyes might betray him. He finds nothing but brasswork corroded by salt air. There is no way he can see himself . . .

On Tuesday, 16th of October, Mortimer reached Shoreham. The weather was damp and cold; sea mists obscured all beyond the harbour buildings. Pushed and buffeted by ceaseless refugees, he disembarked with a curiously uncertain sensation, as if the ground was sinking beneath his feet.

He kept his face well inside his coat collar, having already seen several faces he thought were familiar. To begin with, he turned away on each occasion; then he began staring as if to challenge anyone to recognize him. He passed from the quayside into the town quite unremembered.

It was about five o'clock in the afternoon; there would be no coach leaving until the morning. He would have to find a place for the night. Suddenly the thought crossed his mind that Mr Archer would certainly give him a bed. He grinned contemptuously. The very idea of his old tutor filled him with disgust. The dim, skinny fellow would plague him with idiotic questions, overwhelm him with his infantile *enthusiasm* for matters about which he knew *nothing.*

'You know *nothing*!' exclaimed Mortimer aloud. 'Nothing – nothing!'

Several people by him turned and stared. He hurried into the High Street. A man with a wart on his chin begged his pardon for something or other. Mortimer really had no idea for what until he felt the echo of a pain in the calf of his leg. The man must inadvertently have kicked him. Curious, how *that* had passed unnoticed while the man's face and wart were so meticulously clear.

The man, encouraged by Mortimer's indifference to injury, asked him some detail or other about the town.

'I am a stranger here,' said Mortimer abruptly.

Just beyond the High Street lay a district of narrow, cobbled alleyways where there were cheap hostels for seamen. For a few pence he might stay in one of these, either in a bed or on the floor in the parlour for the night.

He found such a place called, in the hope of attracting a better class of trade, the Captain's Cabin. It had signally failed. The grim little stone-built tavern contained some half-dozen grim little stone-built men, listing, by degrees, over tables or against the wall. Mortimer found himself a corner and immediately fell to studying the intricate mass of initials and obscenities that had been lovingly inscribed on the table-top.

In the midst of these was a crudely incised representation of a naked woman. Either from delicacy or respect for artistic enterprise, it had not suffered defacement. Absorbedly Mortimer began at first to follow the outline with his forefinger and then to dig out the filth that had accumulated in the scratches with his nail. This activity seemed to provide him with physical and mental relief.

He was engaged on this task of restoration when he found himself addressed by a stranger. Instantly he withdrew his hand from the table as if he'd been detected in the most shameful human activity. The man who had accosted him was short and squat with a kind of greasy respectability about him. He reminded Mortimer of a chessboard maker he knew in the Faubourg Saint-Antoine.

'Might I make so bold as to ask,' enquired the stranger, revealing a wide variety of teeth, 'if you and me is in the same line?'

Mortimer, still trembling from having been caught out at his strange action, shook his head.

'Wait for it!' said the stranger, showing still more teeth. 'You don't know what me line may be! I may be a clergyman; I may be a bleedin' colonel of 'orse! It's foolishness to shake your 'ead when you don't know what for. Well, I'm what you might call a commercial traveller. Which is to say, I get me livin' on the road. You looks to me like a man 'oo also gets 'is livin' on the road . . . if you take my meanin'? I thought, maybe,' he went on confidentially, and diminishing his display of teeth by a molar or two, 'that if you wasn't at present occupied, we might go commercialin' together . . . if you take my meanin'? What with bein' a vessel in 'arbour, loaded to the eyeballs, there's many a stranger about what is new to our ways . . . and so there's many a livin' to be picked up on a dark road. If you take my meanin'?'

Mortimer's brain felt as if it would explode; his eyes grew misty with anger and humiliation. This man, this common footpad, had taken him for a criminal! He had come up to him – to Richard Mortimer – as if—

'No violence,' said the commercial gentleman, leaning on the table and pressing his ugly hand over the carvings thereon. 'I don't ask for that. It's just for the company, really. I'll commit what violence is needful. I see you ain't the one for it; you 'ave a tender eye and a soft 'and . . . and I wouldn't want you to vomit your guts up. As I says, it's just for the company. The man's not made what can go it alone.'

Mortimer shrank back and gave his death's-head grin. If this fellow only knew!

The commercial gentleman, taking Mortimer's smile as an invitation, slipped round the table and sat beside him. He nudged him heavily as he did so.

Instantly Mortimer jerked away. The proximity of the stranger was loathsome. He got to his feet.

'I am not,' he almost screamed, 'what you take me for!'

He stumbled outside and half ran down the alley. He turned into another street and came panting to another tavern of more salubrious aspect and joyful sound; singing was coming from within. He thrust his hands into his pockets to see if he had enough money to spare.

His money was gone. He thrust deeper and deeper, forcing his fingers into every recess lest he'd made some stupid mistake. There was nothing. He was penniless. He couldn't understand it. He began to sob bitterly. London, Paris, the Revolution – everything was gone.

He tried to remember where he might have lost the money. In the street, perhaps? But he hadn't heard it fall. He had had it when he'd gone into the Captain's Cabin.

He'd been robbed! The man who'd sat next to him, who'd nudged so intimately against him, had picked his pocket! A blinding, terrifying rage came over him. The very thought of those ugly enquiring fingers . . . !

The man's face with its rows of sneering teeth was vividly before him. So casually, so easily the man had robbed him – of his very life!

Mortimer began to retrace his steps, at first hesitantly and then with frantic haste. He would catch him! He would tear the money out of him! He would smash in his filthy face . . .

'I'll kill you – I'll kill you!' Mortimer howled aloud as he reached the Captain's Cabin.

There was an empty bottle lying against the wall by the door. Having no weapon but his bare hands, he picked it up and entered the grim little parlour. He had mastered himself sufficiently to go in quietly so as not to alarm his victim.

The scene within had remained unchanged, except that the 'commercial gentleman' was now sitting with his back to the door. The folds of his greasy neck seemed like another mouth, sneering at interruption.

'Thief! Thief! Thief!' screamed Mortimer, and smashed the bottle down on the man's head.

He collapsed instantly, falling at first against the table and then sideways into the sawdust on the floor. Huge quantities of blood ran out of his head and were immediately absorbed by the sawdust.

He had killed the man; he saw that at once. The whole scene was as clear and precise as a landscape in a raindrop: the amazed face, the fragments of glass adhering to his head, like a crown of crystal thorns . . .

But it was not the same man. He had murdered a stranger – a man who had never so much as breathed in his face or trodden on his foot. He had smashed in a head that had never contained a single thought of him . . .

He did not attempt to run away. This was a curiosity that, some people supposed, might well be produced in his favour. He allowed himself to be disarmed of the broken bottle without a word.

It was afterwards found out that he had not eaten for three or possibly four days. The two men who carried him to Shoreham gaol declared he had been as light as a weasel.

CHAPTER TWENTY-FOUR

THOUGHTS OF GAOL were peculiarly strong in the Bostons' drawing-room. The count and countess, more than aristocratically pale, stared at the door through which first their daughter and then Henrietta had gone. Mr Boston put down the title deeds and lease signed by M. Robespierre, of the Jacobin Club. He glanced awkwardly at his wife.

'Our child is opset,' murmured the count unnecessarily. 'She 'as nerves.'

Mrs Boston nodded sympathetically; Henrietta had also inherited her share of those burdens.

'She 'as been through too much,' went on the count. '*La pauvre petite.*'

The countess sighed angrily; then she brightened a little and leaned towards Mrs Boston.

'It come – the *agitation* – at a bad time of ze monz.'

Mrs Boston blushed and conceded that Henrietta also suffered at *certain times*.

The count smiled at Mr Boston, who felt suddenly

privileged to be admitted to such female mysteries.

Lewis said nothing. He felt himself to be no more than a spectator of this curiously cruel little comedy that was being played out at the expense of the tortured soul who had left them. Gilberte's cry and her agonized look were still in his mind. This latest lie of her father's had injured her far more than it had touched him. He wanted to go to her—

'Young man,' said the count, as Lewis got up, 'it is better to leave 'er to Mlle Henriette. These are affairs for the women. We, in France, understand this . . .'

Lewis looked at him with angry contempt. The count remained unmoved; not a flicker of shame, guilt or remorse crossed his large face. He was extraordinary. He must have guessed that Lewis was aware of his villainy; he must have known that his very liberty hung in the balance. But all this did not seem to concern him in the slightest. He was capable of denying everything. He had never confessed to anything demeaning in his life. It was as if he did not admit the word 'guilt' to his vocabulary; it simply did not exist. There are such people who, even at the point of death, will deny what is self-evident. Were they to stand before the bar of Heaven, with everything *known*, laid bare, they would deny it. It was the same with the countess. God had placed her in an exalted sphere; He no longer had the right to judge her.

'The count is right, my dear,' said Mrs Boston. 'It is better to leave things to your sister.' She glanced at the title deeds that lay beside Mr Boston. 'I think the house in Paris is a wonderful dowry,' she went on, hoping to comfort her dejected son. 'Perhaps, when things settle down there, we might all go over . . . ?'

'Gilberte! Please let me in! Gilberte – are you all right?'

Henrietta, still outside Gilberte's room, pressed her ear to the locked door. She listened breathlessly, her active mind teeming with fatal doses of laudanum, leapings from high windows, wrists slashed crimson with fruit-knives. The wild and despairing nature of Gilberte's flight from her wedding preparations had captured Henrietta's imagination even more than her pity. Until this moment, life in the Boston mansion had been an open book of surpassing dullness; now high drama had exploded with immense force.

'Gilberte?'

Henrietta fancied she could hear movement . . . and breathing.

'Please may I come in?'

There was a sound of hurried scratching, like mice; then a smell of burning . . . and a sudden exclamation.

'Gilberte! Answer me, please!'

'Henriette?'

'Yes . . . yes! It's me—'

'Are you – alone?'

'Yes. There's no one else!'

Another pause and then the door was unlocked; Henrietta, feeling astonishingly mature to be alone in the presence of some secret tragedy, went into the room. She saw with bewilderment and compassion that Gilberte's eyes were really swollen from crying.

'Gilberte!' she murmured, and put her arm round the older girl's shoulders. With this eloquent gesture she had every right to expect a flood of confidences, tormented questionings and sisterly expressions of regard . . . to all of which she was more than ready to reply with tenderness and understanding. But Gilberte remained quite rigid and silent. Henrietta felt the French girl's shoulders actually stiffen. She experienced a sense of disappointment, even of mild anger. Gilberte seemed to be tolerating her rather than welcoming her . . .

'What is it, Gilberte? Can you tell me . . . about it?'

'I have no intention,' muttered Gilberte, her voice sounding constrained, 'of confiding. You – you must not expect that.'

Henrietta withdrew her arm. She had waited a long time outside Gilberte's door. She had envisaged a great many scenes . . . in all of which there had been expressions of mutual, womanly sympathy. She had counted on it. In no scene at all had she imagined that the wretched French girl would stand on her dignity. Henrietta began to lose her temper. The arrogant bitch had only been upset on account of her pride. At the very last moment she'd been unable to face the prospect of marrying a wine importer's son. She was beneath contempt.

'Very well,' said Henrietta distantly. 'I'll not force any confidence from you.'

'Please, Henriette, do not be angry with me.'

Henrietta, disliking intensely the French form of her name, compressed her lips.

'I am not angry. Not in the least, I assure you. It's just that, as you let me in, I thought you had something to tell me.'

'I – I have.'

'What is it?'

'Will you . . . do something for me?'

'Of course I will!'

Henrietta answered immediately. She couldn't fail to see that Gilberte was labouring under a great strain.

'You do not ask what?'

'Why should I?'

'Ah! You are much better than I, Henriette! Me? I would calculate; I would think, I would suspect . . . But you? You answer at once from your heart!'

'Do you want me to speak to – to my brother for you? Is that it?'

'*Non! Non!* Please, no! You must not suppose I have no feelings for him. I have – I have!'

'Then what is it you want me to do?'

'Is there a *juge – un magistrat* here?'

'A magistrate?' Henrietta felt suddenly frightened. The request for a magistrate suggested something much more real and formidable than anything she'd dreamed.

She began to wish she had not tried to make her way into the young Frenchwoman's life . . .

'Yes – yes! A magistrate!' There was a touch of impatience in Gilberte's voice.

'I – I think so. Yes. Mr Grossmith in Shoreham. He is a magistrate.'

'Will you give him a letter for me?'

'If you want me to. But why?'

Gilberte was now standing by the dressing-table; she was holding out a clumsily sealed letter. At once Henrietta remembered the sound of scratching and the smell of burning.

'Will you take it now?'

She had ignored Henrietta's question as if she had not heard it. Henrietta was on the point of repeating her question, when she sensed that she would have been rebuffed.

'But it's dark already,' she said, and was unable, or perhaps a little unwilling, to keep a certain peevishness out of her voice. At once she saw a look of anguish come into Gilberte's eyes.

'I – I didn't mean that I was unwilling,' she went on hurriedly, 'but I can't leave the house now. I'll take it for you first thing in the morning. It's quite impossible now. But in the morning – terribly early . . . Give it to me—'

She held out her hand for the letter. Gilberte was about to give it to her, when she hesitated.

'In the morning, then.'

'I will be up long before you, Gilberte.'

'In that case . . . would you mind . . . very much if I – I spent the night in your room . . . with you? It is not just the letter, but I – I do not want . . . anyone – *anyone* to come to me . . . here.'

'Of course, Gilberte!'

At once all Henrietta's natural warmth returned. She was tremendously elated by Gilberte's request and couldn't help supposing that, in the recesses of the night, whispered confidences would inevitably take place. She would not ask for them, but—

'You do not mind? I will not disturb you?'

'No, no! Often my sister and I slept together – whenever there was a bad storm, you know . . . when we were children, of course! And one understands,' went on

Henrietta, catching a faint smile on Gilberte's lips and feeling that a more sophisticated precedent was called for, 'I've read, that is, that one woman can be a great comfort to another in times of *inward* storms. And anyway, you *are* practically my sister, Gilberte!'

As she said it, Henrietta really desired the strange French girl to be her sister in fact.

'Oh yes . . . I am so close to it.' Gilberte's smile grew uncomfortably bitter. 'I am a – a *contrefait* sister.'

'*Contrefait?*'

'I do not know the word in English. Perhaps I should say forgery-sister?'

'Oh! You mean counterfeit.'

'Thank you. It is certainly a word I *should* know. Tonight, then, I will be your counterfeit sister. It sounds better than forgery.'

For most of the night Gilberte sat in the window-seat, staring outside. Repeatedly she looked to the bed, catching each time the inquisitive glimmer of Henrietta's eyes. It was impossible not to be aware of the passionate curiosity that was consuming the younger girl – and not to be grateful to her for containing it. A dozen times, Henrietta had made what she plainly thought to be tactful efforts to obtain her confidence; and each time Gilberte had turned her away.

She smiled at the bed and wondered what tangled fancies Henrietta was now weaving about the pale, mysterious Frenchwoman who had come into her brother's life. Whatever they were, she wished with all her heart that she could have lived up to them . . .

Presently the glimmering of eyes vanished; Henrietta was asleep.

The mansion was full of soft noises, each of which sounded like a footfall. Was that Lewis, going to her room? Or was it her father, pale with anger at her outburst against his endless, endless crimes?

Could it be possible that he hadn't realized, hadn't understood how deeply he'd wounded her this time? Or, as always, had he thought it of so little account?

He had turned *her* into one of his forgeries. He had falsified the last thing within her that was real. And with such contempt! The impudence, the very outrageousness of his lie showed all too clearly the indifference with which he looked on the world. The insult he had offered to her, to Lewis, to Lewis's father, was colossal . . . It had only been by the greatest effort of will that she'd prevented herself from shouting out the truth in front of everyone! Perhaps it would have been better if she'd done so? Then at least it would all be over . . .

Again and again she remembered her passionate declaration to Lewis – 'As I believe in God above, there will be no forgery . . .' The memory caused her intense shame – and there was fear, too. Had she not sworn on the Bible?

She had to save herself; at all costs, she *had* to save herself.

The letter she had begged Henrietta to take to the magistrate had contained everything about her family since they had come to England. She had omitted nothing. She had confessed to every crime. She had spared neither her parents nor herself; indeed, she had felt it necessary to blame herself most of all. Everything had been laid pitilessly bare.

The writing of this letter had given her some relief; but then, having done it, having confessed, she had been unable to carry it to its conclusion. She hated herself for her own weakness, but she could not *herself* go to the magistrate and betray her own father and mother. This also would have been a sin. Yet she would have no peace, no happiness in this world *unless* she did so. Surely she was entitled to peace of mind? But not at such a cost; *honour thy father and thy mother* . . .

The course she had at last determined on – of putting the letter into Henrietta's hands and making *her* the instrument – was certainly both devious and ignoble; but then she had had very little experience of nobility other than her family name.

At first she had wondered about addressing her confession to Mr Boston, but she had shrunk from that. The memory of previous occasions in other families – the discovery and then the dismissal in pity and contempt – was still horribly strong. She preferred, infinitely, the cold, dispassionate process of the law.

She laid the letter on Henrietta's pillow, then looked long and hard at the thin clenched hand that had written it; she rubbed her wrist where she had accidentally dropped burning sealing-wax on it.

First thing in the morning, as she had promised, Henrietta took Gilberte's letter and left the house, much to the surprise of a tousled stableboy. She rode into Shoreham and went to the house of Mr Grossmith. On the way, she couldn't help wondering if she should have awakened Gilberte – who had been asleep or pretending to be so – and asking if she had changed her mind. She had the feeling that there was something irrevocable in her journey; a sense of imminent disaster oppressed her.

When she arrived Mr Grossmith had only just returned from visiting the gaol whither he had been unexpectedly summoned. He looked oddly distressed. Before Henrietta could broach her own business, the magistrate felt it necessary to explain that there had been an affray in the town on the previous evening. A man had been killed with a bottle. Mr Grossmith had just come from conducting an examination of the murderer. It turned out that he was a young man of the neighbourhood – a gentleman's son. It was altogether a tragic affair. Surely Miss Boston must remember him? Richard Mortimer . . .

Henrietta uttered a low cry, as if the life had suddenly been drained out of her body. She swayed, and, before Mr Grossmith could stop her, fell unconscious to the floor.

When she had recovered sufficiently to take a little brandy, Mr Grossmith himself drove her back to the Boston mansion. She was put to bed directly; her head and hands were like ice. The letter she had gone to deliver remained in her purse – forgotten.

CHAPTER TWENTY-FIVE

THE EXTRAORDINARY NATURE of the circumstances that attached themselves to the murder – rather
than the crime itself, which had been of a sordid, commonplace type – provoked widespread interest in the little
town. The details had circulated with wonderful speed
and the sudden and unexpected appearance of Richard
Mortimer, after an absence of three years, was discussed
in homes and bar-parlours where, before, the very
name of Mortimer had hardly been mentioned.

It was remembered that the young man had been in
France, concerning himself with politics. It was naturally
assumed that, being aristocratic himself, he had been
involved in the Royalist cause; his dramatic reappearance
in, apparently, a terrible state suggested that he had fled
from the revolutionaries and barely escaped with his life.
But how and why he had come to be in the Captain's
Cabin and there beaten a man to death resisted all
conjecture. Those who knew the truth of young
Mortimer's political leanings were even more baffled;

they could not even explain his flight, let alone the senseless and brutal crime of which he stood accused.

The murdered man had been a local carpenter by the name of Jackson. He had never done anyone any harm, or, it must be admitted, much good either. So far as anyone knew, he and his murderer were entirely unknown to each other; they had never even exchanged so much as a look. Jackson's companions at the table swore he'd not uttered a word during the whole evening, so there could be no question of some imagined insult provoking the attack, such as often happens in cases of drunkenness.

Murder being so extreme a crime, it seemed particularly necessary to find some reason, however slight, and hold to it. Perhaps there lay at the root of this the feeling that it might have been *averted* – that some kind of human control might have been exercised over human affairs . . .

But no reason came to light, neither in the magistrate's examination nor in the discussions that followed it. The prisoner remained obstinately silent and even became aggressive when urged to explain himself. The only conclusion was that he was insane; this was supported by his incoherent cry immediately before the murder and his failure to run away or even to defend himself when he had been taken.

Dr Stump intimated – as discreetly as he could – that here at least was a possible defence; but Mr Mortimer, understandably, shrank from such a course, even though the alternative was for his son to be hanged.

He went to see his son as soon as he had breakfasted. It needed a great effort for him to do so.

The gaol house in Shoreham was a stout building of cobbles and stone, conveniently near the harbour from where most of its inmates were recruited. Mr Mortimer observed with distaste the presence of several curiosity seekers who stared at him and plainly instructed each other in his social standing and his relationship to the prisoner.

The young man was in a cell on his own, furnished with a bed, a table and a wooden bench. Mr Mortimer had some difficulty in recognizing his son; either the cell or the indescribably filthy young man reeked abominably. It was as much as the father could do to remain and maintain a semblance of courtesy.

'I do not want to know how you came to be in this state,' he said. 'Nor do I wish to know why you did not come to your home. As for what you have done – that is a matter for a lawyer. I need hardly say that I will do what I can to have this – this sorry affair hushed up. All I ask is that, whatever happens, you behave like a gentleman.'

The young man did not answer. In fact he did not speak one word to his father during the entire meeting. He stood staring at the stone floor as if the answer to all his problems lay somewhere beneath it. Mr Mortimer went outside into the fresh air where he spoke with Mr Grossmith, the magistrate. He left money for his son to have the comfort of clean bed-linen and the services of a barber; after that he set off for Brighton to consult his lawyer.

He had not gone far when a stone was hurled through his carriage window, smashing the glass and cutting him slightly on the cheek. A piece of paper had been wrapped round the stone with the crudely pencilled word 'PIG' inscribed on it. Mr Mortimer was startled and angry; he was also a little frightened. He supposed the attack was related to the terrible events in France where no person of quality was safe in the streets. He could imagine no other reason.

In point of fact, the stone had been thrown by the widow of the murdered man; she was one of those women whose strong feelings and lack of education often lead them into absurdity and public spectacle. She had prepared the missile some hours before. Although the word 'pig' was hopelessly inadequate to express her hatred, bewilderment and intolerable despair, she knew she could spell it properly and so not expose herself to ridicule.

She had been intending to throw it through the window of the gaol, but when she'd seen Mr Mortimer get into his carriage, and learning who he was, she had run after him with the confused idea that the father was as guilty as the son.

Although she had been taken up almost immediately, she was only cautioned. Mr Grossmith felt to impose any punishment on the widow might well turn the murdered man into a martyr.

Among those most deeply disturbed by young Mortimer's strange crime was Mr Archer, his old tutor. The poor man, on hearing the news, was reduced to a state of feverish terror and grief. For a time, he was frightened to show himself anywhere, feeling that, somehow, his own influence was to blame. He sat in his room, crouching over a meagre fire, at times actually praying that his own soul might be guiltless.

By chance he met Dr Stump once, when he was out purchasing necessities. The doctor stared at him with compressed lips; then, seeing the unfortunate tutor's misery, relented and invited him into The Ship for some refreshment.

'I suppose I must blame myself,' said Mr Archer unhappily. 'I can see no other way. Had I not encouraged him, talked to him, given him ideas . . . ?'

He hoped to anticipate Dr Stump's reproach and thereby take a little of the sting out of it.

'You cannot be held responsible for a madman,' said the doctor curtly. 'No one, not even his physician, could have known.'

'But I *should* have known! I should, I should! I was very close, you know. I knew his mind – his enthusiasm – his fine spirit! I should have *sensed* if there was anything unbalanced!'

'If you will forgive my saying so, Archer,' said the doctor impatiently, 'there has always been something a little unbalanced about your own ideas; so it's not to be wondered at that an unbalanced young man should be taken in by them.'

'That is unforgivable of you!' cried Mr Archer indignantly. 'Do you call a man like Tom Paine un-balanced?'

'As far as I am concerned, he is a scoundrel.'

'And as far as *he* is concerned, you are a – a lackey! A lackey, do you hear?'

'Don't you dare call me a lackey, Archer!' For reasons best known to himself, Dr Stump was acutely sensitive to the expression. 'I won't have it! The trouble with men like you – heads full of cloudy rubbish – is that you can't tell the difference between a gentleman and a lout! I'll tell you one thing, Archer – a good, old-established family like the – the Latours, for instance, are worth a hundred of your plebeian Tom Paines!'

'Lackey – lackey – lackey!' jeered Mr Archer; and so the two gentlemen continued their discussion, moving along oft-trod paths and countering each other, very much as two chess players who are guided by memory rather than imagination.

At length Mr Archer went back to his lodgings; he felt quite stimulated and made up a small parcel of books that he thought might be of use to his old pupil in his time of distress. He took them to the gaol, but came away bitterly hurt. Mortimer had refused to see him. This last blow had struck him to the heart. He dreaded the approach of Friday when Mrs Coker would come and, no doubt, have heard all about it. He resolved to be out.

The Septemberer in prison, quiet, subdued ... A sense of relief has overwhelmed him, like one who has come to a hard journey's end. His feeling of peace is immensely strong; the stone walls comfort him, the bars give him security of tenure. He looks up and is troubled by no sky; he is perfectly preserved from the world.

In a desultory way, for want of other occupation, he attempts to piece together the events that have led him to this place; but there are so many gaps that he is like a drunkard struggling to recall huge fragments of time from which he is inexplicably absent. Scenes recur: the man he killed, the man he meant to kill. Of this latter man he has said nothing. Indeed he has forgotten everything about him except his smile and the touch of his probing hand. Under no circumstances will he talk about it.

People come to see him. Whenever he is allowed, he refuses them. He is not arrogant; he is not even ashamed. He is excessively tired and hoards his solitude like a miser grasping a jewel. Lewis Boston comes . . . and is sent away. He comes again – this time with his sister. The prisoner does not wish to see them; the prisoner has nothing to say. He hears a girl's voice calling out his name, then he hears her crying – then no more.

He returns to the deep satisfaction of being alone, with all responsibility taken from him and with his life itself in others' hands. He knows he will be punished for his crime; but as he killed the wrong man – a man he wished no harm to – it was not really a crime at all. Therefore the punishment must be unjust and he will be in credit with the world for ever after.

He had but one duty left. 'Whatever happens, you must behave like a gentleman.' He smiles as his father's ridiculous words come back to him; but they are not inapposite. He must certainly behave in a fashion that will not degrade his ideals.

Many better men than he had died for causes less inspired than his. Great souls had gone to shameful deaths in dignity and silence. Christ Himself had worn a crown of thorns and been murdered by the law.

The prisoner frowns. A complex chain of thought and association brings back before him the man he killed; he sees the glass splinters adhering to his head. He, too, they said, had been a carpenter ...

But this is arrant nonsense! Twist it what way one would, there is no meaning, no relevance in it. For example: Christ was innocent, Jackson was innocent. Rome killed one; Richard Mortimer killed the other. Does that make Jackson Christ or Mortimer a Roman?

'When in Rome, do as the Romans do,' says Mortimer aloud.

Brutus, the noblest Roman of them all, cast himself upon his sword. Mortimer looks about his cell where there is nothing sharper than a spoon left behind from his last meal. He shakes his head ruefully and returns to contemplating the punishment he believes he will face. By now he is becoming resigned to it and even experiences a sense of exaltation at the thought of the martyrdom he must undergo.

★ ★ ★

Next morning a Mr Purser came to the gaol. He was Mr Mortimer's lawyer from Brighton and so had right of admission. He had thick spectacles which seemed to have no eyes behind them and he wore his legal black as if he was in mourning.

'I want you to understand,' he said, seating himself on the wooden bench and resting his hands on the table as if offering them for Mortimer's use, 'that everything that passes within these walls will be in the strictest confidence. You may speak freely. Nothing will proceed further than what is necessary for your defence. Do you understand me?'

'I have no defence,' said Mortimer calmly. 'I want none.'

'What were you doing in Shoreham on the night of October 16th?' pursued the lawyer, ignoring his client's dismissal of his services.

'I don't know. I don't remember.'

'Good. Why did you leave France?'

'I don't know. I don't remember.'

'Better still. Why did you not go home? Why did you go into the Captain's Cabin?'

'I don't know. I don't—'

'Come, come, young man! We mustn't overdo things. We mustn't be seen to obstruct justice.'

'I'm not obstructing anything. I confess the crime. All I ask is for punishment.'

'What crime are you talking of?'

'Why of – of killing that man, Jackson. I hit him with a bottle ...'

'Oh? You remember that, then?'

'Yes. I remember that.'

'But nothing more? You don't remember why? You don't recall an argument – a quarrel? You don't recall that he insulted you?'

'He didn't!' exclaimed Mortimer quickly. 'I'd never seen him before!'

'That's not true,' said the lawyer, turning his eyeless spectacles full upon Mortimer. 'You had been in the Captain's Cabin minutes earlier. There are witnesses. The man insulted you. You came back and killed him for it.'

'It was another man!' burst out Mortimer wildly, before realizing he'd betrayed himself.

'I thought as much,' said the lawyer quietly. 'You murdered the wrong man. Now listen to me: to kill the wrong man is no less a felony than to kill the man who had injured you. Malice is the great criterion by which murder is distinguished from every other kind of homicide. There was malice in your heart when you entered the room; whether towards the dead man or

324

towards another. The law demands no more than that. Let me impress upon you, young man, there must be no mention of this other person. Do you understand that? He no longer exists. I do not wish to hear anything more about him. Never again—'

'Then why did you make me tell you?'

'Young man, if I, your friend, obtained this from you in a matter of minutes, consider what a prosecuting counsel – your enemy – might not obtain, with all the time in the world, in open court? Why did you leave France?'

The question was rapid and totally unexpected. Mortimer stammered, but before he could answer, Mr Purser continued: 'You had committed a crime there! Another murder, was it? Come, answer! You are a murderer, are you not? A habitual thief, a brutal scoundrel!'

'No – no!' shouted Mortimer, incensed by the lawyer's cold, biting words. 'I'm a – a—'

'Enough,' said the lawyer coolly. 'I don't want to know what you are or have been. And I advise you to forget. You do not know why you killed the man Jackson. You remember nothing about it. You must have been mad. Do you understand? You – were – insane. Insane. *Not responsible*. Stick to that, my young friend. Stick to it like glue. It is your only hope. But I warn you, don't try any tricks with the prosecuting counsel. Give him the smallest chance and he'll ferret out the very secrets of your soul. Everything you have done in your life will be dragged out into open court.'

When the lawyer had gone, Mortimer pleaded with the gaoler for writing materials. He had been severely shaken. He was now genuinely frightened that he could be trapped into betraying Mr Dignam-Browne and those mysterious friends of the Revolution whose wealth had been employing him and others to such striking effect.

He wrote, with great circumspection, explaining his present situation. He ended his letter with the follow-words, scored so deeply that in places they actually tore the paper.

I am not afraid of dying for our cause. You must know that. My fear is that I will not prove skilful enough to avoid betraying, in open court, *those who matter more than I. Please help me. R.M.*

He sealed the letter several times over and begged that it might be delivered to the Cock Tavern in Fleet Street. He had addressed it to a Mr D.B.

Although he had never been guided by self-preservation (at times the reverse seemed to have been the stronger impulse), once the letter had gone it was impossible for Mortimer not to feel a revival of hope.

Almost unwillingly he found himself returning to life with all its anxieties, impatience and the prospect of ultimate light. He no longer welcomed solitude; his own company became a burden to him. He asked that his friends might be allowed to visit him.

CHAPTER TWENTY-SIX

HENRIETTA REFUSED TO go. Not for anything would she again endure the horrible comedy of dressing with feverish care, of contorting her bosom, darkening her eyes and whitening her hands; or perfuming herself with intimate care and sucking hideous sweets to 'render her breath wholesome and desirable to the opposite sex' ...

'Not for anything will I go to that place again and then be told he won't see me! I'm not a child any more. I'm a grown woman! Oh Gilberte – tell me, what ought I to do?'

Gilberte shrugged her shoulders wearily. Since the discovery of Mortimer's imprisonment, she had done the best she could to comfort the distraught Henrietta.

The days that had followed had seemed curiously unreal to her; she felt by-passed by time, left in abeyance ... peripheral to thoughts and feelings that were drawn inexorably to the prisoner in the gaol. Her confession – that great gesture that had been wrung from the depths of her soul – had been undelivered. She had seen it in Henrietta's purse. She'd felt an involuntary pang of anger and injured pride that it should have been forgotten in the concern surrounding the young man in prison. She'd been about to take it back when she realized that if she did so she would cause Henrietta even more distress; also it would leave her, Gilberte, with the agony of having to begin all over again.

She tried to persuade herself that the tragedy in Shoreham had been a sign, a working of fate, to prevent her confession being delivered. Was it not possible that God had given her a second chance? On one occasion she actually knelt and tried to give thanks for being granted this respite.

Her state of mind and, by this time, her almost frantic love for Lewis had brought her to this blasphemous condition. As soon as she realized it, she got up and began bitterly reproaching herself for daring to think that a man's death, another's imprisonment and the unhappiness of many people had been devised by God for *her* advantage.

'Please forgive me!' she whispered. 'Please forgive me!'

In penance, as it were, she devoted herself to Henrietta, whose moods ranged like the Alps, from icy desolation to pastures of green passion, in the space of minutes.

'What ought I to do, Gilberte?'

'Go, but expect nothing.'

'How can I expect nothing? What shall I say to him? What must he be thinking of now – in that horrible place? God knows what it must be like! Gilberte – tell me, what was it that Lewis said to *you* when you were in – in that prison?'

'Your brother? He said nothing. He held out his hand.'

'How would it be if I did that? Just held out my hand. Should I do that?'

'Why not?'

'What shall I wear?'

'Blue – blue – always blue! In prison one learns to adore the sky.'

So they talked on, high in Henrietta's tower; question following on answer ceaselessly, leaving no pause, no silence, as if each was afraid to leave space for the unspoken thought that must have been in each of their minds: the young man in prison had committed a murder and must be hanged for it.

Lewis went to see him in the morning. It was raining quite heavily and the bone-dry prisoner in his dark cell contrasted oddly with the dripping, shining Lewis who left awkward puddles wherever he stood.

'You'll catch your death of cold,' said Mortimer wryly.

Lewis was deeply grateful for Mortimer's good humour. God knew what he'd expected; it had been a meeting he'd dreaded as much as desired. He was thankful, too, that Mortimer had shaved himself and wore good clothes that had been sent from his home. Most of all he was relieved that the misshapen greatcoat had been abandoned; it lay on the stone floor at the foot of the bed where it still uncannily retained something of the shape that had filled it. Mortimer caught his friend's glance and frowned impatiently.

'I've brought you some wine, Dick,' said Lewis, seating himself damply on the bench.

'The best? Nothing but the best?' (Why had he said that? Why, at that moment, had he wanted to provoke Lewis?)

'Nothing but the best. Is there anything I – we can do? Is there anything you want, I mean?'

'No. Everything has been attended to. I have a lawyer, you know. Or, rather, a suit of black with a legal tooth-pick inside it.'

'Good, good. I'm glad that's done. Everyone sends their love—'

'Thank you. But you shouldn't have come. Not in this rain. You could have waited . . .'

'Yes, yes . . . I know. But I thought the rain might be settling in for some time so . . . so . . .'

Lewis fumbled for words. The idea of time passing, however indirectly referred to, seemed peculiarly horrible and cruel in the present circumstances.

Apparently unmoved, Mortimer waited; the silence in the room was broken only by the weeping of rainwater from Lewis's clothing.

'Shall I open a bottle of wine?'

Mortimer nodded, smiling slightly at Lewis's abrupt and almost nervous question. He watched the evident relief with which Lewis busied himself with the wine, dispensing it into two handsome glasses he'd been thoughtful enough to bring.

'What shall we drink to?' Mortimer picked up his glass and studied it elaborately. 'To your family? To the House of Boston?'

'If you like.'

'No. Let's drink to something else. What about that countess of yours? You remember?' He raised his glass. 'To the Countess de la Motte-Valois!'

'But she's dead—'

Instantly Lewis wished he'd held his tongue. Mortimer's eyes had grown momentarily bright, as if with dread. Lewis put down his glass; an immense grief had overwhelmed him. He looked at his friend who suddenly seemed breathlessly fragile; a puff of air might blow him away; yet this was Mortimer . . . Mortimer of countless bright times. These present moments, he knew with piercing clarity, were incredibly precious.

'Oh yes . . . yes. I heard about it,' said Mortimer remotely. 'But if we cannot drink to the dead, perhaps some other lady? Who is it, these days?'

Lewis looked indecisive. He shrugged his shoulders.

'Gilberte,' he said finally.

'Another Frenchwoman? You seem fatally drawn to them! Let's drink to Gilberte, then. And may her eyes always shine on you!'

They drank. To Lewis's discomfiture, the wine proved slightly sour; he hoped Mortimer hadn't noticed.

'Who is this Gilberte? Do I know her? Is she beautiful? What a question! Will you marry her? Tell me about her. I want to know everything!'

How could he waste time prattling about his own concerns – *now*? How could he even *think* about anything else when everything about Mortimer – even the tiniest thing – was so desperately important? Yet what else could he do? What else was there to talk of that would not, sooner or later, remind both of them that one was doomed?

He glanced somewhat shyly at the pale, calm face of his friend and felt an aching tenderness for him. He longed to confide in him, as if that would break down the wall of shadows that was rising up all round him. If only he could interest Mortimer, make him a part of his own life, then he might be able to hold him back . . .

He began to talk rapidly and intimately about his own problems. He wanted to give Mortimer the feeling that he was opening his heart without reserve. He found himself asking his advice on this and that – problems that he could quite well have answered himself; but somehow that wasn't the point. The words, questions, were nothing; it was as if he was asking reassurance from a companion who was a hundred years older and wiser than himself, and that somehow Mortimer would know what was meant. (Perhaps, in a way, it was an unconscious deference to one who stood already at the latter end of his life.)

He told Mortimer about Gilberte and his troubled love for her. He talked freely about the count and countess and the evil times he'd had since he'd been saddled with them. Because the cell had become like a confessional, he confessed everything, including his own guilt in having brought such criminals to his home. He talked wildly and bitterly about the irony of having rescued them—

'You didn't tell me you'd rescued them?' Mortimer, seated on his bed, looked at Lewis keenly.

'Yes – yes! It was—'

Unconsciously Lewis's eyes had strayed to the greatcoat on the floor. He faltered.

'When was it?'

'When I was in – in Paris.'

Lewis was unable to keep his eyes off the huddled coat. The pockets still bulged. He wondered what was in them.

'That was in . . . September.' Mortimer also looked towards the coat.

'Yes.'

'Where did you . . . rescue them from? Where were they?'

'I forget. One of the – the prisons.'

'Which prison?'

'I – I think it was La Force.'

'On the Sunday?'

'It – it might have been . . .'

With the utmost reluctance Lewis withdrew his eyes from the coat and looked at his friend. This was the last thing in the world he wanted to happen . . .

A feeling of the most extreme terror clutched at Mortimer's heart. He experienced a sense of falling – falling into some amazing pit of screams and flashing fire. He raised his eyes to meet those of his friend.

Until that moment he had felt immeasurably superior

to Lewis, as, indeed, he had to everyone and everything unconnected with his great cause. What he had done had sanctified him, as it were, and set him apart; his loneliness had been that of a saint or a prophet. He had known precisely how Lewis had felt throughout their meeting, had sensed exactly every thought of pity and grief; and he had been content to humour them.

But now, as he stared into the stupid, amiable eyes of Lewis Boston, he saw such a depth of sorrow that he shrank from it. He *knew*, beyond all doubt, that Lewis had seen him on that night, had watched him tearing and hacking the young princess into senseless, bloody fragments. This unbearable knowledge Lewis had carried in his heart. He saw also the pain in his friend's eyes that this secret should not have to be shared. The glimpse of this pain caused him terrible distress.

He attempted to rise from the bed but found that his legs would not support him.

'Pardon me . . . pardon me,' he mumbled, and moved awkwardly sideways until he could reach down to his greatcoat. He began to pull and tear at the pockets, scattering his treasured refuse of the Revolution everywhere in the agitation of his search. Presently he found what he was looking for: the twist of silk containing the lock of hair.

He knew it had been in the nature of a pledge; now

it seemed to be infinitely more. It expressed, in his mind, both the extremity of his guilt and the beginnings of his atonement. It united them.

'Look, Lewis, look . . .'

He reached out and laid it, with shaking hands, on the table. Silently Lewis put out his hand and touched it; as he did so, Mortimer gave a cry of desolation and flung himself face down on the bed.

Lewis rose; the tragedy of this meeting seemed to him more awful than anything he could have imagined. Sadly he knew that his own mind, his own intellect, was woefully inadequate before the scope of his friend's despair. He could not begin to grasp it. The only thing he could feel at that moment was a terrifying compassion that blotted out the hideousness of all crime.

He put his hand on Mortimer's shaking shoulders. He had never touched him before; he was amazed by how frail and bony his friend felt. Suddenly Mortimer seized his hand; he gripped it with painful intensity. He would not let go. He pressed it to his cheek, cry-ing helplessly in the manner of a child after a storm of forgiveness. He kissed Lewis's hand over and over again.

'I love you,' he whispered. 'I love you as I should love Christ. Do you understand that?'

'Yes . . . yes.'

Mortimer released his hand. He sat up, smiling almost radiantly.

'Will you come again?'

'If you want me to.'

'I want you to.'

'Will you . . . see my sister?'

'For your sake, yes.'

Henrietta came that afternoon, when the rain had stopped. She was at her loveliest, filling the little gaol with sky-blue silk and a bitter-sweet perfume calculated to 'make the wearer an interesting object to the opposite sex'.

In spite of all this, however, she was excessively nervous. She was frightened that she would make some horrible mistake, would betray her inexperience, and that Richard Mortimer would laugh at her. Her concern for the impression she would make caused her to forget entirely the desperate situation of her lover. She was trembling when she entered the cell; her clothes felt stiff and awkward and her eyes were blinded with tears of embarrassment and distress.

Quickly Mortimer took her hand and kissed it, saying with warmth, that he would have liked to kiss her lips but prison life had made his breath foul. Then he stepped back to admire her and declare how beautiful she'd become. Although he'd been told, he'd had no real idea of the truth of it.

Her awkwardness increased as she attempted to thank him; she was amazed and shaken by his emaciated and intense appearance. The image of Mortimer she'd carried in her heart had been so very different. She struggled to overcome a disappointment and, in doing so, released a flood of tenderness within herself for Mortimer. She felt an overwhelming need to hold him in her arms and keep him from the shadows that were surrounding him and threatening to engulf him.

Eagerly she told him she would help – she had money – there were many things she could sell . . . It mattered nothing to her that Mortimer's defence had already been set in motion. She wanted to save him herself. She began to talk of escape . . .

Although she was desperately serious and was experiencing emotions she had never known before, her youth and bookish imagination led her into strange, muddled fantasies that, inevitably, caused Mortimer to smile. Yet he showed himself willing to enter into the spirit of her plans, even elaborating on or disputing their more exotic details.

They talked a good deal of the future, and in a way that took it for granted they would be together. They became quite animated, as if they were discussing a fact, an actuality . . . yet, at the same time, underlying it all, their deeper selves kept glancing out at each other as if wondering which of them would be the first to abandon the pretence.

Mortimer fought hard against these moments that overcame him like waves of lethargy. He kept seeing Lewis in Henrietta's features. There was a great resemblance between them. He found himself imagining he was talking with Lewis through Henrietta. Brother and sister were one; the relationship bewildered and fascinated him. Henrietta became boyish; her femininity faded . . .

'I have always loved you, Richard Mortimer,' she murmured as at last she rose to go.

'And I you, Henrietta Boston. Truly.'

When she had gone, Mortimer felt wonderfully revived. He asked the gaoler that any money remaining from his father's provision for his comforts should be given to the widow of the man he'd killed. He knew it to be an insignificant, even patronizing gesture; but the expansion he felt of everything within him demanded that he should act in whatever way he could. The knowledge that one human being had found it in his heart to forgive him was almost unbearable in its relief and joy.

He wished he had not written to Dignam-Browne.

The need had gone. He knew he had the strength to stand his trial and betray no one. For the first time in many years he found himself coming back to life with all its golden hopes ...

CHAPTER TWENTY-SEVEN

MR DIGNAM-BROWNE, fresh from his bath and smelling decidedly antiseptic, sat by the door of the smoky upper room of the Cock Tavern. As usual, news of France filled the air; but nowadays, Mr Browne was pleased to detect a certain wafting away of sympathy for the Revolutionary cause. There was even some despondency over the crossing of the Rhine by the Revolutionary Army. Since the September massacres, in fact, ideals had hardly been mentioned at all. Mr Dignam-Browne might well have felt a glow of satisfaction for a difficult task well done, had he not felt an uncomfortable tingling sensation due to too much sulphur in his bath.

'Guv'nor!'

Mr Browne looked round. A waiter from downstairs was addressing him from the doorway. He frowned; he'd warned this fellow several times about calling him 'governor'. The term suggested a financial relationship between them that Mr Browne was anxious to be kept discreet. The man grinned and handed him a letter. It was addressed to a Mr D.B.

'Where from?'

'Dahn sarth. Seaside.'

Mr Browne opened the letter. He read it rapidly, folded it and tucked it into a compartment of his purse.

'Is the messenger waiting?'

'Nah! Sent 'im orf. Told 'im I didn't know a Mister Deebee, but would arst arahnd.'

The fellow was good; no doubt about it. He was worth putting up with . . . Mr Browne gave him a shilling.

'Goin' on yer 'olidays, guv'nor?'

Although he did not show it, Mr Browne left the Cock Tavern in a state of considerable uneasiness. The letter he had just received from Richard Mortimer, now of Shoreham Gaol, threatened the most disagreeable possibilities.

As soon as he was alone, Mr Browne reread the letter. There was no doubt, it was a threat. The foolish young man was capable of causing a good deal of damage in the world, and of making things uncomfortable for more people than himself. How and why he'd turned up in Shoreham Gaol, though mildly interesting, was of no consequence; what mattered was that he should be removed from there. The very thought of the past transactions – in the Haymarket and the Rue Saint-Honoré – between himself, M. Paré and Richard Mortimer coming out in open court caused Mr Dignam-Browne to perspire painfully. The Ministry would be haplessly involved and not only Under-Secretaries would feel the cold wind of change.

There was no help for it; he would have to go to Shoreham himself. Briefly he'd considered sending some trustworthy individual – of whom he knew several – but he'd been too severely shaken in finding his trust in Richard Mortimer misplaced to risk further disappointment. In plain words, he could not afford to be wrong again. He was within a very few years of retirement; his masters would have no mercy.

Curiously, as soon as he'd decided on his course of action, he experienced a feeling of great energy and youthfulness. He had not been 'active in the field' – as the expression went – for many years. Of late he had led rather a sedentary life, which might well have been bad for him. It certainly was the thing to do, once in a while, to renew oneself . . .

He went back to his rooms where he began to pack night clothing, shaving things and several changes of undergarments. He went to his desk, from where he took certain other necessities for his journey, and stowed them in his purse.

All these preparations, carried out with methodical care, increased the sensation of being young again. He was interested to note that the infernal itching and tingling seemed to be in abeyance. He felt almost childishly excited. Lastly he opened a cupboard and took out a hat he'd not worn for years. Although a little old-fashioned, it made him look rather raffish and even dashing. He nodded familiarly to his reflection and hastened outside.

He made for the coaching-office in the White Horse Cellar in Piccadilly. He consulted the latest road-book and found that he could board a coach to Bagshot in Surrey almost directly. This he did, arriving late in the evening. He stayed the night in Bagshot and, next morning, travelled to Farnham and thence to Alton, changing his conveyance each time. At Alton there happened to be a coach standing in the yard, about to set off for Arundel. But Mr Browne preferred to wait till the following morning. He did not want to be seen and possibly remembered, changing from one coach to another.

Perhaps these precautions were a shade fantastic in their elaboration, but Mr Dignam-Browne rather enjoyed the exercise of an old skill . . . even to the point of overdoing it. The last part of his journey – from Arundel to Shoreham – he accomplished on horseback, hiring an animal from the busiest stables in the town.

He reached Shoreham just before dark. He left his horse at a ramshackle inn, that looked to be falling into a creek, on the outskirts and walked rapidly into the town. He traversed the wet, cobbled streets, searching inquisitively, but asking no directions and invariably giving way to other passers-by. He became, as it were, a most courteous shade of the night.

Presently he found out the gaol. In vain the turnkey attempted to discern what manner of person had come to see Richard Mortimer. (The man had been no better than a shadow, with his daft hat pulled down so low over his eyes that nothing was to be seen of them.)

'Who's asking for him?'

'A friend. A well-wisher. He will know.'

'Come along this way.'

He led the shadow to Mortimer's cell and began to unlock it.

'We can talk through the bars,' said the shadow. 'Leave us.'

The turnkey shrugged his shoulders and departed.

'I knew it would be you,' said Mortimer, rising from his bed and standing by the table. He looked extra-ordinarily cheerful.

'Very bad business,' whispered the shadow. 'A sorry

affair. Come closer, young man. Can't shout our little talk to the world.'

As if to emphasize the need for shouting across so narrow a distance, a sudden uproar of banging and swearing broke out from some nearby place of confinement where several seamen, of unknown language and country, had been restrained for the night.

Mortimer shrugged his shoulders and moved closer to the bars.

'It's fortunate,' breathed the shadow, 'that I could get here before matters went too far. I take it I am in time, young man?'

Mr Dignam-Browne seemed to have abandoned his formal habit of addressing Mr Richard Mortimer at full length. It was as if a sense of delicacy impelled him towards the anonymous 'young man'.

'I have said nothing. I promise you that.'

'Good – good. A gentleman's word . . .'

'I wanted to see you . . . about the money.'

'Ah! The money.'

The shadow produced two dazzlingly white hands that proceeded to dance, apparently independent of human agency, with a purse – a large purse of many compartments. One hand plunged into so deep a black recess that it seemed to have been chopped off at the knuckles, leaving a somewhat ghastly mitten, working in nothingness.

'The money stopped,' said Mortimer, watching the hand curiously. 'I thought your friend in Paris was cheating you.'

'Cheating me?' The mitten convulsed. 'Oh no, no! Young man, please do not think that! You really must not – ought not to think ill of anyone!'

'What are you looking for in your purse?'

'Ah! Here it is!'

The mitten jumped. Mortimer saw something shine. Then he felt a sharp pain in the left side of his chest. He tried to ask what it was, but he could not move his tongue; he could not even draw breath. He saw the purse growing larger and larger. One particular compartment seemed to be yawning at him.

'I would like you to know,' whispered the shadow, 'that you are dying for your country. You are a . . .'

The black compartment swept upwards and suddenly engulfed Mortimer.

'Patriot,' finished the shadow, and withdrew his knife from the murdered man.

No one saw the visitor leave; the body of Mortimer was not discovered for a good half-hour. By that time Mr Dignam-Browne might have been on his way to Arundel. Actually he was still in Shoreham. He had observed that, despite the lateness of the hour, several shops were still open – as is not uncommon in harbour towns where business thrives at unlikely hours.

Taking fearful risks, Mr Dignam-Browne had gone in search of a haberdasher's. At last he found one. He had needed a clean pair of white gloves, his own having been stained with blood.

He left Shoreham almost as the discovery was made. He returned to Arundel and thence to London by a different but equally circuitous route. On the morning following his return, he was back in his customary place in the Cock Tavern. The waiter nodded to him.

'Been on yer 'olidays, guv'nor? You look as brisk as the ole Cock 'imself!'

CHAPTER TWENTY-EIGHT

FOR MANY DAYS after the death of Mortimer, Lewis was unable to think of him without great pain. Even when the shock and sense of outrage had died away, there remained a horrible bewilderment and a melancholy disbelief that Mortimer was dead. The child Mortimer, the youth . . . Mortimer at fourteen, lying in the grass and grinning at him – all this filled his thoughts rather than their last meeting.

Together with his father he had gone to the funeral. Mortimer had been buried in Bramber, in the family vault. During the interment, Mortimer's father had stood between his lawyer and a distant relative he'd asked to be present. So rigidly had he held himself between these two that Lewis felt that, were either of them to have moved away, Mr Mortimer would have toppled, like a cloth colossus, to the ground.

The perpetrator of the crime had not been discovered, and there seemed little prospect of ever doing so; the reason for Mortimer's murder was buried with him. For this, Lewis became ultimately relieved. He could not help suspecting a fearful darkness in the affair; perhaps even another secret. There had been moments when he'd dreaded that Mr Grossmith's painstaking enquiries would bear fruit. He did not want such fruit. He believed, with all his heart, that Mortimer himself would have wished matters to have been left likewise; that is, with his friend as they had parted, with nothing more to be explained, forgiven. Lewis felt that it would be wronging him indeed to drag him up to face what he could no longer answer. Little by little, Lewis began to feel a sense of peace for Mortimer, whom he saw now as a restless spirit, often in such pain that he was driven to extremes; but now thankfully at rest.

He knew nothing of Mortimer's life in Paris before the latter end of it. He tried to imagine that passionate feeling for the good of all mankind finding some true expression before it had been finally corrupted. Mortimer must have been like Icarus, who'd flown too high for the strength of his wings, and been burnt.

Poor Mr Archer had taken it badly. Lewis had seen him skulking round Bramber church, not daring to join the mourners openly, but most miserably looking on from a distance at the burial of his pupil.

The memory of quarrels with Mortimer often recurred . . . and particularly the desperate one on the stairs of the house in the Haymarket. He wondered how Mortimer had felt afterwards. He remembered his conversation with Mortimer – that had also terminated badly – in the Café de Foix. His eyes filled with tears as he realized what must have been in Mortimer's mind then – and what was being prepared.

All these attempts of Lewis's to find some coherence, some lasting importance as it were, in his friendship with Mortimer were confused with fragmentary wonderings of how he must have seemed in his friend's eyes. Inevitably he came back to their last meeting when Mortimer's solemn words, 'I love you', had actually struck panic, dread and then a sense of acute unworthiness into his heart. Mortimer had asked him if he'd understood; he'd said 'yes', but it had not been true. But his 'yes' had released such a flood of peace that he'd known it must have been right.

So Lewis, in this odd, drifting fashion, composed his own requiem for Mortimer that was, somehow, more fitting than the nondescript words of the parson over the coffin. 'Tragedy of a young life cut off . . . bereaved family . . . dust to dust . . .'

The air had been full of dust as the October sunshine had streamed through the windows of the church onto the small congregation. When it was over Mr Boston had murmured a few words of consolation to Mr

Mortimer, who had barely acknowledged them. He'd inclined his head and then glanced round the church with a fleeting expression of humiliation. So few . . . so few . . .

The Count de Latour had asked if he might attend. Lewis, feeling the bitter irony of the count's presence at the burial of Mortimer – with all Mortimer, in his finer moments, had stood for – shook his head. A look had passed between them, and the count had flinched a little as if, suddenly, he suspected his heart had been laid bare. Then he'd smiled at Lewis, rather timidly.

'I – I understand,' he'd murmured. ''E was your friend. And we 'ave no place . . . I meant only to be respectful . . . but I understand . . .'

How strange it was that one such small, kind action could sometimes outweigh a great deal of villainy. Lewis had felt deeply moved by the count's gesture.

When they left the church, Dr Stump had come up and shaken Lewis by the hand; his grip had been surprisingly firm.

'I know,' he said quietly, 'how you must be feeling.'

Lewis returned the doctor's grip and smiled sadly. Did he know? Did anyone know how he felt? He would have liked to have talked a little with Mr Archer; but the tutor was nowhere in evidence. Strangely enough, Lewis derived most comfort from the presence of someone who had never known Mortimer: Gilberte. Perhaps this was because her own unhappy spirit awoke a sympathy in Lewis that was in danger of becoming drowned in dreams.

He felt it was possible that she alone might have been able to understand his complex emotions, his fears, his sometimes painful attempts to piece together a comprehensible life.

There were times when he found himself longing to tell her that her own self-torment was not necessary. Had he not said 'yes' to his friend Mortimer, and freed him? And Mortimer's need had been ten thousand times greater than hers. But Mortimer had asked. Mortimer had said: 'I love you.'

Abruptly Lewis recoiled as he realized the spiritual vanity of his thoughts. What right had he to imagine that his own wretched little forgivings were enough to set the torment of another's inner world at rest? The griefs and disturbances of the spirit – like the griefs and disturbances of the state itself – could only be solved from within. To impose a cure from without must always end in anger, violence and rejection – even of what is most good and just.

Who can know what is *really* needful, even for himself? 'Do you understand?' Mortimer had asked. 'Yes,' Lewis had answered; and only then, only when the question had been asked and answered, had either of them understood. His friend had known no more than he; the moment and its aftermath had been created not out of knowledge but out of need.

If only Gilberte could bring herself to give him some sign, he thought, some gesture of *need* . . . But whenever he felt that he himself might make the approach, his own deep feeling of humility and very real fear of trespassing in the profoundest regions of another's heart always held him back.

Gilberte spent a great deal of her time with Henrietta. The younger girl had been hysterical with grief for several days; Dr Stump had dosed her with sedatives so that at least she had managed to sleep. In spite of this, Gilberte had insisted on sitting beside her; almost certainly she was afraid that Henrietta would do something irrevocably foolish. She had begged for the window of the bedroom to be nailed up.

Then, one day – it must have been a week or ten days after the funeral – Gilberte asked Lewis if he would come and talk to his sister. She felt it might do some good. She herself, although she had real sympathy, was unable to talk as Henrietta wanted to talk – about Mortimer.

Henrietta, sitting up in bed, her counterpane a battlefield of cosmetics that had been used to stem the ravages of sorrow, smiled feebly at Lewis and then burst into tears.

'Shall I go, Henriette?' murmured Gilberte.

Henrietta shook her head and extended an arm demandingly. Gilberte held her hand and sat on the bed beside her.

'Don't – don't tell me about the – the funeral,' sobbed Henrietta. 'Just talk about – him as you . . . as we remember him. He loved me, you know. He really did.'

Lewis nodded and, walking about the room, picking up odd bottles, pots, scarves, pins and the general litter of his sister's superfluous apparatus of charm, began talking about Mortimer. He talked at random, calling up memory after memory until Henrietta joined in, even correcting him on something Mortimer had said, or what he'd been wearing . . .

From time to time Lewis would glance at Gilberte and she would nod to him. If only, thought Lewis, the same understanding could be awoken between him and her. But without words. The appalling technicality of words defeated him. And yet, if the moment were right, any words would do.

'Poor Mr Archer!' said Henrietta suddenly. 'Richard was everything to him, you know. Remember how proud he was of Richard's letters? I suppose, in a way, Richard died for ideals?' She smiled at Gilberte. 'My lover was really a hero, you know. That must make me a heroine by proxy.'

'Proxy, Henriette? What is that?'

'A – a – oh! I can't explain! Lewis! There – on my table! My little French dictionary. It's a tiny book . . . next to my purse.'

'No. It isn't there.'

'Look inside my purse, then.'

Lewis looked in the purse. He saw a folded letter. Curiously he took it out, wondering if it could have been from Mortimer. But it was still sealed. He held it up.

'It's Gilberte's,' said Henrietta, flushing guiltily.

Much surprised, Lewis looked at Gilberte. She was trembling visibly. Feeling obscurely frightened, he began to put the letter down, when he sensed that she had shaken her head. The movement had been so small as to be almost imperceptible. Her expression was desperate.

Lewis's fear increased. He broke the seals and read the letter – the terrified confession, the utter self-exposure it contained.

'It's for Mr Grossmith,' said Henrietta uncomfortably.

'No,' mumbled Lewis, crumpling the letter in his fist as if he would crush it into nothingness. 'It was for me. Isn't that so, Gilberte?' His eyes were full of tears.

For a moment Gilberte did not answer. Her lips parted as if she was unable to find the words she needed.

'*Tu comprends? Tu comprends?*'

'Yes . . . yes. I understand.'

'*Je t'aime, Louis. Je t'aime, mon cher.*'

Chapter Twenty-Nine

ON JANUARY 17TH, 1793, the National Assembly in Paris found the King of France to be an enemy of the people and condemned him to death; four days later, at twenty-two minutes past ten o'clock in the morning, to immense applause, they chopped off his head.

From that moment onward, the Revolution burst its bounds and exploded in wildness, enthusiasm and cataracts of blood. War was declared on England and, after that, all the world was to be freed from its chains. Leaders, huge as children's pasteboard cut-outs – and, like them, capable only of slow, enormous gestures – swayed and toppled in the whirlwind they'd sown; while before them and behind them unseen humanity roared its head off, stole money, committed adultery, starved, drank too much and got into debt.

In a certain inn near the Porte Saint-Denis, a mottled cat called Danton had its name changed a dozen times . . . but, as usual, only answered to '*minou*'; while in England, in consequence of a great mobilization to defend the shores, one Lieutenant Philips of the Royal Navy, devoted and patient admirer of Elizabeth Boston, was put upon full pay with every prospect of a ship.

Following on this sudden and totally unexpected improvement in his circumstances, all objections to the lieutenant's union with Miss Boston melted away and the patriotic Mr Boston gave the couple his blessing.

The wedding had been solemnized in Hanover Square in the presence of several other naval officers whose prospects had been similarly brightened. The Army had been represented by Mr Boston's younger brother, the quartermaster, who had gone down vigorously defending the military in a sea of his brother's best wine. ('Ships?' he'd shouted. 'What's the good of ships on dry land? Answer me that, if you can!')

At the beginning of May, the new Mrs Philips visited Lancing and exhibited her prize; to celebrate the occasion Mr Boston gave his first out-of-doors function of the year.

It turned out to be a warm, burgeoning day that brought out the best of last year's summer to stalk and flutter across the mansion's lawns. Servants, laden with glasses, circulated impeccably, and were duly mindful of instructions to visit Warrior Boston as infrequently as possible; Mr Boston did not want another scene. Of all his functions, this, to honour his own family, was perhaps dearest to his heart.

His cup was full to overflowing. One child married to an English hero, another betrothed to the daughter of a French count. In addition to this he seemed to have acquired the stray nobleman and his wife as eternal guests; they had settled in as if to the mansion born. What was it Lewis had said? We cannot turn them out. He had been quite firm on that. It was almost as though, by marrying into their family, he was accepting them as his own responsibility. Generous soul! thought Mr Boston, with a wry smile; but then the sons of comfortable men could afford to be. Well, well . . . the house was big enough; and lately, Boyd and Kerr, his new bankers, had done rather well for him with Swiss and Dutch currency. The wine trade, it was true, was passing through difficult times; but men must always drink – and pay for it.

He beamed and bowed to Lady Bullock, who had been at death's door for so long now that one might have been pardoned for mistaking her for its knocker. And there was Mr Archer, a little frayed and shabby, but one was always pleased to see him. Such a cultured man . . . But no one outshone his married daughter!

Elizabeth was looking superb. She was at that peak of womanhood beyond which – unless there be special redeeming qualities – there can be nothing but decline.

She looked so utterly ripe in the May sunshine that one might have supposed her to have been the model for many a fine ship's figurehead.

She kept glancing about her with splendid satisfaction, noting the grandeur of her father's house and reflecting that it could hardly fail to impress Lieutenant Philips. Similarly, whenever her roaming eye lighted upon the dashing lieutenant, she felt *he* could hardly fail to impress her family and friends.

He was a good-looking, lumpish young man, just sufficiently stupid to allow Elizabeth – who had suffered for years from a younger sister cleverer than herself – to feel decidedly shrewd.

The lieutenant was in conference with his military uncle, who was giving his newly acquired nephew the benefit of various financial tips he had picked up in the Mess. Elizabeth smiled and the lieutenant looked momentarily hesitant, as if wondering if he'd been signalled to join his flagship. Imperceptibly she shook her head; she was in a mood to cruise alone and revisit the harbour that had launched her.

Dreamily smiling, she moved across the grass, pleased with old familiar faces and confidently aware that she had sailed far out of their ken. She was surprised and touched by how small and humdrum people looked; she wondered how it was that she had ever been a part of it all.

She saw Dr Stump and Mr Archer, and grieved at how old they were getting. Mr Archer looked a hundred; his face was all crumpled like a bad page in an exercise book. And Dr Stump had got so fat!

'I brought you into the world, my child,' said Dr Stump, overcome with sentimental memories.

'And I prepared you for it,' said Mr Archer, with a touch of pride.

Elizabeth smiled. 'You should get married,' she said. 'Both of you. I can recommend it.'

She walked on, leaving the two old gentlemen to resume their eternal debate on how the world should be ordered, and by whom.

'Scoundrel!' said Dr Stump.

'Lackey!' said Mr Archer. As usual, neither was prepared to give way an inch.

The shrubbery was looking particularly fine; Elizabeth paused briefly to admire it. She must remember to show her husband her favourite walk. She couldn't help feeling the lieutenant to be a part of her life, rather than herself to be a part of his. Even though she boasted a new signature, it was he who had married into a family; she had not married out of one.

Henrietta hastened by, looking almost elegant. But the silly child spoiled everything by still wearing black ribbons for that unfortunate youth she'd fancied she was in love with. Henrietta was altogether too fanciful. Elizabeth sighed and made a resolve that, when the lieutenant was away, she'd have Henrietta to stay with her. Since she'd known the joys of love and marriage between sheets rather than book-covers, she felt infinitely superior to Henrietta, and really rather fond of her.

Now she joined her mother and her mother's friends. She began to discuss matters of some intimacy with the married ladies, until Mrs Boston, acutely embarrassed, begged her to go and talk to Mlle de Latour who seemed to be alone. Elizabeth shrugged her handsome shoulders and approached Gilberte.

She couldn't help noticing that Gilberte was wearing one of Henrietta's dresses. It really didn't suit her; but then she was by no means as pretty as the Boston females, and finery only seemed to draw attention to her shortcomings. No real bosom to speak of; she was too thin.

In a way, Elizabeth quite liked her. Lewis could certainly have done worse. As soon as they were married, she would have them to stay with her. She felt that Gilberte might derive great benefit from the visit and learn a little of English customs in the house and garden. She suggested this to Gilberte, who seemed very properly pleased. Elizabeth, warming, felt she would have liked to talk to her about more personal, more intimate matters – even to give her the benefit of her own recent experiences – but she felt that the French girl, being narrowly brought up, might have thought her guilty of indelicacy.

At last the sky began to cloud and the air grew a little chilly. A few guests made as if to leave, but Mr Boston, who could never bear a function to end, urged everyone to continue indoors.

'Lewis,' said Elizabeth, attaching her brother to her side with an imperious arm through his, 'you are looking pale. Come up to town and stay with us for a week or two. We will look after you.'

Lewis smiled but said nothing; it was Elizabeth's day.

'I've been talking to Gilberte, you know. I like her. When are you getting married?'

'Oh, any day now, Mrs Philips.'

'Be serious. You ought not to delay. People are beginning to talk. You should think of *her*.'

'I do. Every waking moment.'

'The waking moments are all very well, Lewis. But you ought to be thinking of the others as well. As your married sister, I feel I have a right to talk to you like this.'

Humbly Lewis acknowledged his sister's right.

'For example, have you fixed on anywhere to live?

There's a house quite near us that might suit you. I'll go and make enquiries about it.'

'But I've already decided.'

'Where?'

'Here. We will live here.'

'In Lancing?'

'In this house.'

Elizabeth paused. Lewis felt her grow rigid with indignation.

'Don't be absurd, Lewis! It's out of the question. You must have your own establishment. Gilberte will expect it.'

'In my father's mansion there are many rooms ...'

'You don't seem to understand, Lewis, that – that there are certain things between married people – certain intimacies that are very private. Being married myself, I can tell you this. I don't want to go into details, but I assure you that – that it is better to be on your own. You would feel so – so *constrained* ...'

Suddenly they realized they were alone on the terrace. Peevishly Elizabeth withdrew her arm from her brother's and stalked in to join the company. For a moment Lewis contemplated remaining outside, but it was not really in his nature to do so. He sighed and followed the married woman.

The guests had been successfully herded into the

great drawing-room where further refreshments awaited them, both for the flesh and the spirit.

The harpsichord stood open; Henrietta was to play. Lewis found himself a place as close to Gilberte as he could and settled down determined to applaud, no matter what.

Henrietta curtsied nervously, and then, in a flurry of mourning ribbons, seated herself and attacked the instrument with tempestuous hands. Whatever she might have lacked in the way of taste or precision, she more than made up for in courage. Sometimes flinging back her head to stare at the gorgeous ceiling, sometimes bending low to glare accusingly at the flinching keys, she played a sonata of quite sepulchral passion and gloom. It was impossible not to feel in it a dream of Mortimer.

As the music rattled and jangled, Lewis's eyes strayed round the room until they rested on the one-time prisoners of La Force. The count and countess were seated beside the huge urn that was emblazoned with the arms of Schleswig-Holstein. In a curious, glazed fashion, they seemed to resemble it – as if they, too, had become no more than crested ornaments in the House of Boston. Lewis sensed the half admiring, half incredulous glances bestowed on them by less exalted guests.

But what was to be done with them? Lewis thought.

Were they not too high a price to pay for their daughter? Yet since the passing of the forged dowry they had committed no more crimes. They had been content to eat, drink and sleep under what would, one day, be their daughter's roof. Had they, then, made their masterpiece? Was this the limit of their ambition – only to secure their old age? Was this the limit of all ambition: food, drink and a roof?

They were thieves, scoundrels, criminals – and you cannot change human nature. This was the fixed opinion, among others, of Dr Stump; and he, with his vast experience of life and death, ought to know. But, when all was said and done, who wanted to change human nature? Human nature encompassed the saintly as well as the devilish.

The count was beating time to Henrietta's pounding; the countess was doing her best to look transported.

Transported! thought Lewis. That is what will happen to them, sooner or later . . .

The count, feeling the slow scrutiny, turned and gazed towards his future son-in-law. He smiled . . .

No, no. He would have to protect them. He knew himself to be too feeble to do otherwise. The moment he had extended his hand to them in La Force, he had sealed his responsibility. Somehow he would have to make them a gentler gaol than the law provided. There must be a way . . .

And yet why should there be? Why look for solutions as if living was no more than a problem in geometry? Sensation was all; nourishment for the flesh and the spirit.

Henrietta, in her exalted state, struck a bunch of wrong notes. Involuntarily the countess winced; the count nudged her; she recovered herself and resumed her look of refined ecstasy.

But they've cheated me! thought Lewis with a rush of anger. They must think us all fools! It would be intolerable to live under the same roof, to be watched and all the time held in secret contempt! One could not bear that! Yet what else was there? He was seized with a fit of overwhelming futility . . .

The room was growing hot. He began to breathe rapidly. Henrietta's playing was unbearably loud. It seemed that she wanted to wake the dead. The very floor was shaking.

Suddenly Lewis saw himself struggling with the hopeless burden he'd undertaken. He saw everything he recognized as good within himself being crushed under the harsh necessity of enduring – of making money to provide. He saw himself, grey and frantic, cheating other frantic men so that he might come home, panting in triumph, and his pockets stuffed with banknotes to keep a splendid roof over worthless heads. Everything would be lost – lost!

The china and glass in the room were vibrating; the whole house seemed to be trembling as if it would fall. The mirrors dazed him. Stupidly he felt himself swaying in his chair. He was falling; he was going to faint. And in the middle of Henrietta's piece! Oh God – he must hold on to something! Yet everything had gone so far away . . .

'*Louis – Louis!*'

Gilberte, seeing his suddenly ghastly looks, had come rapidly to his side. Everybody was staring. He must hold on. That mattered more than anything. Henrietta had nearly finished. He could see the last page of the music . . .

'*Louis – Louis!*'

Her arm was round his shoulders; her face was close to his.

'Too – too much wine!' he whispered.

She smiled: '*Je comprends . . . je comprends.*'

The blood began to return to his shaken head. She touched his brow with her hand. She whispered to him. The words did not matter in the least. They never really did. Once again, for the very briefest moment, he understood . . . He grasped her wrist and drew her hand down and kissed it.

'*Je t'aime. Je t'aime, mon cher . . .*'

He felt better, much, much better.

So was this all then? '*Je t'aime, mon cher*'? Certainly it pleased him very much. Once more he contemplated the life and death of his friend from which he'd drawn the essence for his present state. Was it enough for Mortimer? This – and Henrietta's sonata and a father's stately grief? Question! Would he sacrifice all he had gained to have Mortimer back again? Oh my friend, my friend – forgive me!

Henrietta's piece had come to an end. Perspiring with effort, she took her bows. Her proud father stood beside her. His arms were outstretched to encompass the room; it was as if he would hold everything within them for ever. In Mr Boston's mansion there were many rooms . . .

But already it was dark outside. The guests had grown restless; carriages were called and, despite the host's pleas that the function was just beginning, the melancholy moment of parting had come.

'Next time, please God, for Lewis,' said Mr Boston to everyone as they left. 'Next time for Lewis.'

The function was over. Even Mr Archer had gone; and, as always, Mrs Boston bewailed the mountain of uneaten food. Downstairs, the servants, unable to look another jellied fish in its awful eye, counted their tips and set aside half-eaten morsels for the dogs.

On the kitchen table stood a large hamper into which the best of what had remained had been carefully stowed.

'What about wine? He likes his drop.'

Accordingly, three bottles of the master's best were forced down into the hamper and the top fastened with straps. Early next morning it was taken down to Shoreham where Mrs Coker received it with glassy discretion. The transaction was completed just in time for Mrs Coker to catch the Winchester coach.

It was a trifling but unhappy consequence of the war with France that Corporal Bouvet had been arrested and was now lodged, as a prisoner of war, in Winchester Gaol.

The corporal had accepted his fate with stoical calm. He had long been acquainted with the mysterious effects of government upon his person. It was, after all, the business of governments to oppress . . . Besides, was not Winchester in Hampshire; and was not Hampshire the home of Mr Hoskins? Although no gentleman of that name had, as yet, admitted to knowing one Marcel Bouvet, the corporal still nourished hopes. He had not imagined paradise; it was somewhere . . . He became an exemplary prisoner and was soon indispensable in an astonishing variety of ways.

Learning that Mrs Coker was intending to visit him, he had obtained a tablecloth, a pair of brass candle-sticks (the gaol being excessively gloomy), and had mended, pressed and polished himself till he looked like new. In a modest way, he had prepared 'a function'.

Mrs Coker, who had long saved up for the journey, wearing her good black and her piecrust hat, nodded approvingly and sat down. The corporal saluted gallantly, removed his hat and did likewise. They surveyed each other across the snow-white cloth in complacent silence. Then Mrs Coker spoke:

'You're looking well, Mr Bouvet. All things considered.'

'You also, *ma chère*. You are looking as 'andsome as always. I truly thank you for visiting.'

'My pleasure, Mr Bouvet. I wouldn't have come, elsewise.'

'A 'ard journey?'

'Not good; not bad. Mustn't grumble.'

'True.'

'Young Mr B. sends his remembrances.'

'I thank you. Nice young man. Nice 'ouse. Good people. And yours? 'Ow is your poor lady?'

'Not good, Mr Bouvet. Putting our cards on the

table, I don't think it will be long before I can offer Mr A. another two mornings. If you know what I mean?'

'Ah! *C'est la vie!* But remember, *ma chère*, you only give to Mr A. the mornings. For Marcel Bouvet it is the afternoons and the nights – eh?'

He smiled roguishly and laid his firm, broad hand upon Mrs Coker's plump one. The lady nodded sagely.

'All things considered, Mr Bouvet – and bearing in mind our time of life and not forgetting your disability – I'm content to wait.'

'Ah! When this trouble blows over!'

'Please God,' said Mrs Coker; and opened the basket of food.